EX-Girl
to the
Next Girl

EX-Girl to the Next Girl

Daaimah S. Poole

Kensington Publishing Corp.
http://www.kensingtonbooks.com

DAFINA BOOKS are published by

Kensington Publishing Corp.
850 Third Avenue
New York, NY 10022

Copyright © 2006 by Daaimah S. Poole

All Kensington Titles, Imprints, and Distributed Lines
are available at special quantity discounts for bulk pur-
chases for sales promotions, premiums, fundraising,
and educational or institutional use. Special book ex-
cerpts or customized printings can also be created to fit
specific needs. For details, write or phone the office of the
Kensington special sales manager: Kensington Publishing
Corp., 850 Third Avenue, New York, NY 10022, Attn:
Special Sales Department, Phone: 1-800-221-2647.

Dafina and the Dafina logo Reg. U.S. Pat. & TM Off.

ISBN-13: 978-0-7582-0917-7
ISBN-10: 0-7582-0917-7

First Dafina trade paperback printing: May 2006
First Dafina mass market printing: April 2007

10 9 8 7 6 5 4

Printed in the United States of America

Acknowledgments

I would like to thank Allah for all my blessings.

Thank you so much to my family: my boys, Hamid and Ahsan; my mom, Robin; my sisters Daaiyah, Nadirah, and Najah Goldstein; my dad Auzzie and stepmom Pulcheria Poole; my grandmothers Dolores Dandridge and Mary-Ellen Hickson; my aunts Bertha, and Elaine Dandridge, Edith White, and Cynthia Cargill; my uncles Teddy and Aaron Dandridge, Herbie Kidd Jr., Steven, Julius, Eric and Leon Poole; my cousins, Keva, Iesha, Tiffany and Aaron Dandridge, Leno, and Lamar Quattlebaum, Khalif Mears, and Al-Baseer Holly; all the kids of my first and second cousins; the Pooles, Wertzs, Dandridges, Wilsons, Gibsons, Riddicks, and Goldsteins. I love you all and thank you for being in my corner and telling people wherever you are to go buy that book because that's my niece's, daughter's, cousin's, etc.

And thank you to Karen and Camille Miller for always being supportive.

To everyone at Kensington Publishing, thank you for giving me this opportunity. Special thanks to my editor, Karen Thomas, Nicole Bruce, and Jessica McLean.

Thank you to my readers for your e-mails, IM's and inspiration. Also for your encouragement and, most important, your support. I have readers that were in high school when I started writing that are now in college. I want to say thank you to everyone who has picked up, read, told someone about *Yo Yo Love, Got A Man,* and *What's Real.* Nieces and daughters keep telling your mothers and aunties about me.

Tamika Wilson-Mosley and Nichole Adkinson thank you for taking it to the streets with me, getting the word out.

Thanks to Magna Diaz of Frankford High School, Shashana Crichton, Helena Gibson, Deidra Potter, Robert Saunders, Maryam Abdus-Shahid, Darryl Fitzgerald, Kia Morgan, Miana White, Shawna Grundy, Katrina Elliott, Dena Riddick, Gina Delior, Nikki Turner, Carla Lewis, Tamika Floyd, Shana Higgs, Meosha Coleman, Lerhonda Upshur, and Tamika Harper.

To the book clubs, thanks for supporting me: Mrs. Zina McDowell-Heath of FBI Elite, Thembi Maiden, Vera Leath of Circle of Sisters, Tamara Brown and Laverne Dent of Black Voices, Jenette Carter of Tranquil Moments, Monique Ford Circle of Sisters and For DaSistas.

Thanks to African World Distributors, A & B Book Distributors, The Black Library of Boston, Karibu, and Waldenbooks.

I hope I didn't forget anybody, but if I did I'm sorry, and I thank you.

Chapter 1

Shonda Nicole Robinson

I have been with my man for about a year and some change. He was seeing someone when I first met him. Actually, he was living with her and engaged, with a baby on the way. But I deaded all of that. I had to; I fell in love with him. Malik was going to be mine, one way or another. He was so damn sexy, polished, built, and a delicious shade of brown. We met at my old job at a law firm. He still works there as a paralegal. I was a temporary receptionist. I got fired for punching a bitch in the face who was minding my business. Not like that. But I had to handle my business. Malik still works there as a paralegal.

We snuck around for a few months, going to hotels, having lunch together, and taking days off from work. But then we broke up. He started feeling bad about leaving her while she was pregnant, and temporarily got back with her and proposed to her. I thought I could live without him, but I realized I couldn't. Then I heard that he was about to get married. So, I marched right up into his wedding to his son's mom and was, like, "Hold up one motherfucking moment." That's not what I said, exactly, but to make a long story short, I said, "Malik, you don't love her; you love me." And it didn't take a lot of convincing, 'cause instead of staying there and marrying her, he left the church. He fell in love with me and I fell for him, hard.

After I left the church, I went to the gas station and Malik's baby-mom sister attacked me with her bridesmaid dress on. She snuck me. It was cool, though. I guess she was mad. But that didn't make Malik come back to the wedding. He was at my house that next morning, saying, "Baby, you stopped me from making the worst mistake of my life." And if he would have married Kim, I still wouldn't have left him alone. I probably would have settled for being his mistress. He wasn't really trying to marry her, anyway.

It's been all good ever since. We moved in together a few months after his wedding. Now we have a house that we are renting in Wynnfield. My daughter has her own room, then we have our bedroom, and my back bedroom is the junk room. We keep boxes that I haven't unpacked and the ironing board in there. I'm thinking about making that a gym or office for Malik. I don't know. I have a little Chrysler Cirrus and we are doing okay. Malik already has an Associate's degree and is going back to school to get his Bachelor's in Criminal Justice. Then after that he is going to law school. I'm going to be married to a lawyer. Imagine that! One day I might even go back to school. I need a career change. I like my job as a car salesperson, but it is so hard, working on commission. If I don't sell a car, I don't get paid. It is as simple as that. They have this thing called "the draw" that means you get paid six hundred every two weeks, when you don't sell a car. Then when you sell a car, they take their six hundred dollars back; it is just like borrowing money.

I was at the dealership. *I spend more time here than I do at home,* I thought. My luck has not been that good lately with selling cars, but things should begin to pick up very soon. People are getting their W2's in the mail, and soon they will have income tax return checks. People are just now recovering from Christmas. Trying to sell a car in the winter is like selling vinegar juice to a thirsty person on a hot summer day—very hard. Malik's been holding down the bills, then my daughter's father takes care of her. I don't have to buy her anything, and I still get money every week from my child-support check. So I'm cool, I just have to make enough money to get my hair done, shop, and put gas in my car.

It was so slow, I looked out into the crowded parking lot. There were about a hundred cars that were just sitting there ready to be driven home. There was big print chalk writing that read *No Money Down* on some of them, and the others had balloons and fiesta-colored adornments flickering in the wind. Nobody had pulled in the lot the entire hour I sat at the window. I was next up. We took turns and rotated on customers on slow days. But nobody was coming through those doors. So I went to my cubicle and called back old leads. Leads were people who were supposed to buy a car, but something happened with their credit, they didn't have down payment money, or a cosigner. Basically, deals that fell through. I managed to schedule one appointment. The woman would be in on Friday. I went back to the big window, watching closely to see if anybody entered the parking lot. The first car that rode up was going to the parts department. The second car was coming straight towards me. I put on my navy wool coat and met the man at the door. An older Hispanic man, red from the cold, walked up to me. His brown hair covered half of his bald head. He smiled at me.

"Hi, I'm Shonda. What car did you want to see?" I asked as I reached for his hand. He dug around in his pocket and pulled out a piece of paper. It was a printout off the Internet of a car website. He handed me the paper. I looked down at it and said, "So you are interested in a Focus."

"Yes, I want the same one with all those options. Same color, price, and all."

"Okay, let me see if we have any in stock." I went to look in our computer system. I told the man to have a seat, but instead he followed me. Then he said, "You seem nice, so let me tell you. Shonda, I don't want to play any games. Tell your boss that I've walked out of three other dealerships. If he doesn't give me what I want, I'll walk out of here, too."

"Okay," I said as I continued to type in his selection, knowing this man was going to be a pain in my ass. He explained he wanted a four-cylinder car to get him back and forth to work. He was putting too many miles on his SUV.

I took him out to the lot and found the car he wanted. He said that he didn't want to even look inside the car or test-drive it. He wanted for me to just write the deal up. I began writing the deal, asking him necessary questions like his name, social security number, and employer. I already knew he was definitely going to buy the car. I was happy I had a deal, but I wasn't going to make any money on it because he wanted the car for five hundred dollars over invoice. We made fifteen percent on new cars. That meant I was going to make seventy-five dollars.

I finished writing the deal up and took all the paperwork to my manager, Joe. He was a drunk. I think he put liquor in his coffee. He looked over at the customer through the bottom of his thick glasses. He then yelled at me, "Did you give him this number?"

"No."

"Where did he get it from?" he asked.

"He's been to a few other dealerships. He told me to

tell you don't play any games. Give him the car for this price or he is walking."

"Did you take him on a test-drive?" he asked, looking down at me.

"No."

"Why not?"

"He didn't want to test-drive," I said, exhausted.

"Give me a minute," he said as he sipped his dark, alcohol-tainted coffee. I went back and had a seat. Joe pulled his pants up that were falling off his butt. Then he walked over to us and said, *"Señor estoy contento que usted aquí deberá negociar con nosotros hoy."*

"Como no Espanola," the man said.

"Okay, brother," Joe said as he patted his back. "Let's sit down." I looked over at Joe clown-ass. I hoped he hadn't lost the deal for me. Trying to speak Spanish and assuming that a Hispanic person should know Spanish.

"We would like to make a deal with you today, but if we sell this car at this price, we wouldn't be making any money," Joe said, as he wrote a slightly higher number on the sales sheet.

"Have a good evening," the man said. He got up and added, "I told her to tell you I wasn't playing. I want that car under these conditions or no deal."

"Hold up one minute—let's see what we can do," Joe said as he walked back to his desk, pressed some numbers in his calculator and said, "Okay, okay, Mister—you are a good negotiator. What the hell, Robinson, write the deal." He couldn't let him leave; we needed the deal. We were short eleven cars for the month.

I wrote up all the paperwork and took them to Lester, the lead salesperson they promoted to finance, even though he didn't have that much experience. Lester pulled me to the side and said, "We are not making any money on this car. We got to sell him on a warranty so we can make some money on the back end." I hated selling warranties to people. People that buy warranties financed five hundred dollars for five years, and nothing that you needed was covered, like the transmission or engine. I sold him the car, that was my job. Selling warranties, that was his job. I walked back out to the showroom, aggravated.

"Would you like some coffee?" I asked Mr. Rivera.

"Sure."

I grabbed the coffee, stirrers, a pack of the pink one, a blue one, and one sugar. He could decide for himself which one he wanted.

"Oh, Mr. Rivera, I just wanted to tell you that you should get a warranty on the car. It would only increase your payment by eight dollars a month, but you would be covered for everything."

"Well, the car is practically new, right?"

"Yes."

"So, I shouldn't have any problems. Right?" he said, looking at me suspiciously.

"No."

"Well, why would I need a warranty?" he asked.

"It's just good to have. You know, peace of mind," I said, thinking on my feet.

"I meant to ask you, Shonda. Did this car have one owner?"

"Yeah, just one owner," I lied. His eyebrow raised and he said, "Any problems?"

"No problems. I can do a CarFax for you."

"You sure? I don't want to have to replace the transmission or anything."

"No, not at all. It had one previous owner." I neglected to tell him the previous owner was a rental car agency and that the car had been run up and down the highway by different drivers for two years. I turned my head and saw Lester coming toward me. I was saved as he introduced himself to Mr. Rivera and they walked into Lester's office.

He bought the car and I was done for today and off to pick up my daughter, Brianna, from her father's house. I pulled up and tooted my horn.

"Brian, I'm outside,"

"Bree will be out." Bree came running to the car with her pink Bratz doll book bag. I gave her a quick hug and we were on our way home.

"Mom, guess what?" Bree announced.

"What?"

"Daddy said we are going on vacation," she shouted excitedly.

"Really, where are y'all going?" I asked.

"Daddy said me, him, and Andrea are going to Disney World."

Is that right? I thought. I don't know why, but I got instantly jealous. He was not taking my child to Disney World. Especially not with his wife. I was going to take her. She needs her first Disney World trip to be with her mother. I already started pricing it. Me and Malik were going to take his son and her. He wanted to take Kim's other son, Kevin, too, but she said no. If she didn't, I would have said no. I didn't want that little boy to go, anyway. It is one thing being nice and loving Malik's son, but I'm not playing stepmommy to a little boy that ain't even Malik's. But that was another story. I had to deal with Brian. I dialed his phone.

"Brian, um, when y'all supposed to be going to Disney World?" I asked.

"I bought tickets and we are going over Brianna's spring break," he said.

"Well, let me tell you something. You did not ask me. So Brianna can't go."

"What do you mean, she can't go? She is my daughter—I bought the tickets."

"Like I said, she can't go because you didn't ask me. And I want her first Disney World experience to be with me."

"Shonda, you are ridiculous!"

"Whatever, get a refund." I hung up on him. Me and Brian have been broken up for over two years, and I still hate him. Brian thinks he is doing so much better than me, but he ain't, and his wife is ugly. Big, tall, yellow bitch. She looks like Big Bird. I can't wait for Malik to propose to me. Then we are going to get a big town house with a driveway. The only reason I let Brianna go over as much as she does is because I be needing a break and be working. I rather her be with her dad than with a babysitter. Otherwise, he would not have my child so much.

I walked into my house and it was a mess. Brianna's Barbie dolls were scattered around the room. I had started decorating the living room, but haven't had the time or money to finish. I walked into the kitchen. I had a sunflower scheme going on. On the stove there was smelly broccoli in a pot that I had cooked three days ago. I rinsed it out, poured bleach into it, and washed it. The smell still lingered a little.

It is hard trying to clean, cook, and work. I took a look in our freezer: there was steak, a whole chicken, and frozen hot dogs. I continued to stare like something else was going to appear. It was too late to thaw out a steak, and I didn't want a hot dog. I took one more glimpse in the freezer, then I decided I wasn't cooking anything. I cleaned the kitchen and then snatched the Tri-Town delivery menu off of the refrigerator. I worked all day, too. But I was the one who had to find the energy to cook for everybody. *Not tonight,* I thought. I was going to order me chicken fingers and Malik a cheese steak. I picked up the phone and Brianna was on there, talking. I listened for a moment to see what she was talking about. Her and her friend were talking about what they were going to wear to school the next day. I had to cut their convo short.

"Who you talking to?" I asked.

"My friend Leah."

"Tell Leah good-bye and come here."

Brianna told her friend she'd see her at school. She ran down the steps and shouted from the living room, "Yes, Mom?"

"What do you want to eat?"

"Where are you ordering from?"

"Tri-Town."

"I don't know what I want," she said as she looked over the menu.

"Brianna, hurry up and decide—I'm placing my order now," I said as I dialed the number.

"I'll take a salad."

"A salad? I'm not paying seven dollars for a salad."

"Me and Andrea always order salad."

"Bree, you can get some fingers or a burger. Or you can go and fix yourself a peanut-butter-and-jelly sandwich."

"I'll fix a sandwich," she said with an attitude.

"After that, get your homework done." She was only ten, but getting so grown. People were starting to tell me that I needed to sit her down. I found a note she wrote to some boy, talking about meeting her after school under the steps. She said it wasn't hers, it was her friend Erica's. So I told her she couldn't be friends with her anymore.

Malik came in the door around nine. "Hey, baby," he said. My baby made me proud to say I was his woman. He looked so handsome in his white shirt, navy blue tie, and navy slacks.

"Hey," I said as he came and kissed me softly on the lips.

"Where is Bree?"

"She is in the room asleep."

"What you cooked?" he asked as he looked around the kitchen for a sign of food.

"I didn't cook anything, baby. Me and Bree got in here so late." I could tell he was a little disappointed. "I ordered you a steak, though," I said, trying to make up for not cooking.

"A greasy cheese steak and soggy French fries with ketchup in the microwave. Damn, Shonda, cook for your man once in a while," he said as he looked in the microwave. "Why can't I come home to a decent meal?" he said playfully, but I knew he was serious.

"Baby, I'm sorry. I was tired. I promise, tomorrow I will cook for you." I said as I got close to him and put my arms around his waist and kissed him.

"It's okay. Baby, I know you're tired, but you got to feed your man. Look at me, I'm getting skinny," he said as he took a step back from me and raised his shirt to reveal his flat stomach.

"I think you look fine, baby."

"You about to get in the tub?"

"Yeah, I want to relax a bit," I told him.

"I'm going to eat. Then I'll be up there to get in with you."

Malik met me upstairs and we turned the lights out and I lit a candle. The water was hot and the bubbles were high and feathery. We sat in each other's arms. It was so relaxing, ending the day with my man. I took the wash cloth and wrung it out over his back, letting the warm water trickle down his spine.

"Thank you, baby, that feels so good," he said as he sighed. I then began to massage his temples and reached for the Suave apple shampoo and lathered it in.

"When we get our new house, we have to have a Jacuzzi in our bedroom," I said. Malik agreed, and then said, "Let's get out of here." After thirty minutes of soaking, we stood up and let the water out. I took a towel out of the closet and dried Malik off. He came behind me and held me. I went and lay under my warm rose comforter. Malik followed me. My baby positioned me down on the bed and we got in our favorite arrangement: the sixty-nine. I was on the top, he was on the bottom. I put his massive dick in my mouth and tried to take every inch as far as I could. He opened the lips of my inside and twisted his tongue back and forth. Malik was ready to make his way into me, but I wanted him to finish stroking my breasts and to suck on me harder. I loved his touch. He could make me come just from slobbing my breasts. He then entered me. I felt all of him in my stomach. I kept squirming so that I could be able to take it.

"Baby you got some good—" I couldn't get my last thought out.

"I love you, girl—Don't you ever leave me," he screamed out and came as his juices trickled down his leg and we both closed our eyes and fell asleep.

Chapter 2

Kimberly Vanessa Brown

The sound of the grumbling, noisy trash truck awoke me. I hastily jumped out of my bed and looked out the window to see the truck a few doors away from my house. I slid on my slippers and robe and went down the steps. I opened my back door and ran down the steps and grabbed the trash cans. The cold January weather greeted me at the door. I hated the winter. It was always too cold. I looked over at the trash spilling out the trash can. I momentarily thought about letting the trash stay in the yard one more week. Instead, I grabbed the can and pulled it into the house. Just as I opened the front door, I saw the trash truck passing my house. I pulled the can down the steps as fast as I could. The trash man saw me coming and stopped the truck. The sanitation worker had on a blue jumpsuit and layers of clothes with orange gloves.

"Any more, pretty lady?" he asked as I dragged the can toward him.

"Yes, just one," I said as he took the can from me.

I raced back through the house to get the other trash

can. I grabbed the last can and dragged it through the house. Out of breath, I handed him the can.

After the man dumped the cans, I pulled all the empty cans back through the house and then to the backyard. I washed my hands in the sink and grabbed a paper towel and dried my hands. I then put water in my *World's Best Mom* mug, put it into the microwave and pressed one minute, fifteen seconds. I grabbed a tea bag out of the cabinet and the Equal. *I don't want to go to work. I want to go back to bed,* I thought as I reached for lemon juice. It was behind the multiple rows of salad dressing. I needed to go food shopping. There was a container of orange juice, bread, and a jar of apple-sauce, and not much else. I checked the date on the eggs; they were expired, so I threw them out.

I sat down at the table and sipped my tea. I looked over at the time on the microwave. It was 6:30. I had ex-actly one hour to get out of the house if I wanted to make it to work on time. Last night I knew if I didn't pull the kids' clothes out, I was going to be late, but knowing that didn't make me prepare for the next day. Some days I couldn't make myself care, even though I would like to. I needed to start getting my clothes out the night before and make the boys wash up. Actually, I should have taken their clothes out and ironed for the week. If I had done that, I would have been ahead of the game. It was 6:45, and I was still just sitting, sipping my tea. No motivation, no reason to move forward or faster. It was times like this when I felt so alone. When I was all alone, it dawned on me that there was only me. I was by myself. If I didn't wake the kids, feed them, and dress them, then it wouldn't happen. Nobody else would pay the mortgage. Nobody would take the trash out, take them to the barber, or make dinner. It was me, only me. Kimberly Vanessa Brown: the middle child, the shy one, the girl who was a virgin in college. Me. I was on my own, and Malik Moore—my ex—is gone.

It's been almost a year since my fiancé stood me up at our wedding. Well, he didn't exactly stand me up. He did show up; he had the decency to come in and walk down the aisle with his best man, Jarrod. He let my father walk me down the aisle, we recited our vows, and right before the minister said, *Does anyone see why this man and woman should not be joined in holy matrimony?*, Malik's other woman crashed my wedding. I mean, this bitch came in a-shouting from the back of the church, *Malik, you know this is wrong. You love me.* Everyone turned around. Malik had a firm grip on my hand, and then he let it go. I fainted, and hours later I awoke and Malik was nowhere to be found. I asked for him as soon as I awoke. I should have known something was wrong when my mother turned her head and my little sister Kianna ran to my side and said, *Take it easy.*

I left the hospital that same night in my white wedding dress. When I came home, I never took it off. I sat and pulled every bead off my five-thousand-dollar dress, one by one. The phone rang and rang, and I didn't answer it. I felt like a big failure. My parents spent twenty-five thousand on a wedding for nothing. My mother had the cops come bang on my door when they didn't hear from me after two days. They thought I was suicidal or dead, but I wasn't. I wanted to be dead, though. The only things that kept me from going over the top were my boys, Kevin and Kayden. Kayden is the only thing worth anything that came out of my relationship with Malik. Kayden is one and Kevin is eight.

My wedding was so embarrassing. Everybody was there, and they all saw my heart break. My mom's friends, my friends, and just *everybody*. Then his little girlfriend came in and ruined everything. I still think about Malik; it is hard not to. I see his face every day, even when I don't want to. When I look into our one-year-old son's face, I see him. I still wear my engagement ring—it's just so hard to move on.

After the wedding that wasn't, I gave most of my gifts back and got a refund on our honeymoon. Since then, everyone has been so nice to me. Even Karen, my sister, and we rarely get along. But I now have more of an appreciation for her. When it was all said and done and the bitch ran in and stopped my wedding, my sister was the one who was right there, chasing after her. She chased her all the way to the gas station and knocked her out. We laughed about that. My uncle and other family members started calling and telling me about their heartache. Some of it helped, but most of it didn't. People constantly calling you, trying to make you happy, makes you more depressed.

And what really upsets me is, Malik didn't ever tell me face-to-face that he didn't want to be married. He sent me flowers and a note saying that he would always love me, but he wasn't ready for marriage, and he hoped I understood. I didn't understand then, and I understand now. I kept asking myself what I did to make him stray. He betrayed me and our family. He betrayed our son. We were supposed to be together till death do us part. Now I'm out here all alone. Abandoned. I'm mad and a little bitter even though I try not to be. I'm mad because he left me with dreams, promises and hope for the future. I'm mad that he left me for another woman, and because he is not the man I wished he could be.

My last year has been all meshed together. It seems like just yesterday I was pregnant with Kayden, and now he just turned one last month. I hate Malik and I hate men. I hate Malik so much I changed our son's name from Malik Moore Jr. to Kayden Brown. Malik tried to protest, but he isn't entitled to an opinion or choice in the matter.

I hate men so much I became a lesbian temporarily. It was very brief. I think, like, an hour. I said I was going to get a woman and treat her like I would want to be treated. I was going to buy her nice things and take her out. Then, when the thought of sex came to mind, I changed my mind. Unfortunately, I still like men. However, Malik really has put a sour taste in my mouth. If I can't trust him—and I knew him for over four years and he hurt me and I had his only son—what would a man I didn't know do to me? I think losing Malik has been worse than death. Death is permanent and you have no control of that. But Malik is still walking the earth and claimed he loved me, and treated me like this. I guess I'll never know, because I will never love another man again. You give everything, and no matter what you say, the other person doesn't get it. You try to make it work. I thought I would be married for thirty years like my parents, but things don't always go the way you plan them.

My mom has been trying to get me to see a doctor about my depression. I have been fighting it by myself all these months. Nobody sees how difficult it is to be in my situation. All my sisters and my mom say is, *Get over it. You are not the first, and you won't be the last single mom.* They don't get it. Nobody does. I'm trying to pick up the pieces of my life. A whole year has gone by, and I haven't moved from the place in my mind where Malik left me.

I got up from the table. Enough thinking and rehashing old memories. I looked around my living room. There were toy cars and building blocks scattered all over the place. I didn't have the energy to clean up. I went up the stairs to tell Kevin and Kayden to get up. It was now seven—I had to be at work by nine. Kevin had to be at school by eight-fifteen, and I dropped Kayden off after that.

I went into Kevin's room. I had everything decorated with red, blue, yellow, and green crayons, a red dresser, multicolored fan, toy chest, and desk set.

"Wake up, sleepyhead," I shouted as I began to lightly shake Kevin up. He turned over and tried to pull the covers back over his head.

"Kevin, get up now," I said as I searched his drawers for matching socks. I pulled out two navy socks that looked like they matched close enough. I grabbed his white T-shirt and underwear and laid them on the ironing board in the hallway. Now all I needed was to find a clean school shirt and pants. Kevin still wasn't up.

"Kevin, this is my last time calling you." He got up and headed for the bathroom as his head and body swayed sleepily back and forth. I heard him turn on the shower. I looked at the clock again: 7:10. Time was moving too fast.

I walked into Kayden's room; it was decorated in a mint-green and pine wood. Mint-green was the only color that went over the color pink perfectly. Kayden was supposed to be a girl, so I had to paint over the pink without having a dark room. Kayden was already awake, standing up and looking at me. He had a few teeth and couldn't talk that much yet. He knew how to say "mommy" and "bottle." I grabbed him and he grabbed his bottle. I took him into the bathroom and sat him in the sink. Kevin was in the shower, just about to come out. I handed him a towel. I washed and dressed Kayden. Kevin had put on his clothes.

I sat them at the breakfast table and turned the television on to *Caillou* and they ate breakfast. Okay, it was now 7:45; I had fifteen minutes to get myself together. I showered, turned on my curling iron, and curled my hair. I parted my hair in four sections and curled each section one time. It was a loose curl, but it would do. It was time to go.

"Kevin, do you have your book bag?" I screamed.

"Yes."

"Come on, let's go. Where are your gloves?"

"Upstairs," he said as he skipped up the steps in search of them. A few moments later, Kevin yelled down the stairs, "Mom, I can't find my gloves."

"Look around," I yelled. Every morning with Kevin was the same old thing. He couldn't find his book bag, coat, or shoes. Then he screamed down the steps, "Mom, I found it."

"Get your hat, too. Brush your hair while you are up there," I said as I put on my coat and started the car. I had to scrape the ice off my window. The kids waited by the door.

I buckled Kayden in his car seat and Kevin did his own. We were down the road at five minutes after eight. Traffic was unbelievably slow for a Friday morning. That's when I realized it wasn't Friday—it was Saturday, and I had got dressed and ready for nothing. *Damn it*, I thought.

"What's wrong, Mom?"

"Nothing. Nothing at all," I answered Kevin as I turned my car around and headed home. Martin Luther King's birthday threw my entire week off. The trash men collecting trash made me think it was Friday.

Chapter 3

Nadine Clark

I stood over him. *Him* being Erick, my boyfriend of two years. When he was asleep, he was so funny-looking. His ears looked extra big. His cashew-brown skin appeared oily. He is just okay in the looks department—some days he looks better than others. Sometimes he catches me looking at him. He will look up at me and ask me, *Why are you staring?* I'll say something like, *I'm not staring.* I was asleep with my eyes open. But I was staring because I want to know if he is the right man for me. I know staring wouldn't answer my question, but it might help. I don't want to throw my life away if he is not the one. We are not engaged or anything yet, but we talk about marriage and kids all the time. Erick always said, "Baby, are we having a big or small wedding? Baby, how many kids are we going to have? What are we going to name our kids?" He has our whole life planned out, and I'm still figuring out if I like him or love him. We have been around each other for two years. He knows my family and I know his. We have been on vacations to Jamaica, Cancun, and Japan to visit my parents—they are in the military. If I'm not sure about him, then I'm not wasting any more time. I need to be one hundred percent sure that he is what I want. He works as a lab tech at Graduate Hospital. He makes a very nice living. We would have a joint income of over a hundred thousand, but does that even matter if he doesn't make me happy? I guess it doesn't. I looked over at him again. His nose hairs were blowing in and out every time he took a breath. I was about to break up with him. But I'm going to let him think he broke up with me. At least, that was the plan. I have been scheming for months, telling my Aunt Connie and my cousin that I can't wait to be single. Aunt Connie said, *Don't let that good man go*, but I can't keep pulling him along if I'm not sure. He caught me staring again.

"Are you staring at me?"

"No, I was just thinking," I said as he went to kiss me. I moved away from his kiss and out of the bed.

"Erick, I have to talk to you." He sat right up—he knew it was serious.

"Have you ever heard the saying, 'If you let a bird go and it flys away, if it's yours it will return—if it never was yours, it won't'?"

"What are you talking about? You are not making any sense," he said, rubbing the cold out of his eyes.

"Okay, I think I love you, but I think . . . I want to make sure we are right for one another. I think we need space."

"I don't want to break up, Nadine," he said as his eyes began to water. *Don't do this, please*, I thought. I hate to see men cry. He was making this really hard. I had to be firm with him.

"We need time off," I said as I looked him straight in the eyes and grabbed his hands.

"So you want to see other people?" he asked as he snatched his hands away from me, put on his underwear, and searched around the room for his faded blue jeans.

"No, I don't want to see other people," I lied.

"So why break up if we aren't going to see other people?"

"I just think we need space, Erick. Just a little time off."

"I'm not with this. I don't want to be with any other woman. You're all the woman I need, Nadine. But if this is what you want."

"I do. Let's give each other a little time and space."

Erick, trying to be hard, said, "Okay, if you want it this way." He put on his shoes and gave me a kiss. He took a look around the room to be sure that he was not forgetting anything. He pulled his brush out of his back pocket and brushed his hair in place. He walked to the bathroom and washed his face and brushed his teeth. Then he proceeded down the steps. I stood at the top of the steps with my robe on and my arms folded. He walked out, and I began a dance of freedom. I am free.

Growing up, I lived all over the world. My parents are in the military. We were in Virginia Beach most of my life, but we also lived in Hawaii, Germany, Colorado, California, and Japan. My dad and mom separated right before I got to eighth grade. My mom remarried instantly to this man named Mr. Richard. Me and him didn't click. My mom, being so in love, didn't see that this man was mistreating me. He tried to make me do everything around the house and have a curfew and get off the phone by 9:00 P.M. and go to the library every Saturday. He was a real military dude. I moved in with my dad and his new instant wife, Cynthia. At first, me and Cynthia were cool, until she started thinking she was my mom. I moved back in with my mom.

*   *   *

Whatever Mommy wouldn't buy, Daddy would. People worry about children of divorce, but I think we turn out just fine, actually. We might come out a little better, if you ask me. You have two parents that overcompensate and try to buy your love. Tragically, my situation came to an end when my father and mother remarried each other my last year of high school. As soon as I got adjusted to them being apart, they got back together. Most people would be happy about that—I wasn't. They were better apart; that's when I could get away with everything. I was tired of both of them, and I begged my mom to let me stay with Aunt Connie and she did. Aunt Connie and her husband, Chuck, let me move in with them my senior year of high school for stability. My Aunt Connie is my mom's sister. My mother, Faye, is the oldest, and she has one brother named Scott. We call him Uncle Scotty. He is a drunk.

My mom is tough; she doesn't care about makeup and shopping. Years of the military have destroyed her femininity. She doesn't wear her hair short or look like a butch, but she doesn't play dress-up very often. I tried to give her a makeover, but that was short-lived. She loves sports and I got F's in gym because I'm a girly girl. By ninth grade I was already cutting gym class to go to the nail salon. Gym didn't make sense to me. Get undressed, get sweaty, then put your same funky clothes back on without a shower and walk around school all day. I wasn't having it. I hate working out. I'd rather just watch what I eat and that's what I do to maintain my size 9/10. I like it. Not too big, not too skinny.

I thought if I didn't answer the phone after the fourth ring, the caller would get the hint. Not my persistent Aunt Connie. I answered the phone and she asked from the other end of the telephone, "You want to go shopping with me?"

"Where you going?" I questioned.

"Well, I want to go everywhere. I got my income tax back."

"Already?"

"Yeah, I just cashed it. Just hurry up and get dressed and meet me at my house."

"What time is it?" I asked, still not fully awake.

"Eleven-thirty."

"I'll be right there," I said as I stretched. I went in my closet. *Just what I needed to do: go shopping*, I thought. I looked at all my clothes in and around my cluttered closet. Belts, bags, shoes, boxes. I had gold, big hats, and purple bags and clothes that I never wore. I have a compulsive spending habit. My paycheck is always gone before I get it. I get paid on Friday and I would start shopping by check on Wednesday. Well, I used to be able to start my shopping early until they came out with that Check 21 thing. They started taking the money out of my account the same day. Well, I didn't know about the check law change, and let's just say I had to pay for five bounced check fees at thirty dollars a pop. I learned my lesson real fast. So now I wait to payday and shop 'til I drop.

I always buy shoes, bags, and jewelry, things I don't need. But I still feel like I don't have enough. Last month I bought two pairs of shoes that I couldn't fit into. One was stiletto heels that my foot slid down into. The other pair made a corn on the side of my toe grow back because they were so damn tight. Sometimes if they don't have a medium in something I want, I'll buy a small or extra-small, knowing that it looks young on me. I just buy anything. Kids selling M&Ms or bottled water at the light, kids raising money for their drill team—they always get my dollar.

I buy people gifts, doing a lot of shopping, and spending credit cards like I didn't have to pay them back. Now I'm twenty-five and I make okay money and have nothing to show for it but clothes and a house. I feel like I should have more—I don't know why, but I do. If I'm not shopping for myself; I'm always giving my money away to someone for some reason. I always have to give the best present at a shower, wedding, or birthday parties. Even Mrs. Pierce, another teacher, who wasn't my friend—I didn't even like her that much. I had to bring the best, biggest gift to the shower they gave her at school. Like I'm always treating my aunt and cousin to dinner. I like nice places. One time I got a thousand-dollar bonus check for perfect attendance at my school. So I put up another sixteen hundred and I took me and my cousin, Toya, to the Virgin Islands. Besides my house, I have a new car. But I feel like I deserve all of it and much more. I got seventeen thousand dollars in credit-card debt and about sixty thousand in student loans. I'm going to pick up a second job to pay all of my bills one day.

I took my jeans off the hanger and then separated the other hangers. Erick's shirts were still in my closet, his porn collection, belts, hats, and a couple pairs of boots. I pushed his stuff to the side. I located a blazer with a little flower on the lapel. I was going to wear a white shirt underneath. I laid my clothes out on the bed and jumped in the shower.

On the weekends I try to sleep as long as I can. I have to be up and in the classroom every morning by eight. I'm a seventh-grade Social Studies/English teacher. I hated English growing up. I hated the red marker with a bunch of squiggly lines everywhere. Now I'm the one writing squiggly lines. I kind of fell into teaching. When

I was in high school—and even college—you could not have told me one day I would be a teacher. I love my students but sometimes they get on my nerves and I wonder why I am a teacher.

I graduated from the University of Maryland with a degree in business, late or early—it was a nontraditional graduation in January. I needed a job badly. I didn't want to be one of those people still working at the mall with a college degree. Nobody was hiring. A classmate told me that the district was hiring, and you didn't need a degree in education to be a substitute teacher. I started as a substitute. The next day, when I came back for round two, the principal was so happy I returned he asked me if I could stay until June. It was on-the-job training. I didn't know the first thing about teaching, lesson plans, or any of that, but other teachers helped me out.

And now that I am a seasoned teacher, I'm getting paid back on a daily basis for every class I cut, every book I threw at a teacher, and every lie I told about an assignment I didn't complete. At least back when I was in school, students cared if you called their mom or threatened to send them to the office. My students test me. They want to see if you play or if they can play you. I don't play with them—I'd give a detention in a minute.

Chapter 4

Kim

I walked into my office Monday morning. It was an office in a strip mall storefront. Some days I just looked at all the other people going about their day and wished I was them and not me because I had too much responsibility.

"Your baby father called," Nicole said as I walked in the office.

"What did you tell him?" I asked as I sat at my desk with a grande latte in my hand. I placed my change purse in my drawer.

"I told him that you weren't here, like you said to do."

"Good," I said as I sat down and began checking my e-mails.

"But then he said he wanted the baby for a couple of hours, and if you didn't call him back he would be up here."

"Forget him—he is not coming anywhere. He can leave me and my son alone," I said. Nicole was cool; she had been working with me for two years and she knew everything about me. She was like a little sister. We did things outside of the job together, like have drinks and go to shows. It was good to have someone in my office that I could trust. I hired another woman, Jacqueline Stevens, but she went out on maternity leave four months after I hired her. If she doesn't return soon, her and her baby are going to be in the unemployment line. I needed somebody else in the office to help us make calls. We are inundated with all this work. I'm a manager, which is basically a nice way to say customer-calmer. Every day there is something different and difficult going on. Do you ever see those signs that read "zero percent interest"? Well, that's us. The furniture companies go through our company to get the people financed. We also do plenty of refinancing. People need money to remodel their homes and send their kids to college. But they don't always tell the truth about their credit. I love when people say their credit is great, and I see that they have a Capital One credit card that they stopped paying on. When people are not lying about the condition of their credit, they are lying about how much money they make. I had a customer that said she made fifty-five thousand, and when she gave me her W-2 form it showed she made thirty thousand. As I speak, I have to call a customer, Mrs. Saunders, now about a check mix-up. We accidentally sent a three-thousand-dollar pay-off check to Wal-Mart and a ten-thousand-dollar check to Home Depot. She didn't even owe Home Depot ten thousand, but they cashed the check. Anyway, I wasted my day going back and forth, debating with their reps about the confusion, and still didn't get the problem solved.

"Kim, pick up line one," Nicole screamed.

"Kimberly Robinson speaking," I said as I held back a yawn.

"Yeah, listen, I'm in the parking lot. I'm tired of playing the games with my son." I automatically caught the voice. It was Malik.

"What games, Malik? I don't know what you are talking about. When Kayden is ready to see you, I will call you. Until then, leave us alone."

"Listen, I just want to see my son—that's all, Kim."

"Well, when do you want to see him?" I asked.

"Today!" he yelled into the telephone.

"Well, he is busy today, tomorrow, and any day you call, Malik. You're not going to have my son around your trashy-ass ghetto girlfriend. If you don't like it, take me to court."

"I will take you to court. She is not trashy or ghetto. Grow up, please," he said, irritated.

"I don't give a fuck about that bitch—she doesn't have anything on me."

"You have let me see my son three times in a year, and I'm tired. Shonda already told me to take you to court. I'm trying to be nice to you, Kim. But I need to see my son."

"Really? Well, do what you got to do, my brother," I said as I grew increasingly angry.

"I will do what I have to do because Malik needs his dad," he shouted.

"You are not a good example of a man for my son, and his name is not Malik anymore, it is Kayden—and he doesn't need you in his life."

"Don't tell me what kind of man I am, Kim. Go 'head with the foolishness. How you going to change the boy's name at three months?"

"It was really easy. Um, when I'm ready to let you see him, I'll call you. Bye." I had to laugh when I hung up the phone. I looked up to Nicole, staring at me.

"What?" I asked as Nicole looked at me accusingly. I

looked at my computer screen and tried to regain my composure.

"You know you bein' petty, right?" I looked over at her and told her to mind her business. A few moments later, the phone rang again. This call was from my mother.

"Kimberly, I just got off the phone with Malik. Why aren't you letting Malik see Kayden?"

"Because I don't feel like it."

"Are you going to be bitter your whole life? It is so very unattractive. What's done is done."

"Mom, please, I don't have time. You are supposed to be on my side, not his," I said, trying to block her words out. I wasn't going to let her upset me.

Then she shouted, "Kim are you listening to me? Don't you get it? There aren't any sides. You are handling this situation all wrong. I think you should see Dr. Burrows."

"For what? There is nothing wrong with me. I'm not going to see anyone. I don't want to talk any more. Good-bye, Mother. I have work to do."

Nicole flipped to the horoscope section and asked me my sign.

"I got to read yours to see what's going on with you. You're a Cancer, right? Y'all is some overacting, drama-filled people. I'm going to read your horoscope to you. *You will be put in an adult situation.* Will you be able to handle it?"

"Let me see—it doesn't say that," I said as I grabbed the newspaper. It did say I would be put in a very difficult situation and asked what steps would I take to right a wrong.

"I don't care what it says—I don't believe in that, anyway."

* * *

When Nicole wasn't giving me advice, she was busy reading a self-help book. Every week there is some new method or way we should eat or live our life.

I instructed Nicole to take messages the rest of the day. I had to look at a few résumés and set up interviews. Mrs. Jacqueline "Maternity" Stevens better come back to work, and soon. My boss was on me about firing her and hiring someone else. She claims she is suffering from postpartum, but I doubt it. There was so much that needed to be done. I wanted to bring her back, plus hire someone new.

After a long, exhausting day at work, I went home and started dinner. I was cooking my specialty spaghetti again. It was easy, the boys liked it, and it took under thirty minutes. Kayden was in the living room chasing Kevin. He just learned to walk, so he was still wobbling away. Kayden just kept screaming every time Kevin got too close to him.

We ate dinner and I began to do the dishes. I don't know what came over me, but I felt so hopeless and tired. Then a pain came over my eye; it was so sharp, and it kept hitting me like a punch. Everything was too loud and bright. I went into the bedroom and put my head down under the covers. I found some Tylenol and took a few. It wasn't working. I felt nauseous, then I started throwing up and my body went into an involuntary jerking motion. All my spaghetti was all over the floor. I hadn't eaten anything else, so nothing was coming up. But my body refused to stop stripping the lining of my stomach. I didn't know what to do. I just lay there, hoping it would stop, and it did. I just wanted to sleep and stop thinking about everything that was going on.

The next day after work, almost the same thing happened again. I started feeling really sleepy and my head felt tight like it was going to explode. I placed Kayden in his room—he had fallen asleep on the way home. I told

Kevin not to bother me. I opened up the Oreo cookies and gave him a few.

"Eat those and drink some milk and start your homework. I'm going to lie down."

"Okay," he said as he reached in the cabinet for a cup.

I got in my satin, soft, raspberry-colored bed, popped another Tylenol, and just closed my eyes. I was awakened several hours later by Kevin announcing, "Mommy, we hungry."

"Kevin, here I come." I looked up at the clock and it was 10:00 P.M. I had slept for the last four hours. I went down the steps and saw that my curtains were pulled apart and you could see right into my house. The light was burning my eyes and I could barely see. But I opened my eyes wide enough to see that there was popcorn and cereal all over my tan carpet. Juice spills and an open applesauce jar were strewn across the dining room table. They had all the lights on in the entire house. I pulled a chair up to the window, stood on it, and put the curtains back in place.

"Kevin, why didn't you wake me?"

"You told me not to wake you. Because your head was hurting. I didn't want to bother you, Mom."

"What did you eat?" I said, looking around at the mess.

"I gave Kayden applesauce. I ate cookies and popcorn."

"Are you still hungry?" I asked him.

"Yes."

"I'll fix you some Spaghetti-O's." I grabbed some out of the cabinet and warmed them in the microwave. I tried to feed Kayden, but he was full from junk. I washed him and got him ready for bed. His eyes were bright and he was still bouncing around. I tried to force myself to eat, but I still wasn't hungry. I then checked my messages. I had a reminder call from Kayden's pediatrician's office that he had to have his one-year-old shots. I had totally forgotten about it. I had about another year of these shots. I didn't want to risk my son's health, but I hated taking the day off to go sit in the doctor's office. They triple-book appointments and you sit and sit. I had to reschedule.

My district manager, Elizabeth Reddy, was already in my office when I arrived. She had a nasty disposition. She was short with gray roots and red-colored hair. Her skin was damaged by the sun, with little brown spots on it. She was the kind of person, when you asked her a question, she said, *What?* instead of *Excuse me,* like you interrupted her entire day. She was all in my office, searching through my files. "What's going on with that Saunders account?" she asked.

"I have been in contact with the stores involved. There was a little confusion. Someone sent the wrong checks out."

"That's not a little confusion. You need to get a grasp on this situation, because your customer contacted corporate. And corporate asked me what was going on, and I had no idea. So get to the bottom of this," she said, as she gathered paperwork folders and headed toward the door.

Chapter 5

Nadine

Ipulled in front of Aunt Connie's row home. There was a green weathered awning hanging over the porch. The porch had white lawn furniture on it, and she had bouquets of fake flowers in her windows. I rang the bell, and Rodney, my Aunt Connie's stepson, answered the door.

I walked into my Aunt Connie's home. It smelled like spring laundry dryer sheets. She had a thing for leopard and cats. Leopard carpet and a tawny brown throw blanket with a leopard swung over it. She had her dining room table set with glasses, napkins, silverware, and a floral arrangement. Nobody ever sat at that table, not even during the holidays; it was just a decoration. I stepped in the kitchen and smelled breakfast—eggs, grits, toast, and sausage.

"It smells good. Did you make all of this?" I asked Rodney.

"No, I think she made it for you." Rodney said with his mouth full.

"Where is she?" I asked, getting a plate.

"Upstairs, getting dressed."

"Auntie, can I have some breakfast?" I yelled up the steps.

"Yeah, go ahead. I made extra for you," she yelled. I took a seat at the table and looked over at Rodney, my step-cousin. I wanted him to be a stranger since I was eleven, so I could date him.

"What's going on, Ms. Nadine?" he asked as he munched on toast.

"Nothing. What's up with you?" I asked as I reached in the refrigerator for orange juice. The yellow refrigerator had magnets from every vacation she had ever gone on.

"Nothing much—down here trying to close a deal," he replied.

"Look at you making money," I said as I poured the juice in my glass.

"No, my mom is moving to Georgia, so I sold the house for her. I'm just in town to the end of the day. I'm trying to catch up with my dad while I'm here. I was trying to see him before I leave. What's up with you?"

"Nothing—can't wait until June gets here," I said.

"June will be here before you know it. Y'all always off. How do the kids learn if you guys are always out?"

"We find a way." I stared at Rodney—he was five-eleven, and cute. Rodney was always cute and fly. When we were in high school, he already had a car and girlfriends who were older. He was just that decent boy who everybody wanted to talk to. He had every pair of new sneakers, a clean ride, and a job. He worked in the sneaker store on Germantown Avenue and hung out with other older guys. Girls would come up to me and ask me, was he my cousin? They wanted to be my friend to get closer to him. I used to lust after him, but in a different way. I wanted him to take me to my prom. I wanted us to get a convertible, and have everybody there to see us off. Now that we were older, I still wanted him. I loved him then and now. He looks even better now that he is into real estate and making money, looking good. I wish he wasn't my step-cousin.

My Aunt Connie walked down the steps. Aunt Connie was a beautiful woman, and she made sure you knew it. She had clear, soft, oatmeal-brown skin—not one trace of a wrinkle or bag under her eyes at forty-nine. Her favorite pastime was pointing out other women in her age bracket and saying, *That's a damn shame—can you believe that such-and-such is the same age as me, looking like that?* Even if someone looked comparable to her, she would find a flaw. Her other pleasure was requesting the manager in any and every store. Meat undercooked? Manager. Slow service? Manager. Waitress or teller got an attitude? Manager. She put ice in her glass from the automatic ice dispenser on the refrigerator and poured orange juice into her glass.

"Rodney, your daddy at work," she said as she sipped her orange juice.

"I know, I was just stopping by," he said as he stood up and cleared his plate into the trash.

"Your mom moving, I heard. That's nice," she said, somewhat sarcastically.

"Yeah, she said she can't take the city life and weather anymore."

"Too bad—everybody coming back to the city now."

"Well, my mom's going to Savannah to take care of my aunt."

"Okay, well, you staying? Because we're about to go out. I love you," she said as she hugged him.

"No, I'm going to get out of here." He gave Aunt Connie a kiss and said that he would stop by again before he left.

* * *

After Rodney left, Aunt Connie said she was happy Uncle Chuck wasn't home yet.

"Why?" I asked as I stood up and put my coat on.

"I don't want that man to know I have any money. He wants us to put our money together and get the basement finished. I told you I have my income-tax check. I did a rapid refund. This guy down on Walnut Street, he got me back forty-five hundred. You should let him do your taxes. He is so good. I usually don't get but five-hundred dollars, but that man found all these deductions I could get."

"That's good."

"I know, isn't it?" she said excitedly as she put her earrings in her ears. She continued on. "At first I saw his butt. He looked dirty, so I said to myself, *this man can't do taxes—he barely looks like he washes.* But it was so crowded, and I wanted to get it done and over with. So I took a chance with him and it worked."

"That is so good."

"I know, and this money is right on time. I'm going to pick up a few gifts for Monet's birthday. It's a shame Toya didn't give her a party. I should give her one, shouldn't I?"

"Well, you know Toya knows if she doesn't do it, y'all will."

"I know. That's what's wrong with my child. Let me get my other bag. I'll be right back."

I sat back down and waited for her. My little thirteen-year-old cousin, Ariel, came down the steps in her pajamas, braces, and big rollers in her hair. She picked off what was left of the eggs.

"Where y'all going?" she asked.

"We are going shopping. Where are you going?" I asked.

"Me and my friend are going to the movies, then we

are going to the arcade." I guess she remembered she needed money and screamed, "Mommy, can I have some money?"

"Ariel, I just gave you thirty dollars yesterday."

"Mom, I got my nails done with that money. See?" she asked as she showed off her decorated, long nails.

"Ariel, here," she said as she placed a hundred dollars in her hand. "Don't ask me for any more money." Aunt Connie had Ariel when we were about thirteen, and all she ever did is complain about her. I guess she was an unexpected blessing. Poor Ariel, every time she asked to go somewhere or do something Aunt Connie said, *I ain't got time for this shit* or *I'm too old* or *I did this shit already.* Ice-skating shows, the zoo, school plays, and double Dutch. She was burned out from doing everything with Toya. By the time Ariel got here, she was sick of everything. She was upset because her daughters were twelve years apart, so Ariel always got stuck with the short end of the stick. I try to take her out and I am more of a big sister to her than Toya because she has children of her own now. Their house phone rang. "Get that, please," Ariel said with her mouth full of food.

I picked up the phone. "Hello?"

"Hey, cousin, what's up?" Toya sang. "What are you doing there?"

"Me and your mom about to go shopping." My Aunt Connie came down the steps, waving her hands in front of her, whispering, "No, don't tell her." It was too late. I had already said something.

"Ooh, ask my mom, can y'all come and get me?" Toya said.

"Okay, hold on—I'll ask her." I gave my aunt the telephone. She took the telephone and handed it right back to me. I took the phone back and said, "Toya, she said she don't have time to come and get you."

"All right, then. My mom be tripping—she can come and get me. It's cool, though. Bye." I placed the cordless phone on the charger.

Without any guilt, my aunt said, "Come on. You ready?" while she put her coat on and we walked out of the door. "Make sure you call when you get to the movies and when y'all make it back to Angelique's house," she told Ariel.

"Yes, Mom. See you, Nadine."

"Bye. Have fun," I said as we walked out the front door.

Aunt Connie checked the door to make sure it was locked. "We taking your car or mine? We can take mine. That way, I can leave all my bags in the car."

We got in her 1999 Buick LeSabre. She took her coat off and adjusted her chair and said, "Nadine, remind me to buy some minutes for my phone," she said as she plugged her phone in the charger.

"You need to get a plan and stop wasting your money. I don't know why you got that stupid prepaid phone."

"I like my phone. I don't have to worry about having a thousand-dollar cell phone bill or getting cut off. I buy the minutes when I need them. My friend at work got Sprint and her phone gets cut off every other day," Aunt Connie said as she put on her seat belt and lifted the sun visor.

"But that doesn't make sense—you have to keep running to the store, getting cards."

"It makes sense to me," my aunt said as she handed me two hundred dollars.

"Thank you," I said.

"You're welcome."

"Buy yourself something nice, and buy that boyfriend of yours something."

"I thought I told you—I broke up with Erick."

"No, not Erick. I liked him—he was so nice."

"I just didn't know if he was the right one for me." I sighed.

"Girl, that man has a good job and no kids. You shouldn't have never let him go. Some woman going to find him, dust him off, and marry him before the summer."

"I don't care—she can have him." Changing the subject, I said, "Why didn't you want Toya to come with us?"

"Because she is going to spend all my money. Why, was she upset? She wanted to go. I guess I should go get her, huh? It is her daughter's birthday." She questioned me and answered her own question in the same breath. She picked up her cell phone and dialed Toya's number back.

"Toya, I'll come and get you. You better be ready, 'cause I'm not waiting for you. Who is going to watch the kids? Okay, I'll be there."

"Who's watching the kids?" I asked as we rode down the street.

"Nate."

"Really?" I said as I laughed.

"You know it is not funny. One day, Tony, the next day, Nate," she said as she took a deep breath. "She has to get herself together."

My cousin was a pimp. She has dealt with the same two guys for the last three years. The guys have fought and threatened each other, and she refuses to leave either one alone. She has a baby by both of them. It is hard when one of your male relatives stops dating a woman and she gets all attached to the family, but imagine two men fighting over who can come to the family reunion or cookout. Both trying to play the position of Toya's man. It is so funny.

She met Tony at her first and last semester of college,

and Nate is the childhood sweetheart. When she met Tony, the family almost gave her a party. Like, *Yes! No more bummy Nate*, but somehow Nate wiggled his way back in the picture, and now Toya got Monet by Nate and Destiny by Tony. Destiny is one and a half and Monet is four. Everybody likes Tony because he has a job and takes better care of his daughter. He is from Jamaica. Nate plays with the kids and cooks for them, but never keeps a job. He hardly does anything financially, but he is always available to watch them.

I'm pretty close to Toya. I don't have any girlfriends, just an aunt and a crazy cousin. Me and females don't get along. You probably heard it before, but most girls who say they don't like girls are girls who like being around men, because they are gay or out there. I'm neither, but even in high school, I was always fighting them. My last year of high school it got ugly. Mean girls to a whole other level.

We pulled up to Toya's apartment. We got out of the car and rang her bell, but she didn't answer. She lived in the lower-level apartment, so I knocked on her window. Her cream blinds were broken and bent on the edges. I could see Monet sitting on the sofa in her Dora the Explorer underwear with her hair sticking up. Little Destiny was lying on the carpet with a bottle in her arm. When they heard the knock, they jumped up and ran and got Toya. She came to the window and peeked through the mini-blinds. "One minute," she said, like we didn't just call her and tell her we were on our way.

Toya came to the door in tight red boy shorts and an oversize white t-shirt. She was incredibly thin. Toya is one of those people who could eat a whole extra-cheese pizza and never gain a pound. She was tall—five-eight—

with brown skin and long, natural, thick black hair that reached her shoulders.

"Toya, I told you to be ready," Aunt Connie yelled.

"Mom, I'm getting dressed!"

"It smells like cat in here," Aunt Connie said, sniffing around with her nose turned up.

"Oh, I know. I have to clean the litter box," she said as she went into the bathroom and dumped the litter box. She sprayed orange-blossom air freshener into the air. It covered the smell a little.

"Does it smell better?" she asked.

"Yes, now get dressed."

We sat down among the empty Bacardi Apple Twister bottles, a pizza box, and condom wrappers. *Well, at least she is protecting herself,* I thought. I tried to save my cousin some face and kicked the wrapper under the sofa.

"Nadine, I already saw it. I don't know who this girl is. She is not my daughter," my aunt said as she turned her head away from me in disgust. "Why couldn't you be my daughter, Nadine? You're more like me. You got a drive. Maybe Ariel will be a go-getter like us, 'cause that damn Toya don't want to do shit. Look at this place." My aunt loves bragging about me; she tells all her friends she raised me. When anyone asks about Toya, she will say, *Toya's okay, but do you know my stepson is a mortgage broker and my niece—you know, the one I raised—is a teacher.*

"She'll get herself together," I said.

"When? She can't decide on a man, a career, or anything else," she said, loud enough for Toya to hear her.

The kids ran back into the living room. They climbed up my Aunt Connie's legs. Monet had silver caps on her front teeth—too much sugar and drinking a bottle for too long. She had red, green, and yellow barrettes in her hair, and they clapped as she ran over to Aunt Connie. The girls gave us an impromptu booty dance. They were doing the tick and popping and locking. "I ain't no holler-back girl," they said as Monet did half of a flip. She was trying to follow her sister.

"Stop, Monet, before you break your neck," Aunt Connie shouted.

"Y'all were good," I said as I applauded them.

"Very good, now sit y'all butts down and watch TV." The kids had a seat and we continued to wait for Toya.

Finally Toya walked in the room with a tiny t-shirt that looked like it belonged to Monet. She didn't have a bra on, and was trying to put her hair in a ponytail.

"Where are you going with that t-shirt on?"

"What's wrong with my shirt?"

"You are not going out with me looking like that. Go put on a bra, and hurry up! I would like to leave!" Aunt Connie yelled.

Toya changed her shirt and put her little bomber jacket on. As we headed for the door, Destiny started crying. "I go with you, Granma."

"No, I'm going bye-bye," Aunt Connie said.

"Nate, come grab her—I'm trying to go to the store with my mom," Toya said. Nate came out with his boxer shorts on and said, "How you doing?" grabbed Destiny, and shut the door.

We all got in the car.

"Where we going?" Toya asked. Aunt Connie didn't want to tell her she had money, but somehow Toya already knew.

"Mom, can I borrow, like, a hundred dollars?"

"No!"

"Mom, why you frontin'? You know you got money."

"How you know I have money?"

"You gave Ariel a hundred dollars."

"So what? Ariel is thirteen. How are you going shopping if you don't have any money?" It was obvious that Toya was on her freebie mission. Whenever one of us got money, we would always treat to a restaurant or a little shopping trip. It was mostly me and my aunt taking each other out and Toya coming along for the ride.

"Is there a Wachovia Bank around here?" Aunt Connie asked.

"Why?"

"Because I need to use the ATM machine to get more money."

"There is an ATM machine right there in that gas station," I pointed out.

"I'm not using another bank—they are going to charge two dollars!" I looked at my aunt like she was crazy. "You're going to spend two dollars' worth of gas riding over to the bank."

"I just don't like giving my money away," she insisted.

"I think they take only fifty cents." She went into the gas station and came out scratching a lottery ticket. She had no problem giving her money away to the lottery, though.

We went to the King of Prussia Mall. I didn't need anything else, but I still found myself in the shoe department of Bloomingdale's. Sometimes I don't like shopping with my aunt because she was always trying to search and dig for sales. I don't have any time for the clearance rack. I like this-season clothes and shoes. I'm going to spend this two-hundred-plus to do some damage to my credit cards.

We took the shopping experience down a notch and hit the Target. I loved Target; they had everything. I bought towels and a digital camera. After Target, it was on to my other favorite store: the dollar store. This was

a place I loved and hated. I loved that everything was so
cheap and that you could walk out of the store with a lot
of bags and only spend twenty-five dollars, but I hated
the fact that some people thought it was the damn super-
market. Spending a hundred dollars in the dollar store
and tying the line up. Toya filled her cart up. I didn't say
anything. I wasn't paying for her stuff.

"Mom, I need some more money."

"What, you mean to tell me you been laying up with
that man and don't have money to get something out
the dollar store?"

"Mom."

"Don't Mom me. You ask me, you ask your father and
everybody else for something. But scared to ask that
man you sleep with."

"Mom, stop playing."

"I'm not playing with you. If you don't have a dollar you better get it. Shit, when I was single and
young, I didn't play that shit. A man couldn't even be
in my face without some money."

"We just paid the rent, Mom," Toya whined.

"Girl, you owe me," she said as she placed a fifty in
her hand.

After shopping, I went home by myself. My house
was a spacious, two-bedroom house. It was a three bedroom house, but the previous owner knocked the divid-
ing wall out for extra space. One room was my office/
dressing room/closet. I kept all my grades, my computer, my rows and rows of shoes in there. I ran out of
closet space, so I had to buy extra portable closets. I
took off my clothes and ran a hot bath. I checked my
voice mail—Erick was on there a few times telling me
how much he loved me and didn't want us to be over. I
erased them. I was already just enjoying being alone. It
felt so good to have all my pillows to myself. I spread my
legs across the bed and stretched my legs wide open. I

was single and loving it. And now that I'm single, I can go out and have fun and not check in with anyone. I'm beautiful, fun, sexy, and I don't mind paying for a date with a guy I like. So I should have no problem finding Erick's replacement.

Chapter 6

Shonda

Tae called me up and asked me, did I want to go out with her to get garlic Dungeness crabs from this bar around her way called Scooter's.

"No, Malik wants to chill—we went to the movies the other night."

"Yo, you tripping. I would not be staying in the house for no man."

"He ain't *some man*. Let me talk to you later, okay?" I said, irritated as I disconnected the call. Tae is so jealous of my relationship with Malik. She really misses our days going out. I missed them, too, but she had to understand that I have a man, and every time there was a party, I couldn't just jump up and go. She goes out all the time, but once she gets a man she won't be worried about me. She is going through a little drought; I need to find her a man. Then she will understand that I can't run the street like I used to. I felt a little guilty for not being there for my girl, though. She was always there for me when I needed her. I didn't want to completely neglect her. It was still early, only eight o'clock. Malik wasn't here yet, and Bree was with Brian. Maybe I could go out with her real fast. I looked real quick at the clock in the kitchen. Even though I was really tired, I called Tae back and told her I would go. She was so happy. If I go out with her, she'll find a man and won't be mad at me. Then I called Malik to fill him in on my plans.

"Malik, what you about to do?" I asked.

"I was going to hang out with Jarrod for a minute. Why?"

"I think I'm about to go out with Tae real quick. Okay?"

"Go ahead. I'll see you in the house later on," he said.

"I love you, baby," I said.

"Love you, too!"

I met up with Tae at her mom's house. I beeped the horn once and Tae came out in jeans, timbs, and a black leather jacket. She had a sandy brown short weave that went with her complexion.

"I just need to meet a man. I want to be in love. I want to get married," she said, once in my car.

"What, get married?"

"Yeah, girl, it's time. I need to settle down."

"It will happen. You got to take your time."

"It's not happening fast enough," she pouted.

"You weren't like this before. What is happening to you? Why are you so caught up with having a man?" I asked, looking over at her.

"I don't know. I just want a husband. I'm looking around and all my friends are settling down."

"Well, calm down—maybe you'll meet your husband tonight."

Judging by the bar scene, Tae was probably not going to meet her man. It was a bunch of regulars hanging around on a Wednesday night. I don't know how many new people Tae thought she might run into in a neighborhood bar. Everybody in the bar was real laid-back—smoking cigarettes and eating fried fish and Dungeness garlic crabs. I wasn't drinking since I had to work in the morning, so I ordered a Coke with lemon. An older man with gray hair and young clothes on approached Tae. I knew she was about to shoot him down real fast. But to my surprise, she gave him conversation.

"How are you, sexy?" he asked by sliding up beside us.

"I'm fine," Tae smiled. Why Tae was giving that Pop-Pop the time of day, I didn't know. He was old and disgusting with a big, gray beard. He looked like Papa Smurf. He pulled out his cell phone and began to enter the telephone number Tae had given him. When he walked away, I said, "Tae, I know you gave him the wrong number."

"No, I gave him the right one."

"What? That old man?" I said, turning my lips up.

"Look, maybe that's what I need, a sugar daddy to take care of me," she said, sipping a piña colada.

"You are tripping," I said in disgust.

"No, I'm not. That old man might teach me something. Or I might teach him something new, like some butt action."

"I'll be twenty-eight and I never took it there."

"You don't know what you missing, girl. Don't knock it till you try it."

"That's so nasty. I'm not missing nothing," I said.

"Girl, it feels better than the front."

"I won't ever find out." I began to clench my cheeks together at the thought.

Once again I was at work trying to summon some business. "Hi, this is Shonda Robinson from Mancinni

Ford. I was calling to tell you that you are approved for a new car." The customer on the other end of the phone said thanks, but they already had a car. Then I saw Mr. Rivera, my customer from the other day, and he didn't look happy. He approached me so fast I couldn't get up and run to the bathroom.

"Yeah, Shonda, you sold me this car and my engine went last night!" he shouted across the showroom floor.

I walked over to him. "Please have a seat and let me find my manager," I said, looking around for help.

"My engine is done. And you want to know the reason I didn't know it? Huh? You want to know why I didn't know something was wrong with my car? I'll tell you why. Because your mechanic took out the bulb for the check-engine light," he screamed at the top of his lungs. He ranted on and on, shouting, "I called Saturday and you were closed." All the customers were listening to what Mr. Rivera said, rethinking their decision to buy a car from us. I tried to calm Mr. Rivera down and do damage control. He was fuming mad and I didn't know what to do. I went to get management so they could sort everything out. Lester came out and took him in his office. I can't keep going through this kind of drama on a daily basis. I sighed.

"Shonda Robinson, you have a call on line four." I picked up the phone, and it was Brianna.

"Hi, Mommy."

"Hi, Bree."

"Mom, Daddy said I'm coming home tonight, but I want to stay with him. Andrea is going to take me to the pet store. They are buying me a dog."

"You don't want to come home with me?"

"No, I want to get my dog, Mommy. Please. Please."

"All right. Well, I'll see you tomorrow," I said, disappointed my daughter was choosing a dog over me.

"Okay, bye, Mommy. I love you."

*   *   *

Today was my day off. I didn't have to get Bree ready
for school, and Malik had already left for work. I snuggled under the covers since I had nowhere to be today,
and I couldn't have been happier. I'd probably clean
the house and go to the market and catch up on my
laundry. I hated cleaning, cooking, and all that domes-
ticated stuff. I wish I had a maid. Instead of wishing, I
took a load out of the dryer and put one in. While fold-
ing my clothes, the phone rang. I ran upstairs to answer
it.

"What you doing today?" Tae asked

"Nothing. Why, what's up?" I asked.

"Ride with me downtown."

"Why? Where you going?"

"To pick up this application, and I don't feel like paying for parking or getting a ticket."

"All right, come and get me," I said.

Tae picked me up in a new Toyota Solara.

"Tae, this is nice. I didn't know you rented a car."

"You like it?"

"Yeah, this is real cute. How long you keeping it to?"

"It's mine."

"Really?"

"Yup—you remember Pop-Pop from the bar last
week?"

"Yeah."

"He gave me the down payment. And he is going to
pay the $479 a month."

"And what if he doesn't pay for it?" I asked.

"He is going to pay for it—he is crazy about me."

"Why didn't you come and get a car from me?"

"It was spur-of-the-moment. He took me to the Toyota dealership and was, like *Pick out a car.*"

"Okay, baller."

"Plus, I don't want one of those lemons you be selling."

"So where are you trying to work at anyway?" I questioned Tae as we exited the Schuylkill Expressway.

"Working at the prison."

"Doing what?" I asked as I rifled her CD collection. I found an Amerie CD and put number six on.

"As a guard."

"A prison guard? You not going to be scared?"

"No, Donate's girlfriend said you make good money and you can get overtime."

"I need to put in an application, too! Because I hate my job. Working on commission is starting to become the worst. I got deals falling through and customers looking for me."

Tae laughed and said, "Well, as far as I know, it is sweet. You just got to take a test—then they call you back and you go for training for six weeks."

"It's paid training?"

"Yup, and your benefits begin after sixty days."

I decided I was going to apply, too.

We entered the Municipal Service Building across from City Hall. We had to fill the applications out right there. Tae went and put a few more quarters in our parking meter. I sat down and began filling out the application. I had to lie on a couple of answers. I didn't remember any of my previous jobs' dates or I wasn't there long enough for them to count. The next question was, Could we contact your current employer? *Hell no,* I thought. I looked up and saw that Tae was still filling out her name and address. Ten minutes later, I completed my application and handed it in. The woman said I should receive something in the mail about the testing process. I told Tae I would go check the meter to make sure she didn't get a ticket. Too late—she already had one.

Chapter 7

Nadine

I was at school Thursday morning. One more day and it would be the weekend. I couldn't wait. I was going to go home and just relax. I was writing on the board to read chapters 14 and 15. By the time the students finish both chapters and we go over the lesson, it would be time for lunch.

"Stop talking," I said as I surveyed the room to find the talking students.

"I was asking her if I could hold her sharpener."

"Raise your hand if you are finished." Nobody raised their hand.

"Okay, nobody is finished, so I don't want to hear any talking."

"Ms. Clark, can I go to the bathroom?" Erica asked. I told her she could go. She rose out of her seat and ran out of the classroom. I sat back down and looked around the classroom to see if I had any talkers. Erica came back in and had a seat.

"I'm finished, Ms. Clark," another student, Samara, said. I went over to check her paper. In her mind, she thought she was doing the greatest thing by hurrying through her assignment. Half of it was wrong. I circled half of the page and told her to take her time and do it over. She sat back down.

"Ms. Clark, I need you now." I walked to the door to see what Mrs. Meyers, the nosey science teacher, wanted.

"Yes, Mrs. Meyers. What's the emergency?"

"Okay, we have a definite problem."

"What's that?" I asked as I stepped out of the door.

"Mrs. Ramos quit."

"What? Did you tell Mr. Mitchell?"

"Yes."

"So why are you here?"

"We have to split the kids."

"Split what kids?" I asked in disbelief.

"Her class for the rest of the day. Only for today—Mr. Mitchell has a sub coming in tomorrow." Just what I needed: twelve more students to add to my twenty-eight. Mrs. Ramos's students dragged their desks into my classroom. It was thirty minutes before lunch. Friday, please hurry up and come.

Friday was here. Hallelujah! I stopped and grabbed a big tea. I had a feeling that Mr. Mitchell wasn't going to find a substitute, and I was going to have twelve extra students in my room. I walked into my classroom and my assumption was right. It was crowded. Students were popping gum, standing on their chairs, and playing Game Boys and listening to Walkmans.

"Everybody put everything away. Pull out your social studies workbook," I shouted. All of my students except for one put their Walkmans away. I walked over to the lanky boy and said, "Tyreek, give me the Walkman." I put my hand out to reach for it.

"I'm going to put it away, Ms. Clark," he said as he put the Walkman in his desk.

"Everybody turn to page 284."

Again, everybody was doing what he or she was told, except for Tyreek. He was now playing with Yugioh cards and letting the Walkman play under his desk. I crept up on him and snatched the Walkman. He tried to jump back and said, "Yo, man, you better give me my Walkman back."

"And if I don't?" I asked as I lifted the Walkman high enough so that he couldn't reach it. Tyreek was pouting as he sat down. I tried to begin the class again. Before I could get turned to the right page, I heard Tyreek at it again.

"What are you looking at?" he screamed at Dana.

So then Dana said, "I'm looking at you, you black monkey."

Tyreek jumped up and tried to hit Dana. Before he could reach her, I grabbed him, guiding him back to his seat, and said again, "Now turn to page 284."

"I'll bang you, bitch. Keep playing with me," Tyreek said while cracking his knuckles at Dana.

"You will bang who?" I had had enough of Tyreek for one day.

"I'll bang her *and* you," he yelled as he walked out of the classroom. I made a call to the office. The secretary answered the telephone.

"Office—this is Mrs. Tuner, how may I help you?"

"Where is Mr. Mitchell? Tell him that Tyreek Freeman walked out of my classroom."

"Do you know where he is?"

"No."

"Okay, I'll tell Mr. Mitchell."

I hung up and went on with my lesson. "Start reading, Aniya," I said. As she began reading and the class somewhat got in order, the phone rang.

"Hello," I answered.

"I need to speak to Ms. Clark," a voice shouted.

"Yes, who's speaking? This is she."

"This is Tyreek Freeman's mother. All I want to know is, did you put your hands on my child?" The woman caught me by surprise. I told her to hold and took the call outside the classroom. I stretched the phone cord as far as I could out the door.

"Hello?"

"Yeah, I asked you a question. Did you put your hands on my child?" I could see her neck snapping and going side to side, through the phone.

"Excuse me. No, I did not put my hands on your child. Your son disrupted the class and then he said he was going to bang me."

"What did you do to him?" she asked, like there was a reason that could justify him for threatening his teacher. I was not going to bother rationalizing with the woman. I told her I was conducting a class, and if she wanted to speak to me she could make an appointment.

At lunch I went to the office, where there were phones ringing and students sitting, waiting to be disciplined. There were blue mints sitting on the counter, and I grabbed one and waited for Mr. Mitchell. Most days he was usually very understanding. I hope today he would understand that I could not tolerate Tyreek Freeman anymore.

"Ms. Clark, are you waiting for me?" he asked, grabbing papers out of the holder outside his door.

"Yes," I said as I stood up. He instructed me to come in. The moment he closed the door, I said, "Mr. Mitchell, I can't take it. Get him out of my class!"

"Who?"

"Tyreek Freeman—he said he is going to bang me. The mother? She doesn't think he does anything wrong. And I'm not going to be disrespected."

"Can you just deal with it for the rest of the school year? I really don't want to move him. I'll give him a three-day and get Mom in here and we will see what we can do and we will talk. Okay?" he asked as he took his eyeglasses off and scratched his head. I didn't agree or disagree. I guess that was good enough for now. Nothing was really accomplished by our conversation. *Mr. Mitchell better do something*, I thought. I walked out of the office, grabbing another mint before I left.

Toya asked me to go out with her on a Wednesday night to this reggae club. I hate reggae music. I don't know what the hell they saying. To me, reggae is just fast-talking noise with a good beat.

We went to Olde City. It's a part of town where all races and ethnicities hang out. There are rows of restaurant bars and taverns. We entered the bar and had a seat. I noticed Toya's stomach and told her she better start doing some sit-ups. She had a little gut sticking out of her skinny frame.

"I know," she said while acknowledging her stomach. She ordered a drink and gestured for me to come over where she was standing. She handed me another drink.

I noticed there were a few all-right-looking brothers. The first one who made eye contact with me was smiling super-extra hard. I wanted to walk up to him and ask him, "Do you know me? Why you keep looking at me? You don't know me, so turn around."

"Hey, beautiful." A brown-complexioned brother approached and attempted to grab my hand. His teeth were crooked and his lips were chapped. I walked away like I didn't know he was talking to me. The next guy who approached looked okay, but then he opened his mouth. His voice was weak and squeaky like a little girl. He asked, "Is this seat taken?"

I looked him right in his face and said, "Yes, it is. K-I-M. Keep it moving."

I was tired of the men that I didn't want coming up and saying something. I decided I was going to go up to someone I was interested in and say hello. There he was: Mr. Dark Chocolate with Caramel in the Middle. His face was clean-shaven and he had a mustache. I accidentally brushed against him, letting my firm breast rub against his back. He turned around. His smile looked even better up close. About two inches separated our bodies.

"Sorry about that," I said as I smiled and tried to conceal my intentions.

"It's okay."

"No, sorry. I'm going to have to make it up to you. What are you drinking?"

"Oh, so you're going to buy me a drink?" He took a long look around the bar. "Really? I'm Quentin, and you?"

"Nadine. Here is my number. Call me and we'll talk," I said as I paid for his Heineken and walked away. I was on my way to find Toya when I saw the man from earlier who kept looking at me like he knew me. This time he came up to me and touched my waist.

"Do you know me?"

"No, but I would like to get to know you. I'm Demetrius and I have been looking at you all night. I saw you walking toward the door—are you about to leave?"

"No, not yet."

"Well, dance with me." Demetrius pulled me to the dance floor and pulled me closer to him. I loved his assertiveness. Our bodies swayed as we danced off the hypnotic beat. A woman's voice was singing about waiting for her man to come home. After our dance, we exchanged numbers.

* * *

By the time the night was over, I had met three guys. Quentin was extra sexy, and with guys named Jermaine and Demetrius added to the list, I should have dates for the rest of the week.

Monday morning was business as usual. I didn't want to go in to class, but if I didn't show up, who would? I began writing my lesson on the board as the students began coming in and unpacking. Tyreek Freeman was back, and a man was with him. The man approached me and said, "Excuse me, can I see you in the hallway?"

"Sure, one moment," I said as I instructed my class to pull out their journals. I stepped out of the classroom and closed the door behind me.

"How can I help you?" I asked as a nosey student walked by.

"I just wanted to talk to you and apologize for Tyreek's behavior. Listen, Ms. Clark, I know my wife gets slick with her mouth sometimes. But you're not going to have any more problems out of this boy the rest of the year—is she, Reek?" He turned to his son and stared at him.

"No," Tyreek said as he held his head down.

"No, what?" his father asked as he moved closer to his face.

"No, sir," he said, looking down at the ground.

"Look at her and tell her that you are sorry for disrespecting her."

Tyreek looked at me and repeated what his father had said. His father put his hands up like he was about to grab and shake him but held back and said, "Ms. Clark, one phone call. One phone call is all it takes. Don't call my wife—she lets him get away with too much shit. Call me. I'll be up here."

"Okay, I will," I said. The class was on the other side of the door, listening intently. Mr. Big and Bad Tyreek was crying. This was the perfect time to embarrass him, but I didn't. I felt sorry for him. As soon as his father turned the hall corner, I told him to go to the bathroom and get himself together and then come back to class.

I went home and turned on *Oprah,* while I made out my lesson plan for the next week.

The phone rang, and I answered it and heard Erick saying, "Hey baby I miss you. Can I come over?"

I thought about it for a minute. I could let him come over and spend the night, but then he will think we are back together and I don't want to confuse him.

"I don't think that is a good idea." I said.

"Why not? I miss you."

"No, not right now, Erick. I have to go. I'm doing something," I said as I went back to my lesson plan. He called me right back, but I turned the ringer off.

Chapter 8

Kim

My district manager was getting on my last damn nerves. She was spending too much time in my office monitoring my every move like she is the C.I.A. She was riding me for no reason, saying that she had to check on a few accounts. I was fed up fucking with her *and* my job. I didn't say anything else to her, I just grabbed my bag and car keys and went toward the door.

"Where are you going?" she asked. *You know everything. So you should know why and where I'm going,* I thought.

"I'm taking an early day."

I went home, turned the heat on, and sat on the sofa and opened my bills. I paid everything regularly. My gas bill was three hundred dollars for one month. That was ridiculous! I wanted to wash clothes, but I didn't feel like doing anything else. Not a dish! I went upstairs and got in the bed. What I needed was a nap—a nice, cozy nap. Then I'd wake up and get the boys. I went upstairs and turned the television on because its blare usually puts me at ease. I took off all my clothes and tossed them across the room.

A show called *Amazing Love* was on. The show was about couples who overcame barriers for love. I started to have the show at me and Malik's wedding. I'm glad I didn't. This episode was about a couple who had met in the tenth grade. They were separated for ten years, but recently reunited. They both thought about each other over the course of ten years. The wedding was at their old school's gym where they had their first dance. It was so nauseating. Then they let the doves out at the end of the ceremony. I had had it. I was going to do that at my wedding, but I didn't get a chance. Seeing the white, angelic, peaceful birds fly reminded me of my wedding that never was. I got instantly sick; it triggered something. "Good for fucking you," I said as I threw the remote at the television.

I don't know what happened, but I kept repeating the same phrase. "How could you, Malik? How could you, Malik?" Tears streamed down my face. I snapped out of it and went into the bathroom and looked at my reflection in the mirror. My light brown hair was standing up as if I had been shocked.

"Malik, how could you? Whhhhhhhhy, Malik? Why you had to do this to me? I did everything you asked me to do. Why, why, why, Malik? I didn't deserve this. I was a good woman to you. I did everything. Everything you asked, I did. All I wanted was for you to be good to me, be honest." My head was throbbing. I couldn't think. I looked in the medicine cabinet and took a few Tylenol. I went and lay down. I would get the broken glass up later. I set my alarm for five. I could sleep for three hours. I would then pick up Kevin after school and Kayden from daycare. I just needed to rest a little. *I will feel much better when I awake,* I told myself before I shut the world out.

* * *

It was dark outside when I awoke. It was not just-got-dark, it was pitch-black-dark. I searched around my bed for my cell phone. When I finally found it, I flipped it open. The time read 7:08. I jumped out of bed and grabbed my bag and keys and raced out the door. I put the key in the ignition when my phone rang.

"Where are you?" my mother asked.

"Mommy, I can't talk. I have to pick up the kids."

"I have them. I picked them up. Their schools called me. It was either me go get them or DHS."

"They're okay? Thanks, Mom," I said as I sighed with relief.

"Kimberly Vanessa Brown, I wish you would really snap out of it. You are a strong girl. You can overcome anything. This is nothing."

"Mom, I'm okay. I just was sleepy. I fell asleep and my alarm didn't go off."

"I don't care how sleepy you are. How do you forget to pick up your children? What is wrong with you?"

"I don't know what happened, Mom."

"You shouldn't never let a man break you. You're better than that. Can you hear me?"

"Yes, I hear you," I said.

"We'll be there in a few moments."

A few minutes later the boys were running through the door. My mom used the spare key I had given her to get in.

"Mommy, Mommy," they screamed. They both came up to me, hugging me. My mother gave me a look-over and shook her head.

"Give me a call if you need me. I wish you would go see Dr. Burrows." I walked my mother to the door. Then I fixed the boys a frozen pizza and we watched television before going to bed. I was so happy they were safe. I don't know what I would do without them. I was mad at myself for oversleeping, but thankful because I did get some rest. I felt a little better.

The next morning, I dropped the boys off at school and headed for work. I thought about my life. How nobody cared about me. How I was a loser with my kids and work. *Nobody cares about you. You weren't good enough to marry. You're not a good mother. You're not nothing,* I kept thinking to myself. I dialed my mother to get the number for Dr. Burrows—maybe I did need to talk to him. I pulled over and just started crying. I couldn't stop. Traffic was passing me, and cars were beeping their horns, but I couldn't move. I was immobile—I couldn't move my legs, they were so heavy. I remember my mother begging me to go to the hospital and for me to call her when I arrived there. Then there was a loud crash. I still had my cell phone in my hand. My mother was yelling, "What's going on, Kim? Are you okay?" I got out of my car. My car was not damaged. A man came running toward me, saying, "Are you on drugs?" I didn't know what to say or do—I just kept crying. Did I look like I was on drugs? I caught a glance at myself through the window—maybe I did. I didn't look my best. Apparently I did look like a drug user because the police came and said I had to go to the district so they could check my drug and alcohol level.

"Have you been drinking, miss?"

"No."

"Do you do drugs?"

"No."

"How did you run into a parked car?"

"I was talking to my mother. I need to talk to my mother."

"Are you okay?" the officer asked.

"No, I am not," I said as I attempted to stand, and stumbled.

"Would you like to speak to someone about the feelings you are having?" the officer said in a real calm tone, like I was crazy.

"What feelings? No, I'm fine. I need to speak to my mother." They gave me the phone and allowed me to contact my family. But my mind was clouded, I couldn't think of anybody's number. "I'm so sorry, I'm so sorry," I kept saying aloud. The police officer said they were going to take me for a ride and go to the hospital. I'm thinking, *I'm not sick. What can the hospital do for me?* Then I saw a sign that read MENTAL HEALTH. I opened my eyes so I could see better. I walked through the doors and they shut behind me. There was a guard to my left, and the door was locked. Once you were in, there was no way out.

A nurse came in with a mixture of brown and gray hair in a bun. She handed me a hospital gown and said, "Remove all your clothes." I was reluctant until she said *or she would have someone remove them for me.* She took my clothes and I became petrified.

"What are you doing with my clothes?"

"You get them back after the doctor has seen you."

I sat in a white room with nothing but a chair and a bed in it. While waiting for the doctor to come, my imagination got the best of me. My mind started racing. *What if they commit me? What if the doctor thinks that I am crazy? What if I am crazy and I don't know that I'm crazy? Kim, you are not crazy, and you have to let the world and this doctor know that you are not crazy.*

I peeked out the door and down the hallway. There were real crazy people out there. One older white man was smacking and hitting things that weren't there. His robe was hanging open, exposing his droopy underwear. Another kept trying to chew on the side of her cheek like a dog. I was so scared. If I thought I was crazy,

I knew now I wasn't crazy. I was very sane, and I had to get out of there. I wanted to go home. I wanted to get my life together. My sons needed me. I have to leave.

The female doctor entered the room. She didn't look old enough to drive, let alone be a doctor. She had deep, dark olive skin and black hair, French-braided.

"Any history of mental illness in your family?" she asked with an accent.

"No," I answered quickly, but then I thought of my dad, who was sick in a V.A. hospital. I rephrased my answer.

"Well, yes, my dad was in the military and he suffers from mental illness, but only because of the chemicals from the war." As the young doctor wrote something on her clipboard, I stood up and said, "Listen, I'm not crazy." Me saying I wasn't crazy probably confirmed that I was.

"You're not?"

"No, I'm not. I, I just can't take all the pressure that's building up on me anymore. I do everything without any help."

"Everything like what?"

"Everything. Take the kids to school, pick them up, homework, ironing clothes, dishes, trash—you name it, I do it. And when I try to talk to my family about it, they say, *So what?* I tell them I need a break, but nobody gives me one. I'm always stuck with my kids. They are with me from the time I wake up to the time I go to sleep. The only time I get a break is when I'm at work. And that's another story. They will just say something like, *You are not the first person to raise children alone.* And I just need help. I'm not crazy. I just need a break. I swear to you," I said as tears began streaming down my face. I continued, "I'm not crazy at all. I never think about hurting myself or my kids. It's just, I've been having a hard time since my son's father left me at our wedding. I love my life—not my circumstances, though. Some days I can't stay up; others, I stay up all night and can't go to sleep. I didn't mean to hit that car. I don't know what's wrong with me. I've been having really bad headaches and been very sleepy."

"Your headaches are probably coming from stress. Listen, I don't think you are crazy. You do not belong in here. However, I am going to suggest that you seek out-patient care. I'm going to refer you to a psychiatrist. Every day we bottle up things that we need to get out of our mind and system. And sometimes talking about them relieves us of all the stress that we have inside. I'm going to also give you a prescription for Lexapro and Ambien to help you sleep. Do you have someone who can watch your children?"

"Yes, I'll find someone. I'll pay someone." I wanted to say anything to get out of this place.

"Well, I suggest that you don't return to work for a few days and just take it easy. The nurse will bring in your clothes."

"Thank you," I said as I waited for the nurse to bring my belongings.

I was released after I was given my prescriptions and signed a release form. I called my mom and she said she would meet me at my house. I caught a cab back to my car. I tried to think about everything that happened. *What could be bottled up inside of me? I released all my pain from Malik. I think. I cried every tear that I am going to cry for him. Who knows?* I thought to myself as I drove toward my house.

"So what's the verdict?" my mom asked as I walked in the door.

"The doctor said I had a mental breakdown."

"Those doctors don't know what they are talking

about. You are in control. That's why it is called mental mind over matter. What I do want is for you to take it easy."

"I have been."

"No, you haven't. I'll come over and help you. And we have to teach Kevin how to do something like dishes."

"He's too young."

"No, he is not. It is time to put him to work. So you can get a break."

Chapter 9

Shonda

I got a card in the mail to take the exam. Me and Tae went to the test site, and it was a whole lot of people out there. *We ain't never going to get this job if all these people are our competition.* It was old and young, white, Hispanic, Asian, and black. Everybody was trying to get a new job. It was like I was back in school, taking a city or statewide test. I think I did really good; it was really easy. They gave us two hours and I took the test in forty-five minutes. After I finished, I checked my answers twice. Tae was still taking the test, so I whispered to her that I would call her later. I went home and spent some time with Bree.

I walked into the bathroom and I smelled my Paris Hilton perfume—it was strong. "Did you spray my perfume, Bree?"

"No."

"Don't lie," I said as I sniffed her clothing. "Yes, you did."

"Andrea lets me spray her perfume."

"Brianna, I don't care what Andrea lets you do. You

keep telling me what they let you do over there. Daddy has his rules and Mommy has hers. You understand?"

"Yes," she said, tilting her head down toward the floor.

"Now go get dressed so we can go to the hairdresser."

I knew how to do Brianna's hair, but most times I left it up to the professionals. It was very thick and long. I didn't have the patience or time to deal with it.

I started going to a new salon not too far from our house. It wasn't the most stylish salon—the hair stylist of the moment didn't work there. I liked the shop because it wasn't a fashion show or car show outside the shop. No "such and such is balling. Look, she mess with the boaw and his car is outside." Nobody cared what I was wearing, and most importantly, I didn't sit half of the day to be styled. My new stylist, Cece, was about my age and into church. She didn't gossip or ask me about my business, and she didn't mind tackling Bree's hair. Most importantly, my hair always looked great when I left her chair.

I sat in the waiting area and flipped through a *Glamour* magazine. Brianna's face was into her Cheetah Girls book.

"I'm ready for you, Shonda," Cece yelled across the salon. She was wearing a black cape with her name embroidered on it. Her tattoo with a pair of scissors and barber clippers decorated her arm. Big Cece was in parentheses.

"How you been?" I asked.

"I'm good," she replied as she pumped the bottom of my chair up with her foot. "Okay, girl, what have you been doing to your hair? When was the last time you had a perm?"

"I put one in myself, like, two days ago."

"And before that, when did you put a perm in?" she asked.

"Like last month."

"Shonda, your hair is overprocessed. You have to cut this mess."

"But I don't like short hair on me."

Cece was looking and acting like cutting my hair wasn't debatable. I was sure she could just curl it. I didn't want to cut my hair. It was just starting to grow and getting to a multipurpose length. I could get ponytails, wraps, rods. There was no way I was going to cut my hair.

"Cece, I'm not cutting my hair."

"You have to!"

"How much?" I asked, seeing that no was not an option.

"This much," she replied firmly with one hand on her hip and the other hand in the form of a large C.

Parting my hair, Cece snapped, "Your hair is overprocessed. You have been putting perms in your hair every month. Your hair doesn't need to be permed that often. And on top of that, you put a permanent black dye in. It is all damaged. It all has to go."

"You can't save it?" I begged.

"No! It's only hair—it will grow back and this time it will be healthy." Cece seemed like she was getting irritated by me. She did good hair, so I would have a cute short style. My hair would look like the singer Fantasia. Or maybe like Halle Berry when she wears her hair short. With that, she got to chopping. She said she was making my hair healthy, but I felt so ugly. When she was done she handed me a mirror. I took a look in the mirror and almost cried. I tried to hold back my tears. When she said she wanted to cut my hair I should have got up and left. She slapped some mousse in my two-inch spiked hair and said, "It even looks nice like this— just short and wild." The other stylists were cosigning for her, agreeing with her that my hair looked good. To me it looked messed up.

"No, I think I'll get it curled," I murmured as I viewed my hair at different angles in the mirror. Every which way, it looked a fucking mess.

After the hair salon I took Bree to get her nails polished while I got acrylic tips and a pedicure. I looked in the mirror in the nail salon, and my hair still looked ugly. I should have known better. *I don't understand; she does medium-length hair so good and short hair so bad.* But she hadn't mastered the art of short hair because my hair looked a hot-damn mess.

I couldn't let Malik see my hair looking like this. He would laugh at me, then leave me. On my way home I took a scarf and put it over my hair. At every light I glimpsed my hair in the rearview mirror. Luckily, Malik wasn't home yet. I had time to get in the bed and pretend to be asleep before he came in.

"I thought you went to the hairdresser," Malik said as he entered the bedroom.

"I did." I said, acting like I was too sleepy to talk.

"So why do you have a scarf on?"

"Because she messed my hair up," I said, looking up from my fake sleep.

"You are exaggerating. You always don't like your hair, and then it grows on you. Let me see," he said as he pulled at the scarf on my head.

"No," I exclaimed.

"I won't laugh, let me see," he said.

"No, I'm going to sleep—turn off the light."

I awoke and my scarf was off of my hair. I felt around for the scarf and I tried to cover my hair before Malik came out of the bathroom.

"I already saw your hair. It is short. What made you cut it that short?" he asked as he brushed his teeth.

"It was breaking off and she said I had to." Malik said just what I thought he'd say. Nothing. He didn't say it looked good. He said it will grow back.

I looked at my hair again on my way to work. I looked like a major butch. I wouldn't be surprised if girls started asking me what was up. I looked so ugly. I just didn't feel feminine or sexy enough. I tried to put some eye shadow on, and I bought some long, dangling earrings, but nothing was making this hair work.

I had just picked Bree up from Brian's when Malik called me. "Baby, you want to watch the fight at Jarrod's? Then later we can go get drinks?"

"No, Malik. I look a mess," I said.

"Baby, you look good. It's not that bad—trust me."

"Let me see if I can do something with my hair. I'll call you back." I had to do something. I wanted to look good. When me and Malik were out, I liked to look dressed-up and sexy. I liked him to be proud to have me on his arm. I spotted Bree in the backseat, looking at my hair. Then she said, "Mom, won't you get a wig? Andrea—" she stopped before completing her sentence.

"That's a good idea, Bree." I immediately went to a beauty-supply store in search of a wig. I walked inside and mannequin heads were evenly lined against the wall with expressionless smirks on their faces. Each had a wig set on top of it, ranging from Dolly Parton white-blond to short, curly Afros. I was greeted by a young woman with a long brown-and-auburn wig on. The girl said hello and asked me, was I looking for a wig? I told her I was. Then she informed me that I had to buy a wig cap for a dollar if I wanted to try on a wig. I gave her a dollar and then tried on a bunch of ugly, wiggy-looking wigs. Most of them looked synthetic or were too thick. Then I found a basic, plain black wig that looked just like my hair before it was cut. After I left the wig store, I went to pick up a sweater and matching boots.

I dropped Bree back with Brian and headed to Jarrod's house. Malik should have come home so we could have driven in one car. I waited outside in the car until he got there.

"Your hair looks good," he said as he kissed me. Jarrod had a girlfriend now. Her name was Heather, and she was older. She was a registered nurse dating his bum butt. He had just purchased a duplex. He was living on the second floor and renting out the storefront. He had cleaned up his act a little, but to me he was still a bum. We used to be cool, but now I don't really care for him. I caught him staring all the time. And it was not a lustful stare. It was like I stole his boy away from him. He was probably jealous of the relationship I had with Malik. I didn't know, but it was something up.

We sat and watched the fight. Javier knocked out Palmer in the third round. We drank and played cards for a little while. I wanted to ask Heather her age so bad. I knew she had to be at least thirty-eight. She could pass for about ten years younger. She was thin, but proportioned properly. Nothing was sagging and everything was sitting up. Actually, she made me feel bad, being twenty-seven and looking the way I did. I have never been fat; I am a comfortable size 12, but looking at her body made me want to work out. "I never thought I'd see you settle down, man," Malik said.

"Hey, all you need is a good woman to lead you right. One day you will have that," he said as he kissed Heather on the top of her head. I didn't like how he said that. He didn't think I had caught on to that. *Shut up—she's just old, and any man will do. I don't like you, Jarrod,* I thought as I gave him a fake smirk. We stayed for about two more hours, but I had been ready to go.

"I don't think you should drive home," Heather said.

"We're cool—I do this all the time," Malik answered. "I didn't drink that much."

"Okay, be safe," Jarrod said.

An ambulance was flying past us. Malik barely got out of the way. Maybe Malik had one too many beers. Now I saw what Heather was talking about.

"Are you okay?"

"Yeah, I'm fine," he said. I continued to follow him until we reached the house.

I opened the door and began to undress. I was tired and just happy we made it home safely. I told Malik to bring me something to drink, but he never brought it to me because he was still on the sofa the next morning. In the place I left him the night before.

Chapter 10

Nadine

I have been keeping in contact with my future prospects. Usually I meet five guys. One doesn't call. I don't like one's conversation, the other one has a girlfriend answer his phone, another has a disconnected number because he didn't pay his bill. And then I'll go out with the last one, but we won't be on the same page. I just won't like him.

I talked on the phone to Quentin once. He called me while I was at work, and I told him I would call him back. Demetrius wanted to take me to dinner today. And I had talked to Jermaine—he wanted to take me out.

Jermaine came and picked me up at my house. He beeped his horn, like, five times before I got to the door. I was a little irritated. His excessive beeping was unnecessary. He had a black Pontiac Grand Prix with silver rims on it. I got inside of it. He seemed a little juvenile. The car had a gray leather interior and smelled like vanilla.

"What's up, Miss Teacher?"

"Nothing, I'm okay," I said.

"All right, all right. So you ready to have fun?"

"Fun? I guess. Where we going?" I asked.

"I wanted to stop past my man party. Then take you to get something to eat. You okay with that, Mami?" I told him okay and observed his erratic driving skills. He kept riding people's bumpers, then braking hard at every other light. I looked at him and smiled as I put my seat belt on at a red light. When the light turned green, nobody in front of us moved. So Jermaine went around the other cars and beeped his horn. There was a funeral procession riding past. Instead of stopping like a normal person, he began beeping his horn at them to tell them to hurry. Jermaine cut in front of the funeral and then made a wide left turn. I was at a loss for words. How ignorant can you get?

"Did you know that was a funeral line?" I asked.

"It was? No, I didn't know." *How could he not have known—there were orange stickers on each car,* I thought. But hold up, it gets better.

We went into Erie Lanes, a crowded bowling alley. All you heard were balls rolling. Pins were being knocked over and people were guzzling pints of beer. They were having a beef and beer. Jermaine walked me in front of all these men and said, "Let me introduce y'all to my friend Nadine. She is a teacher. Go 'head, baby, tell them about how you a teacher." They looked at him like, how did he pull me, and then they started asking me questions.

"What grade you teach?"

"Sixth grade."

One said, "You know you out with a crazy man."

Then the other said, "Jermaine can't read—you need to give him some private lessons."

They all started laughing and drank some more beer. Jermaine came back with beer for both of us. I didn't even like the way beer smelled. I wasn't about to drink it. He then joined in with the jokes. I didn't find any of the jokes funny. The next thing I knew, he punched his brother, whose birthday it was, in the face. His brother walked away without doing anything. That meant to me that he was about to get a gun. I wanted to run and go hide under a table. He came back and I was ready to duck when his brother came back with a busted lip and a wet paper towel held up against his face and said, "Good one. Motherfucker." Then they all started laughing again. But it stills gets better.

Jermaine was five minutes away from my house, but he insisted that he had to make a stop. He stopped in a 7-Eleven to get something to drink. I hope he wasn't wasting his time buying condoms. Jermaine got back in the car, smiling. I peered into the nearly sheer bag. Sure enough, there was a box of Magnum condoms. I guess he didn't know that our date was awful, and I couldn't wait to get on the other side of my door and be on safe territory so I would never have to see him again. I decided when we stopped past the bowling alley—this was our first and last date.

We pulled off so fast, my body jerked and I couldn't wait to get home. He stopped at the stop sign and I noticed the police behind us. I saw him glance in his side mirror. Then he glanced at his rearview mirror, and at the next light he made a right. He should have made a left.

"Where you going?" I asked.

"Nowhere. I just wanted to shake this cop."

"What's wrong? Is everything okay?" I questioned him. He was making me really nervous. Was the car stolen? Was he wanted? Did his brother call the cops on him?

"Yeah, I'm good. All my paperwork is cool and legit. I just get nervous when cops get behind me."

We rode a few more stop signs and I saw the red and blue lights flashing. He pulled over. The cops got out of the car. They flashed a bright light in our faces and said, "License and registration," to him. I just sat there, being careful not to move too much, but also trying to shun the bright glare out of my face. The cop had one hand on his radio and the other on his gun. He looked around in the backseat with his light. He didn't say anything, he just kept looking. Meanwhile, the other cop took Jermaine's information and went back to the patrol car. The cop on the passenger side with me followed.

"Sorry this had to happen. Cops be tripping on any black man with a nice car. I get stopped all the time." I wanted to tell him his Pontiac was not all that nice.

The cop on the driver side came back to the car. Jermaine reached out to grab his license and registration. The cop said, "I need you to step out of the car."

"Why, man? What's going on?"

"Step out of the car now."

"I didn't do anything," he shouted.

"I'm going to ask you again. Step out of the car." Jermaine looked at me, then got out of the car. They then pushed him up against the car and said he was wanted on warrants for child support and bank fraud. They put him in the back of the wagon. They came back to me and asked me how well I knew him. I told them I just met him. They said I was free to go and I left him, the car, and the cops in the middle of the street. I got out of the car and began walking toward my house. I guess my wish came true: I wouldn't have to worry about Jermaine calling me for a long while.

* * *

I called Toya and told her what happened and she was dying laughing. I then called Demetrius to set a date up for Saturday. If at first you don't succeed, try, try again.

"Hey, this is Nadine."

"Hello, hey. I was waiting for you to get back with me. What's going on?" he asked enthusiastically.

"Nothing much."

"Okay, well, I'm on the other line. I'm going to call you right back. Okay?"

"All right, then," I said and hung up the phone.

A few minutes later the phone rang. It was Demetrius.

"I was trying to get off the phone with my pastor," he said.

"Oh, okay," I said.

"Do you go to church?"

"No, not regularly," I said.

"Why not?"

"I try to get there when I can."

"When you can? Naw, sis, you got to do better than that. The night I met you, even though I was out in the streets, I still made it to church the next morning."

"That's good." I was thinking, *what does that have to do with anything?* but okay.

"Yeah, the Lord's great. Without Him I wouldn't have been able to get through my dark days." *Dark days?* Now he was really getting interesting, so I had to ask, "What were your dark days?"

"My dark days were when I used to be in the life."

"What life?" I asked. *He better not be talking about what I think he is,* I thought.

"I used to be gay."

"Really," I said as I took the phone away from my ear and shook my head in disbelief.

"Yeah, I believe in being honest with people in the beginning."

"Well, you got to respect that." I didn't let him say another word. I disconnected his call and deleted his number out of my phone.

Two down and one to go. A gay guy and a felon. How nice. I was down to Quentin. I put on a crinkled, sand-colored dress. I met Quentin at the Aston Restaurant on City Line Avenue. Quentin was better-looking than I remembered. No wonder I approached him.

"Hey, beautiful," he said as he came and kissed me on my cheek. That was different. He greeted me like we were old friends. I smiled. We sat down and had an extensive conversation about his life working as a detective.

"How long have you been on the force?" I asked. He paused and asked the bartender to come over, ordered our drinks, and then he answered my question.

"I have been on the force six years."

"So, I might feel safe with you?"

"You could."

We sat and drank three rounds. I kept it light, since I had to get up and go to work the next day. I wasn't tipsy, but I felt very horny. I just wanted to take him home and fuck him, but he was the kind you have a relationship with: good job, intelligent, and so handsome. He could be my future husband. I should have called him first instead of those other two losers I wasted my weekend on. But I didn't know. Quentin was so, so cute. That wasn't the liquor talking, either. I wasn't drunk. I had a few drinks but I wasn't drunk. I wished I was. I needed some excuse as to why I was having thoughts of sticking Quentin's dick in my mouth and just loving him down.

"Look, we can get a room," I said without thinking.

He seemed surprised. "I don't get paid until Friday and I'm tapped on cash."

That should have been the moment I said, *Hell to the no*, but I didn't because he had a big dick—it was peeking out through his pants. Our sexual energy was so high. He kept massaging my fingers, the palm of my hand, and blowing in my ear. I wanted him bad. I wasn't paying for a room, so we went back to my house.

A man I just met was in my house about to sex me up and down. I could not wait. He was so gigantic. I could feel him through his pants. *Damn him.* He was playful, slamming his pelvis into mine, simulating a sex act. I wanted him just as much as he wanted me. I was about to explode off of that alone. He pulled my dress over my head and began rubbing my pussy. He licked it raw, but I stopped him. I wanted him to continue to let his fingers tap and massage the lining of my vagina. He played with my body until I reached the best moment of pleasure. No more foreplay, I told him, just stick it in.

He pulled me away from him and put on a ribbed condom. As soon as he put it on, I began kissing him. I wanted it—I needed it now. He placed his condom-wrapped, deliciously thick and firm body in me. I waited for the feeling of pleasure and pain to overwhelm me. I waited. Then I realized it wasn't working anymore. It had deflated. Was I anticipating too much? Because what was presently inside me was not the dick that was trying to escape his pants. This one was limp and weak. He pulled his body out of mine and said, "Um, I can't stay hard with the condom on."

"Why not?"

"I don't like condoms. Plus, this one is too small. Do you have a bigger condom?" *You not that big*, I thought.

"You can't take it off. Make it work or nothing is going down tonight."

He removed the condom. Well, that was it. We had to get together another time because this man was out of order and he was running out of time because I was sleepy. He dressed as I yawned, and I told him good night.

Friday we got together again. Okay, no games. We knew what we came for. We met at the Loews Hotel downtown. I liked this situation. No pressure. I didn't have to worry about him getting comfortable all in my house. We didn't have to rush anywhere, just sit back and unwind.

I met him in the lobby, and after three drinks we were on the elevator, kissing and hugging. He slid the credit-card-like key in the door. The light turned green and he opened the door. Everything was dark. He turned the light on.

I was ready. It was still built up from the last time. The first round. We went round for round. He won the first two rounds and the second I rode him so hard and fast he fell asleep instantly after I jumped off of him. When I awoke, Quentin was already showered and dressed. "You want to get some breakfast?"

"Sure, I'll be dressed in a little bit."

I went in the bathroom, took a shower, and I felt a little funny. I didn't even think to bring a change of clothes. After I showered I just looked in the mirror and tried to make myself as presentable as possible. I walked out of the bathroom with the same clothes from the night before and he asked was I ready. I told him I was. He stood up and inspected the room. I opened the door and he cupped my butt. I laughed. It gave my body a little tingle.

The next day Quentin called me to tell me that he had a great time and that we had to get together again. We talked for a little while, then he asked me what I was doing.

"Sleep. I have to get ready for work tomorrow. Why?" I said.

"I wanted to stop by and see you."

"No, it's too late. Just call me tomorrow," I said. He said okay and that he would call me. That was the last time I talked to him.

Tuesday morning I was in class. I had assigned all my students two states to research. One student was already finished. They were supposed to draw the state and tell me population, agriculture, and economy. One student had his hand raised.

"Yes?" I said.

"I'm finished, Ms. Clark."

"Let me see," I said as I grabbed his project. "Okay, you can do something quietly," I said. I looked to see if anyone else was done. They weren't. I walked all around the room. I noticed one student reading the dictionary.

"What are you doing?" I asked.

"My mom said I have to read three pages of the dictionary a day to improve my vocabulary. She said I play too many video games."

"That's nice," I said.

I continued to walk around my class. My mind began to think about Quentin. I bit and chewed at my fingernails. *Why hadn't he call me since Sunday? He didn't call me yesterday.* I kept thinking about everything he said and what I said and what I did to see if there was a reason why he wouldn't call me. It seemed like it was going so okay. We got together two times, and they all were very nice dates. I'm not his girlfriend, but damn, I deserve a call. Maybe he's upset I didn't let him come over that night. Oh well, I was asleep.

It had been one week and Quentin still had not called, not one time. I was too old for this shit. I would have more respect for him if he would have hit it and quit it. But no, he had to string me along. There had to be a logical answer, but what could it be? There I was, asking Toya for advice, and the girl couldn't even figure her own life out.

I was like, "Should I call him?"

"I don't know. I wouldn't call him. That's just my opinion," she said.

"Why?" I asked.

"Because I would wait."

"It has been a week."

"So, let another week go by. He knows your number, right?"

"Yeah, I guess you're right."

I called Quentin anyway. I had to see what Mr. Detective was doing. I was so mad at myself as soon as the phone started ringing. I cleared my throat.

"Hello," he said, all cheery. So he wasn't dead and he could have called me. *Okay.* I took a deep breath. I had to not sound mad, not sound irritated. But *how dare you not call me, bitch?* I adjusted my temperature and sounded as relaxed as I could.

"Um . . . hey, Quentin. It's me, Nadine."

"Nadine, I know your voice. Hey, how you doing?"

"Fine." I answered. His conversation was so laid-back, like he just wasn't at the hotel licking me raw. "Did I catch you at a bad time?" I asked, trying not to pry.

"I'm out having dinner with a friend."

Out having a date with a friend translated to: *I forgot whose number this was, and that's why I picked up. I'm on a date, so I'm trying to holler at her now, and I got to downgrade both of y'all to make it seem like it's not that serious so that I can still get with either one of you when I get ready.*

"Oh, you're at dinner. Okay, well, I'm going to let you go," I said, disappointed and hoping he would say, *Hey, no, it's my friend Charles from college,* or *No, I'm with my brother.* Instead he said, "All right, talk to you soon."

Chapter 11

Kim

I was at my psychiatrist's office, Dr. Olivia Weltz, waiting for her to enter. This was my third visit, and I was becoming comfortable discussing my problems. When the doctor entered the room, she sat down and began recording our visit.

"Kim, have you been taking it easy like I suggested? Have you?" she said, tilting her head to the side, trying to evaluate my answer.

"I try to take my children out when I'm not working. I signed my oldest son up for karate lessons and we have been to the aquarium," I said.

"That's good. But what have you done for you? Something outside of your children. I know that you love your children, but you have to love Kim. You have to get better to take care of them."

"You're right."

"So what do you like to do? What makes you happy? When was the last time you were totally happy?"

I pondered her question.

"I don't know. I haven't done anything for me in a long time."

She handed me a journal and told me to write down how I felt about Malik, Demetrius, what I could do to change my situation, and five things I used to enjoy.

"Like a hobby?" I asked.

"Yes, like a hobby, and go do two of the things and the other three schedule for the next month."

I thanked the doctor and said I would see her next week.

"Okay."

What did I like? What made me happy? I'm going to love me. I like music, relaxing, perfumes, and body washes. I like to smell things. I went to the Strawbridge's perfume counter. I loved music. I went to a FYE music store and browsed. I decided to buy myself some CDs. I loved the Mary J. Blige *My Life* CD. Okay, then I went and found Erykah Badu's first album. I loved it. That was a good CD. 'Kay, who else? I like Kelly Clarkson from *American Idol.* I picked up her CD. Okay. I thought that was it. But then I saw the *Ready to Die* by the Notorious B.I.G.

I opened my CDs in the car. The music took me to another place back in the twelfth grade, the summer before college, before the kids and the relationships, when I was just Kim that didn't have to worry about anything but me. Wow, that was a great time. I even sprayed the coconut fragrance all around my car. It was all about me.

I drove to my mother's house. She was in the kitchen, washing the dishes. The smell of beef ribs permeated the room.

"Where are the boys?" I asked her.

"Kianna came and took the boys to the movies."

"What?"

"Yeah, she playing stepmommy to her man's kids."

"Man? Kids?"

"Yup, her new man got three, and one she said was a possibility," my mom said sarcastically. "I'm only repeating what she told me," she said, correcting herself and hunching her shoulders.

"Well, that's nice."

"How was your session?"

"It was great."

"That's good. I'm going to finish fixing my dinner and after that I'm going to feed the boys and bring them home."

"You sure, Mom?" I asked.

She said, "Yes, and go home and get some rest."

Once I was home I couldn't rest. I got to sit in the bubble bath without somebody screaming, *Mommy, he did that. Mommy, I'm hungry. Mommy, Mommy, Mommy.* The house was quiet. I was having my break. I listened to my Kem CD. The telephone was ringing. I didn't bother answering it until it rang again. I jumped out of the tub, all wet and naked, and answered the telephone.

"Kim."

"Yeah?"

"Hey, sis. Um, Karen said she was going to keep the boys for you."

"Tell her she doesn't have to."

"She already put them to sleep. Do you need anything?"

"No, I'm good. I'm just going to relax."

"You have to give Malik the baby sometime. You are not hurting him. You are hurting you. You know that, right?" Now even Kianna was giving me advice.

"I'll talk to you later, Kianna."

"You need to get back out there and have a social life and have fun, Kim. Me and Karen are going to take you out and reintroduce you to the world."

"Okay, thanks for thinking of me. I'll talk to you later," I said.

I got up and realized I had fallen asleep on the sofa. I turned the television off. I made myself some coffee. Then I just sat and wrote a list in my journal. I listed what was going right in my life and what was going wrong and what I needed to change. I tried to think of everything. I wrote down that I have to find Kevin's father. I have to find Darius. Darius date-raped me back in college. I got pregnant, dropped out, had Kevin, and never saw Darius again. Father's Day came and went every year. I almost was in tears. I was in tears just thinking about all the people who don't have dads. My sons don't have fathers. I don't let Malik see Kayden and I have no idea where Kevin's father is. I didn't even know if Darius is aware that he has a son. I was determined to find him.

I called a private detective. He told me that to start he would need at least a thousand dollars down. I didn't have that type of money. I didn't know where else to begin, so I called down to Delaware State University. I told one of the administrative staff my real story. She said she would pray for me and gave me his last known address. I then called directory assistance.

"Do you have a Darius Miller at 8427 Highstown Place?" I was stunned when she began to recite a home telephone number. I copied the number onto my hand. I thanked the operator and stared at the number. I called the telephone number. An older man with a shaky voice answered.

"Hello, may I speak to Darius?"

"Who's calling?"

"Kimberly Brown."

"Kimberly, are you from the congregation? He moved, honey. Him and Jocelyn moved to Detroit. I'll tell him you called. Bye." He hung up the phone and then I called back.

"Hello."

"Yes, I am a friend from college."

"Well, give me your number and I'll pass it along."

"Okay, thank you."

I was tired of taking care of Kevin by myself. If Darius didn't want to have a fatherly relationship with him, the least he was going to do was pay for my son every month.

Chapter 12

Shonda

I called Tae and decided to bother her. "So what's up with Poppa Smurf?" I asked.

"I had to drop him. He can't do it unless he popped a Viagra," Tae said while sniffling.

"Iiillll! I can't believe that you had sex with that old man."

"He was forty-seven—that is not old."

"That's disgusting. I wouldn't talk to anyone over the age of thirty-four and younger than twenty-five."

"Love don't have no age limit. But fuck that old bastard. He didn't pay my car note yet. I wouldn't have got this stupid car if it wasn't for him. I don't even have a job."

"You will soon."

"I hope so. The first time in my life I want to work, and I can't find a job. Well, the good news is I got this young boy and he is the truth."

"How old?"

"Not that young."

"How old is 'not that young'?"

"He's twenty-three—his name is Kenneth."

"You have five years on him."

"I know, but he's young enough for me to school him. Listen to the message he left me." Tae dialed her answering machine and I heard her young boy professing his love.

"Tae, I'm so glad you came into my life. I can't wait to see you this weekend. I think I'm falling in love with you. I hope you feel the same way. I never felt this way about anyone so soon."

"Girl, he wants me to be his girl," she gushed. I wanted to tell Chantae she was twenty-eight—she was too old to be someone's "girl." And she had only been dating him a few days, so what if he was leaving cute messages now? That doesn't last. It is always like that in the beginning.

"Tell me you not falling for that," I asked.

"Yes, I am. Matter of fact, I'm about to call him now."

"Well, what does he do? What are you going to do with a young boy?"

"He is twenty-three—that's old enough. I mean, it's not like he is twenty-one. I'm going to mold him. He already got his mind straight. He work for FedEx as a driver and he hustle CDs on the side."

I received my correction officer's test results back in the mail.

"Baby, I passed the corrections officer's test! I got a ninety-one," I yelled to Malik.

He came out of the kitchen and said, "Shonda, I don't think I want you working at a prison full of rapists, murderers, and robbers. I'm going to be putting those kind of people away, and you're going to be tending to them."

"It is a lot of opportunity."

"What opportunity? You are going to go to the top as a prison guard? I'd rather you go to college and get a degree in something."

"Well, I want to try it. They have full benefits and I would have a set schedule. I am going to at least try it out."

I called Tae.

"Girl, I got my results. I got a ninety-one."

"That's good! I'm out with Kenneth. I'll call you back."

I had to go for an interview. If I get this job, I'm quitting. I'm not even going to give them two weeks' notice. I'm going to be out with the quickness.

The next step was for them to conduct a background check—like if I ever been to the jail to visit anyone. Then you had to list all the people in your household. That was easy: just me and Bree.

Jarrod was over our house. Malik and him were sitting back, watching a basketball game. I tried being nice and making small talk and asked, "How's Heather doing?"

"She's okay," he said, without even looking up at me and sipping on a Corona.

"Tell her I said hi."

"Uh-huh," he said.

I left them alone and went upstairs to get ready for bed. Tae was calling me back on my cell phone.

"Girl, that is crazy, you got a ninety-one."

"Yeah, did you get your results?"

"Yeah, I got a damn sixty-seven. If I would have three more points, I would have made it."

"Dag, that's messed up."

"Yeah, especially 'cause I got this car payment and I put you on. I'm not going to worry about it. Something will come through for me. I'll talk to you later." It sounded as if she was jealous of me getting in. It wasn't my fault she didn't pass. That was some real hating shit.

They called me in for three interviews, a mental analysis, and did a thorough background check. They wanted to make sure I didn't have a relative I was trying to help escape. I got a call-back and they said that I was hired and had been selected to enter the academy.

Chapter 13

Nadine

Ariel called me early Saturday morning—I was just getting myself together.

"Hello."

"You haven't heard, have you?" Ariel whispered.

"No, heard what?" I asked.

"I heard my mom on the phone this morning and she said that Toya is four months' pregnant."

"Toya is pregnant again?"

"Yup, and nobody is supposed to know. My mom said that was on her because she was not helping her anymore and she was on her own." I couldn't believe I was getting the scoop from a twelve-year-old.

"Ariel, you sure?" I asked

"Pos-si-tive," she sounded out.

"I'm going to call her and see if she tells me. I will call you back." I disconnected the call. I couldn't believe it. *That is crazy! She was just shaking it with me at the reggae club.* I knew her stomach was pudgy. I wondered whose baby it was, Tony or Nate? I called Toya casually and said, "What's going on, cousin? What's good?"

Toya paused for a moment, sucked her teeth, and

she said, "You fake and corny. I know my mom already told you. Yeah, I'm pregnant."

"So who is the father?" I laughed.

"Well, Tony want it to be his. But I know this time it is Nate's. So I'm going to stop seeing Tony for good and just marry Nate, because I'm twenty-four and this has been going on for too long."

"How sure are you?"

"Look, I'm sure," she said defensively.

"I don't have to take you on *Maury* to get a DNA test, do I?"

"No, I know who my baby father is. It's Nate."

"So Toya, why it take you this long to leave Tony alone?" I asked.

"I don't know. I liked them both. They both are good for something."

"Poor Tony. That Jamaican man is going to whoop you ass. I feel so sorry for him," I said.

"I don't know why. That's on them if he allowed himself to be treated bad."

"Toya, you just as bad as a man. I'll talk to you later. I have work to do."

It was time for my grades to be turned in. As usual, I had procrastinated until the day before report cards needed to be turned in. I was sweating and using my calculator to average out my grades. I had about a quarter of my grades done, but I couldn't be completely finished because the music teacher hadn't sent hers down.

"Did you meet the new teacher yet?" Mrs. Meyers asked as she walked in my classroom unannounced.

"No, I haven't. I have been really busy, trying to get these grades together," I said as I looked down at the numerous papers scattered around my desk.

Mrs. Meyers still rambled on. "She has the students

under control and in check. I don't know where Mr. Mitchell found her, but he needs three more like her."

"Is that right? I have to meet her," I said.

"And she is so pretty and really nice." Sometimes Mrs. Meyers went on and on. Like if you asked her about her day. A simple question like *How's it going?* could send her into a fifteen-minute rant about her arthritis and the misbehaved student in her class. I wasn't for it today.

"Okay, Mrs. Meyers, I have to get back to my report cards. I'll see her."

"Okay, see you. You want me to bring you up some lunch?"

"No, I have a yogurt and Diet Coke."

"You sure? They're having open-faced turkey sandwiches."

"I'm okay—really," I said as I forced a smile. This time she got the hint and left.

I had five more report cards to complete and after that I would be done. I swore I would never wait until the last minute to do report cards again. I was dismissing my students. The yard was loud. School buses were revving. Students walking with their friends. Parents searching for their children. "Bye, Ms. Clark," I heard ten times or more.

"Bye, see you tomorrow," I said countless times. Then I heard my name being screamed. I turned around and saw Mrs. Meyers.

"Ms. Clark, Ms. Clark, I want you to meet Mrs. Dorsey."

One way or the other, Mrs. Meyers was determined to have me meet this new teacher. She took my hand and pulled me over to the new teacher. She tapped the woman on her shoulder. She had maroon, neatly locked dreads that were tossed around her shoulder. *Very pretty,* I thought.

She turned around and I couldn't believe it was her. I hated her. She reminded me of my past—the life I left behind.

"Nadine—hey girl, how are you?" she asked while attempting to hug me.

"Hey," I said, shocked and unable to move.

"I walked past your classroom the other day. I started to say hi, but you were teaching."

"Oh, so you saw me the other day?" I wanted to spit on her right then and there. She knew who I was and never said anything. Mrs. Dorsey was Brandy Henry in high school—the best friend of the bitch who ruined my senior year. She wasn't the ringleader, but a conspirator just the same. Right then and there, the hate I had for her seven years ago reappeared. I smiled, told her welcome, and walked to my car as fast as I could. I got in my car and pulled off. I hated that Brandy Henry knew what I was doing with my life now. I felt like she would go and file a report to all the girls that used to sit at the lunchroom table with her. The call would go something like, *Hey y'all, Nadine work at Johnson Master School and she's not married yet with no kids.* She would giggle. They all would laugh and talk about me for an hour.

Mrs. Meyers entered my class. "Can I see your stapler? Mine is broke."

"Sure," I said, reaching in my drawer.

"It's almost time to pick the students up from prep."

"Yes, I know," I said. Mrs. Meyers was reaching, making dumb conversation. I wondered what she wanted.

"So, Ms. Clark, what's going on with you and Mrs. Dorsey?"

"Nothing."

"Well, why did you run off like that after I introduced you?"

"You didn't introduce us—we already knew each other from high school. It is a long story, and I'd rather not talk about it."

"Okay—if you need something, let me know."

"I will." She left the room and I had a moment to think about why I didn't like Mrs. Dorsey, aka Brandy Henry. I didn't like her because her and her friends had the entire senior class not speaking to me for a year. It was so stupid over a bunch of he said, she said. They told the entire senior class not to talk to me, and everybody listened. Brandy Henry's best friend Tyesha didn't like me for no reason. I went my entire senior year without a friend. I skipped the prom and senior trip, and from that point on I haven't had any girl-friends.

Chapter 14

Kim

"Hello."

"Yes, may I speak to Kimberly Brown?"

"This is she."

"Yes, this is Darius Miller."

"Yes, this is Kim," I said as it registered to me who I was speaking with. I pulled to the side of the road. Kevin asked why were we stopping. I looked at him, and whispered to him to sit down. Kayden was asleep. I got out of the car. Cars were whizzing past. Before I got a chance to speak, he said, "Look, sorry if I caught you at a bad time. My father said you called me." I gathered the strength. I was trying to find the perfect combination of words to say.

"Yes, I have something I need to talk to you about."

"Well, Kim, let me first say I am flattered that you contacted me after all this time, but I'm a man of God now and I'm happily married with three wonderful daughters. So thanks for contacting me, but whatever it is, I'm not interested." I felt a pulse of jealousy come over me. Then I was a little upset that he actually thought I tracked him down to date him or something.

I wanted to go off on him and tell him how he ruined my life. How I had to take care of Kevin myself because he raped me and forced his self on me. So without even thinking, I belted out, "Remember that night in Johnson Hall in my room?"

"Yes, I remember," he said, confused.

"Well, you have a son—he is seven and his name is Kevin," I said while looking at Kevin in the car.

"What?"

"Yes, so I wanted to contact you to give you an opportunity to meet him and build a relationship. I know I never called you before—I just felt like it was the right time."

"I'm speechless. I had no idea," he said.

"I already contacted a few paternity agencies. I'll pay for the test, but I'm sure he is yours. I was a virgin that night you took my virginity."

"Took your virginity."

"Yes—remember, you were drinking gin and juice. You bent me over a chair and told me if I told anyone, no one would believe me."

"No, I don't remember any of that. Um—I'm sorry. Can I call you back. I have to discuss everything with my wife, but I will right now and I'll give you a call back. I'll take a paternity test—I'm sorry I didn't know. What city are you in?"

"Philadelphia."

"I promise I'll give you a call." I thought *whatever,* but I said okay. I got back in the car. Kevin was oblivious to my whole conversation. He was getting to the age when I knew he was going to start asking questions. Right now, I think he thinks Malik is his dad and he is just a child of divorce.

* * *

Part of the recovering process was getting out. I needed to get a break. I wasn't trying to leave my kids with everybody, but I did want to do the grown-up thing. Karen and Kianna were taking me out for drinks and dinner. They said they didn't want me to be upset. I didn't know why they think I would be upset until I looked at the calendar. My one-year anniversary. I would have been married to Malik for one year. I wasn't upset. We met at my mom's house—she was taking Kevin and Kayden to the arcade. It was raining hard outside. I almost decided not to go, but I knew if I didn't, my sisters would think something was wrong with me.

We came in the restaurant Glam and had a seat at an upper booth. I took my wet jacket off and placed it on the back of my chair. I sat my umbrella on the chair beside me.

"Y'all know we supposed to get a major storm this weekend," Karen said. The waitress came over—she had lips that looked as if they had been surgically enhanced. She used a plum liner and bright peach lipstick.

"Ladies, are y'all ready to order?"

"I'll take an order of buffalo wings as an appetizer and a piña colada." Karen looked down at the menu and said she needed a few more minutes, then just decided on a Bahama Mama and mozzarella sticks. Kianna ordered poppers and had a Kahlua and cream.

"This is nice—we rarely ever just all go out. We need to do this more often," Kianna said while looking over the menu.

"So, how is the industry life going?" Karen asked Kianna playfully. We laughed at Kianna because she thought she was the next best thing.

"It's great—I have been in three videos and I'm taping another one next week."

"You got to show us a copy," I said.

She paused and said, "I will. They don't give us copies of the video. They hardly pay us right. I heard they used to pay girls that were in videos, like, six thousand, ten thousand a video. Now we get like a thousand a day."

"Well, that's still good for one day's worth of work," Karen said.

"I guess."

"You guess? I don't make a thousand a week," Karen said.

"I really want my acting to work out. I mean, it really can. All you have to do is be at the right place at the right time. I was at this party the other night. And I'm standing right next to all these celebrities. I saw Jamie Foxx and Beyoncé and Jay-Z. It was like I was a star, just like them. Everybody was asking for my card, and the women that weren't intimidated by me were real nice."

"*Intimidated*—that's a big word," Karen said as she looked over at me. We laughed.

"Why you think people are intimidated by you?"

"Well, one, because I look good, and I would try to speak and they would look at me like, who are you? Or they would try to pull their man in closer toward them. Like I wanted them." My sister was a riot.

"How about they might have thought you were a stranger?" Karen told her.

"That's true," she said while thinking about it.

"I forgot to ask you about your new man."

"Yeah, I have been dealing with him, but I don't know how long it is going to last."

"Why you say that?" Karen asked.

"Because he always wants to have his kids around, and I don't have time for kids on a daily basis." The waitress came with our drinks, placing napkins in front of us. "How's everything?" she asked.

"We're fine," I said as I took a sip of my piña colada.

"Kianna, don't you think that's good he wants to spend time with his children?" I asked.

"Not at my expense. I think I want a guy with no kids," Kianna said.

"Good luck finding one," Karen said in her usual negative tone.

"You call the house to check on Mommy?" I asked.

"No, Mommy can hold her own. She raised us. You better enjoy this time away from the boys," Karen said.

A group of young white guys across from us were making a lot of noise—they were laughing and singing and just being silly. One was turning red and falling out. His blond, short hair was disheveled.

"Excuse me, do y'all know the girl singing that song from *American Idol*?" He started humming and trying to sing the song.

"It's 'Breakaway' by Kelly Clarkson. I actually like her. I just bought her CD," I said.

"Who?" Kianna said.

"The girl from *American Idol*—the one with the dark hair."

"Oh yeah, I like her, too!"

"Thank you—I want to buy him that CD. He is about to get married and he needs to break away."

"Aw, don't say that," Karen chimed in.

He invited his self over to our table. He started shaking his head and said, "I'm Rick." He tried to shake Kianna's hand—she popped gum in his face.

Karen reached in her pocketbook, and I said, "Hello."

"His fiancée is a witch—she takes all his money and is

always shopping. It's my brother—I should look out for him, right? I don't want him to marry her."

One of the calmer guys, he was tall with brown curly hair and rich, dark, brown eyes, walked over to the table, trying to convince his friend to come back to their table. "This guy is out of control. His brother is getting married to his high-school sweetheart, and he is upset. Don't mind him."

"I'm cool, man. I'm cool, ladies, right? I'm not bothering y'all, am I? Can I sit down with y'all?"

"We don't care," Kianna said, answering for everybody while applying lip gloss to her already-shiny lips. The calm guy went back over to his table. Our wings, mozzarella sticks, and poppers came. The waitress gave us small plates and wipes for our hands.

"These buffalo wings are spicy," Karen said, always complaining. We ate and got back into our conversation about Kianna and the world of trying to break into the industry, as she put it.

"Are you a model or dancer?" Rick asked.

"I'm a model and aspiring actress," Kianna said.

"Oh, so you know a bunch of rappers?" Rick asked Kianna.

"Yeah, I do," she said, as if what she did required expertise.

"Why?"

"Because all this time, I have been trying to figure out what 'crunk' means," Rick asked. We all gave him the look, like, he couldn't be serious. Karen, she was not amused. It was like he was waiting to run into a black person to ask them that. Kianna tried to explain, but then got frustrated.

"So is it music or, like, a way of life, because I think I'm crunk sometime, like, I get fired up," he said as his words slurred and he took another swig of his Samuel Adams beer.

"Okay, that's enough," his friend—the tall, tanned one—came over and said. "Say bye-bye."

"He is okay," Kianna said. She was actually amused by him.

"Okay, then I'm going to have to sit here, too, to keep him out of trouble."

"So what were you talking about, music and television?" he asked.

"I'm surprised he is not trying to do a *Seinfeld* impersonation—that's his favorite show."

"I love *Seinfeld*. I didn't get it until it went in syndication," I said. We all started comparing episodes.

"You know what other show I like? *Everybody Loves Raymond.*"

"I can't get into that one. I watch old episodes of *Martin.*"

"Yeah, I do, too, on TV One. What's your name?" he asked.

"Kim."

"I'm Andrew. Are you married, Kim?"

"No."

"Divorced," I lied. I didn't know him and he didn't need to know all my business. I looked at Kianna and Karen to see their expressions. They weren't paying any attention to me—they were still laughing at the drunk guy, Rick.

"Do you have any children?"

"Two," I said as I finished off my piña colada.

"How old? he asked.

"Eight and one."

"I'm sorry if I'm asking too many questions."

"No, it's okay," I said.

"I have a daughter—she is five. My Cianni—she is my little princess," he said as he pulled out his brown leather wallet. He showed me a picture of a beautiful little black girl smiling extra-hard with a tooth missing in the front. I guess he wanted to let me know that he knew black. Karen excused herself and went to the restroom.

"Oh, she is so beautiful," I said.

"Let me see," Kianna said as he reached for his wallet. "Oh, she is cute," she said as she examined the picture.

"Thank you. She looks like her mother, my ex-wife."

"So your ex-wife is black?" Kianna asked.

"Yes, they live in North Carolina," he said as he put his wallet back in his back pocket.

"Why y'all break up?" she asked intrusively.

"It is a long story," he said. Karen came back from the bathroom and asked us were we ready to go. I said yes—we all looked at the bill.

We said our good-byes, wished the guy good luck with his nuptials, said it was nice talking to him, and left the restaurant. On the way back to the car it started raining a light mist. I realized I didn't have my umbrella. I went back to Glam and got it. Kianna and Karen continued to walk back to the car. I saw the white guy, Andrew, with it in his hand.

"I tried to catch you to tell you you left this."

"Thank you," I said as I turned to walk out of the restaurant.

"You think I might be able to talk to you again?" he asked.

"That might be possible," I said.

He handed me his card. I wrote my cell phone number down for him on an extra card.

I opened the umbrella and jogged to the car. They were already waiting. "What took you so long?" Karen said as she pulled the car off before my foot was all the way in the door.

"That guy Andrew asked me for my number."

"He was cute. If I was into white guys, I would have talked to him," Kianna said.

"Yeah, I turned him down, though," I lied.

Chapter 15

Shonda

Valentine's Day was here, and I didn't know what to buy Malik. He had a lot of cologne and shoes. I didn't want to get him a robe or watch. I was clueless. I knew what he was going to get me, and that was an engagement ring. He has been hinting around it. He told me this morning that tonight was going to be special, so wear something nice. I decided to get Malik a gift card to Macy's—that way he could choose whatever he wanted himself.

I shaved every inch of my body that had hair. I put on my new sixteen-inch wig—I felt like a stripper. I already had on my black dress with a silver-sequined collar. My nails were already done. I just had to repolish my toes. I then painted every toe hot pink. Bright colors always make my feet look good. Everything was ready. Malik came home.

"Hey, baby, you ready?" he asked.

"Yes, where we going?" I asked.

"You'll see."

We got in his car. I loved riding shotgun in his new car. I felt like his Mrs. Moore already. This is how we will be growing old, taking trips. Malik will do all the driving and I will sit back and enjoy the scenery.

We arrived at a sushi restaurant on the waterfront by the Delaware River. I looked at the menu. I tried to concentrate on what I wanted. But my mind kept wandering and thinking about Malik's proposal. I could not wait to see my ring.

"Close your eyes," Malik said. When he told me to open them, I opened them and saw an envelope. I opened the envelope and it was a cruise to the Bahamas.

"Oh, this is nice, Malik," I said, confused.

"I know you said you wanted to go away. So I wanted to take you away."

Still hopeful—maybe he wants to get married while we are there, I thought. I gave him a hug and said, "Thank you, baby." I ate a little and then said, "What else do you want to do while we are there?"

"We're going to be on vacation. What else is there to do?" he asked, smiling.

"Nothing," I said as I put my head down.

"Are you okay?"

"Yes, I'm fine," I said, holding my tears in.

"You sure?"

I held my tears back and ate the rest of my dinner in silence. Malik didn't say much. So many thoughts went through my head. Why was he waiting? Or maybe Malik didn't have any intention of proposing. I didn't know. I got up from the table and went to the bathroom. When I returned, there was a white square box on my chair. I smiled at Malik and began opening it up. It was a goddamn heart diamond pendant necklace. *How nice.*

"What's wrong—you don't like it?" Malik asked as a tear escaped my eye.

"No, I love it," I said as I tried to keep my face from falling apart. Then he pulled out another box here. *Wow—nice! The fucking bracelet to match.* "Thank you, baby,

I love it." Okay, a vacation, a necklace, and bracelet—yeah, this was nice and over the top, but I thought Malik was going to say *I want you to be my wife.* The tears started flowing down my face. I went into the bathroom and began to cry uncontrollably. People were walking in and out of the bathroom. I was in front of the mirror, just crying, wiping a tear as another one ran down my face. I soaked the first towel completely, so I grabbed another one. Then I picked up my cell phone and called Tae.

"What's up, Shonda?" Tae said.

"Tae, I thought Malik was going to propose to me but instead he gave me jewelry and a vacation."

"It's okay—he might not be ready just yet. That doesn't mean he isn't going to marry you at all."

"Well, tell you one thing. I'm not sitting around getting old waiting for him."

"Malik is a good dude, and you're a good person. Malik will see the light eventually."

"I hope so. I have to go," I said to Tae. Talking to her did not really make me feel any better. I walked back to the table, still wiping away my tears.

"What's wrong? You okay?" Malik asked.

I couldn't keep it bottled up any longer. I spoke slowly and said, "I thought you were going to propose to me."

"What, Shonda? I'm not ready for marriage right now. I have to get myself together."

"But we have been living together and we have been playing house."

"Baby, in due time we will get there. I'm not trying to rush into marriage. If I wanted to rush and get married, I would have married Kim."

"Huh, what do you mean, if you would have married anyone it would have been Kim?"

"I didn't say that," Malik said.

"You might as well have," I shouted.

"Shonda, I love you. If I didn't I wouldn't be with you. Now, sit down," he ordered me as he grabbed my arms. People began to look from other tables.

"Get the fuck off me. If you should have married her, then go marry her. Go be a daddy to your son and be a happy little family."

"Shonda, people are looking. Please sit down."

"No, I'm not sitting down. I don't give a fuck who is looking at me," I said as I turned around to see who was looking at me. I got angrier and angrier and shouted, "Well, then go marry that bitch. Fuck you, Malik," I said as I stormed out of the restaurant. I threw the necklace and tickets at him. I was fuming—how dare that niggah! I left the restaurant. Shit, I'm not going to be dumb-ass Kim and stay with him all those years and not get married. And I'm not buying my own ring. If Malik's not trying to marry me, and soon, I'm out. No—better yet, he is out!

I wasn't hardly speaking to Malik since Valentine's Day. I wanted to kick his ass out that night. But I sat down that night and figured out all the bills. I couldn't afford our house, electric, cable, food, gas, and all the extras on my own. Not yet, anyway—maybe after I start the academy, I will. I'll only be in training for six weeks. Then after that I'll be getting a regular paycheck. That's when Malik is going to be out of here. Get rid of his ass.

Today I'm going to tell my job to kiss my ass and I'm giving them a verbal two weeks' notice. I went in and saw Joe in his office. He was such a pervert—I could already feel his eyes on my breasts when I walked in the room.

"Joe, I found another job. I wanted to give you my

two weeks' notice," I said seriously while laughing on the inside.

"Really? Where you have a job at?" he said, looking up at me.

"Prison guard for the city."

"Well, to be honest, you don't have to wait two weeks—you can leave now," he said as he took his glasses off and wiped his eyes.

I needed the next two weeks' paycheck, but instead of saying no, I would like to stay the next two weeks, I said, "You know what? You're right—I'll clean out my cubicle now. You enjoy the rest of your day." I was happy to clean my cubicle and go. I threw all my old documents in a shredder, then took the picture of me and Malik and Brianna's picture off my desk. Then I emptied my accumulated change into my purse. I found a box in the coffee room and packed everything else up. Once in my car, I became a little scared. I had really left my job.

Brianna was home with me, getting on my nerves. I told her to clean up her room and she was upset about it.

"Mom, can I get new sneakers? Look at all these scuff marks on my sneakers. I had them for over a month, and I want a cell phone."

"What? You can't have a cell phone."

"You don't have to get me a plan. I can get, like, a prepaid or Boost Mobile. I can get money from my dad to buy cards. All my friends have one."

I looked at her sneakers—she did need a new pair. And she wasn't getting another pair of white sneaks to dog. I told her if she cleaned her room, I would take her to get new sneakers.

We went to the store and I spent my last hundred dollars buying Brianna black-and-pink Reeboks and a cell phone. I guess I was going to have to be Malik's friend for the next week. Then, once I get my first paycheck . . . he is out.

We laid our bags down and were exhausted. Bree went and took a shower and got ready for bed. I came into my bedroom and smelled Curve cologne. I wondered where he took his ass to. I called his cell phone and got his voice mail.

Fuck him, I thought. If Malik is not worried about me enough to marry me, then why should I worry about him? I lay in my bed, snuggling under the sheet. My movie *Crash* was on. I hit the MENU button on the remote to see the time. It was 9:48. Where did Malik go? I began wondering. So I called his cell phone—he picked up and said he would be home shortly. Satisfied that he was on his way home, I went to sleep. Malik woke me by rubbing his rock-hard friend on my butt. I wanted Malik bad, but I had to teach him a lesson. So I acted like I was still asleep.

"It's been two weeks, Shonda—when you going to give me some?" he whispered. I continued to ignore him.

"I know you hear me, Shonda," he said.

I closed my eyes. I could hear very well, but he wasn't my husband so I'm not his wife and I don't owe him shit. No dinner, no money, no sex. He can go to hell. Then Malik took off his clothes and attempted to pleasure himself. It was a lot of smacking and slapping going on. Then it stopped. Thank you—now I could go to sleep. As far as I was concerned, he could do that for the rest of his life.

* * *

I dropped Brianna off at school, and I had to get my uniform together. I needed black shoes. I didn't have any money. I had to break down and speak to Malik. I called him at his job.

"Baby, I need some money."

"How much you need?"

"Like a hundred and fifty."

"Come and get the money."

I went to his office. Technically, I wasn't allowed in the building, because I was fired. My old co-worker Monique was so excited to see me.

We had lunch together at Ruby Tuesday and Monique was the same old crazy chick. She was still the office gossip, happy about other people's misery, wearing a lot of makeup.

"All this time, and y'all still together—that is so nice." If she only knew.

"I know his baby mom is mad. Remember when she came up here and was ready to kick your ass?" She began laughing. *It wasn't that funny*, I thought.

"Yeah, I remember. She is crazy. I don't know what's up with her. She doesn't even let him see the baby. I can count on one hand how many times she let him see him."

"She is going to pay for that in the end."

"I know."

After lunch I went to a uniform store nearby. I tried my uniform pants on. They were too long. I took them to the cleaners to be hemmed. I then went to the grocery store and began to make dinner for myself. I didn't care that Malik had given me money. He was still on my list, so he would have to find his own dinner.

I went to pick up my daughter. I hate Brian's wife. I tell my daughter one thing, she tells her another. She thinks she is better than me because she is married to Brian—big fucking deal. He is no prize. He will cheat on her like he cheated on me. I turned my back to her and told Brianna, "Come on." We got in the car.

"Your hair looks nice, Bree," I said.

"Thank you, Mommy. Andrea took me to the hairdresser."

"Whoever did it did a great job."

"I like it, Mom. Look, it bounces when I walk. Andrea said she had to do something with my hair, 'cause it was nappy and you never do it." I looked at Brianna. And then I began coaching her for more information. "What else did Andrea say about me?"

"Nothing."

"Mom, they put some white stuff that burned in my hair. Then it got straight."

I stopped my car, got out and examined Bree's hair. "Bree, did they call it a perm?"

"Yes, Just for Me," she said while smiling, excited that she had remembered the name of the perm.

I couldn't keep my anger in. I was steaming—she gave my daughter a fucking perm. Who the hell is she? Give yourself a perm, do your own damn hair, bitch. I didn't care if Bree was in the car, I was about to cuss Andrea's ass out.

"Hello, can I speak to Andrea?"

"Yes, this is she."

"Yeah, this is Shonda—you know, Brianna's real mother."

"Did she leave something?" she asked.

"No, she didn't leave anything. Who the fuck do you think you are, giving my daughter a fucking perm without my permission?" I screamed.

"She needed her hair done," she yelled back.

"I don't give a fuck—you are not her mother! And then you talking about me to my daughter like she is not going to come back and tell me."

"I didn't say anything to her about you. How old are you, ten?" she asked in a nasty tone. "She needed her head done. Listen, I'm a grown woman—I'm married to Brianna's dad. You both will have to accept that. Okay? She needed her hair done—you should have done it, and maybe I wouldn't have to." She disconnected the call.

I called right back and Brian picked up. "Brian, you better tell your wife something."

"Tell her what, Shonda? Grow up. I saw Brianna's hair—it looks nice. You are reaching, Shonda." Then he hung up.

That was it—Bree wasn't going over there anymore, at least for a month. I was going to prove to him you don't fuck with me.

Chapter 16

Shonda

I started the academy today. It was a lot of people at training—they said to look around, because everybody wasn't going to make it. Our training uniform was black dickeys, black rubber-sole shoes, and a uniform shirt. We had our training in a building directly across from the prison. The county prison was for inmates waiting to go to trial or get sentenced. We had so much to learn and master in a few short weeks. Intro to Governing Jails, Fingerprinting and Photographing Arrestees, Contraband Searches.

They gave us this big binder with all these codes—ethics, policy and regulations, and report writing—that we had to learn. We were going to have a test every week and one big test at the end. There also were surprise quizzes. They were really trying to act like we were in real school. We had to visit a jail once a week to get OJT—on-the-job training. A few people were trying to be nice and smile and talk about studying together. I wasn't with it. I don't need any more friends. Our instructor was Officer Parham—he told us that we had to keep our hair above our collars, not be late, that we were on probation, and not to think that we were hired just because we had made it this far.

Malik was still trying to be my friend—I was holding out good. He has been tippy-toeing around the house. Being extra pleasant. I have decided I'm not going to get rid of Malik right away. I just know that I have to do me. Since I see that we are only going to be boyfriend and girlfriend, I think I'm going to start going out and meeting people. When somebody asks me for my phone number, I'm going to give it to them. I stopped being mean to him, but I still got my plan ready. I'm going to kick him out, and if he don't leave, I'm leaving. I'll have my first month and security to find my new place.

"How is training going?" he asked.

"It's okay," I said as I underlined a paragraph in my textbook.

"I wanted to tell you I'm real proud of you," he said.

"Thank you," I said, without looking up. Malik was talking, but I wasn't listening.

"Did you hear me, Shonda?"

"No, sorry, I didn't," I said as I got off the sofa and went upstairs to the bedroom. Malik followed me up the stairs. He didn't get it that I didn't want to be bothered.

I had training tomorrow, but I didn't feel like staying in the house with his ass. *Fuck out of here,* I thought.

I wasn't about to stay in this house with Malik. So I called Tae and told her I was about to come over her house, in like, twenty minutes.

"What, you going out?" Malik asked as I began to dress.

"Yeah."

"Where are you going?" he asked, stepping into the cramped bathroom.

"Out," I said, annoyed while plugging in my curling iron.

"What, I can't ask you any questions?"

"Does it really matter what I do?" I said as I looked at him in the mirror.

Malik gripped my arms and said, "Yes, it does. I don't want you going out."

"Malik, maybe if you was my husband, then maybe I would consider listening to you. But since I'm not your wife, you can get off my arm and out of my face." That shut him right up. I showered and came out of the bathroom with the towel wrapped around my body. I sprayed perfume all over my body. I opened my legs and sprayed some in the middle of my thigh. I looked at him through the mirror, trying to see his reaction. He pretended to be watching television. I bent my wet ass in front of his face and dug around in my armoire to find something to wear. I greased my legs up and down with lotion and I put on my tightest, hip-hugging jeans. He watched my every move. I put on jade-green earrings and a necklace.

I made it to my car and looked up at the window to see if Malik was peeking out, and he was. I started the ignition, turned my radio on, and by the time I pulled out of my parking space, Malik started calling my phone. I repeatedly sent him to voice mail. Malik called, like, twenty times. I didn't have a whole lot to say. Niggah, don't try to trap me now that I'm going out.

I arrived at Tae's—she was watching *The Apprentice.*

"What's going on?" Tae asked.

"Nothing, Malik just getting on my nerves and I wanted to get out of the house." We went to the bar around Tae's mom's way. As soon as we sat at the bar, Malik started calling every ten seconds.

"Why he keep calling like that?" Tae asked with her mouth screwed up.

"I don't know."

"Won't you just answer it?" she said as she blew smoke out of the side of her mouth.

"No."

"He is going to keep calling you." She was right, so I answered. "Yeah, Malik, what's up?" I said with an attitude.

"Come home—I don't want you out in the streets."

"Why should I come home? I'm not your wife." I really didn't want Tae to hear my desperateness, but if she didn't hear it now, she would hear it later.

"Shonda."

"Yeah, Malik?"

"Baby, please come home."

"No, for what? You ain't wife me yet. I might as well meet somebody else and stop wasting time with you."

"Shonda, just come home so we can talk."

"Ain't shit to talk about, Malik. Unless you putting a ring on my finger, you can get the fuck out of my life."

"Well, come home, I got that."

"You got what, Malik?"

"We going to get married. Okay?"

"Malik, don't play with me."

"I'm not playing—just bring your ass home." I went and sat back down.

"So what happened?" Tae asked.

"Nothing—he trying to get me to come home, but I told him to get out of my face." I wanted to run home, but I had to talk tough in front of Tae. I sat and drank with her until she was ready to leave, then I dropped her off and sped home. When I walked in the house, Malik was sitting on the sofa.

"Baby, you're the best thing that ever happened to me and I don't want to lose you. What I'm saying is, I want you to be my wife."

"Huh?"

"Yeah, I just want to make you happy. I just want to be all you ever need. And I hope being your husband will make you happy. He pulled out the same necklace he had in the restaurant and a thick gold band—it was plain but pretty. I stared at the ring and burst into tears as I cried, "Oh, Malik—this is beautiful!"

"I love you, girl."

"Malik, you sure?" I gazed up at him. "Are you serious?" I asked him again. I was just ready to leave him. Damn him—I was just looking in the paper to see if I could find another place. I do love him and I don't want to leave him. He is my baby. I just wanted him to marry me.

"Yes, I'm very sure. I called the justice of the peace at city hall. We can go and start our paperwork tomorrow. If you okay with us having a small wedding and saving our money to buy a house."

I was speechless—get married, buy a house! I had a new job—life was going too good. "I love you, Malik," I said.

We had to get a marriage license by going to court and filling out an application. It was a three day waiting period. Malik took a vacation day and we went to city hall and were married. We went before the judge and repeated after him. Malik snatched my hand and said, "You happy now." I laughed and said, "Yes," as he slid the ring on my finger. Malik had the same matching band with chips of diamonds in his. I bought it from a

jewelry store on jewelers' row. I wore a cream dress and
Malik wore a suit. It was plain and simple, just me and
him. I didn't need all the fuss. I didn't even tell my dad
or grandmom. We went to my dad's house—his girlfriend Marjorie was there, playing house. I never liked
her because she told my dad some shit about Malik last
year.

"Frank, come down—Shonda's here," she said. I
walked in without speaking to her. Malik spoke, and I
yelled up the steps. "Daddy," I said, walking around her.

"Where y'all going, all dressed up?"

"Daddy, we got married today."

"What! You took my only daughter off and married
her without asking me?" my dad said as he looked at
Malik. I stepped in between them and said, "Daddy, we
didn't plan it. It was just something we decided to do."

"What do you want me to say? Welcome to the family,
son?"

"Yes."

"Hey, Malik," he said as he shook his hand. "Congratulations—you could have told somebody. Well, now I
don't have to give y'all that ten thousand I was saving for
Shonda's wedding," he said, laughing. He gave Malik a
little man-hug.

"Daddy, you can still give us that money."

"No, I think I'll use that money for a nice vacation."

Marjorie smiled. I guess she thought my dad should
be marrying her ass soon, but that's not going down as
long as I'm breathing.

I called Tae and Brianna and my grandmother. Malik
called Jarrod, who said he was happy for us and him and
Heather would take us out.

"Well, Mrs. Moore, we told everybody about our nuptials—now it is time to go home and consummate."

"We didn't tell everybody—we didn't tell your mother.

You never even introduced me to her. It is like you are ashamed of me, Malik."

"Baby, I know you want to meet my mom and sister, but they real funny-acting."

"Well, they got to accept me now I'm your wife."

"If it means that much to you." He paused and said, "Look we'll go past there right now. I don't know why you care about my family. You know they're on Kim's side. You met my sister. I don't have no father, my brother's in jail."

We pulled up to an apartment building. "Hey, Mom," Malik said as his mother came down the steps in a loose, teal color silk shirt.

"How you doing?"

"Mom, this is Shonda, my wife."

"Your wife?" she said with her eyebrow raised. She put her eyeglasses on to get a good look at me.

"Yes, my wife."

"Nice to meet you. Malik didn't say he was getting married. But my son never ever tells me anything, anyway." Then she said, "Malik, why didn't you tell me you were getting married? I would have come and I would have bought you something," she said as we followed her up the steps.

"Ma, it was spur-of-the-moment."

"We just went and did it," I added.

"Well, congratulations. I'm happy for you. I got some good news for you, too. Omar is coming home."

"How?"

"Well, all I know is somebody was planting narcotics and guns on people, and even though he was one of them, they got to let him out because his case might have been tampered with."

"That's great. When can we go get him?"

"Well, they have to sign some paperwork and he will give me the call. I'm so glad my baby boy coming home." she said as the phone rang. "Hey, baby—well, one of your brothers will be home in two weeks and the other just got married. Yup, Malik is married. Here—your sister want to talk to you," she said as she gave the phone to Malik.

He grabbed it, got on the phone, and said "Hello." In less than sixty seconds he gave the phone back. "Tell her I don't have time for that—bye, Mom—I love you," he said as we walked toward the door. I stood up and said it was nice meeting her.

"What happened?" I asked, once we were out of the apartment.

"Nothing—my sister is just a trip."

"What she say?"

"Nothing, really—just something I didn't want to hear. It don't even matter. You are my wife! Let's go home," he said, as he grabbed my hand and we walked out of the apartment building.

Training wasn't that bad. I wasn't trying to make any friends or be cool with anyone. I was just trying to pass all three of my quizzes and the test. So far, so good—it has been cool. Already three people have dropped out. Two got fired. The two that got fired were smoking a blunt outside the building during our break. These young girls have formed their little group. They order lunch and don't ask if anybody wants to place their order with them. They are very cliquish. I don't care. I take them in doses. Just enough friendly chitchat to get through the day—after training, all of these people will be in different prisons and I'll never see them again. After training I went home and tried to study some of

my notes. I called Malik to check on him to see how his
day was going.

"Hey, baby," I said.

"Hi, Mrs. Moore—how are you?"

"I'm good—studying."

"Is Bree home?"

"No, she is with her dad. Why?"

"Because I want to take you to my mom's house. Be
ready by the time I get home. Okay?"

"I'll start getting dressed now."

Malik's mother's little apartment was decorated with
blue and red streamers. It was weird being there. Everybody was staring. At my family's house, if there was food,
you could have it; a soda, take as many as you like. I
guess that's not the way Malik's family gets down, because they were real funny-acting. They weren't wel-
coming at all. His sister kept looking me up and down.

Every time I took a soda, his sister was all in my face.
She needed to look at the makeshift ponytails in her
bald-spot-edges-headed daughter's hair. I heard her
whisper, "I don't like that bitch." I wanted to say, I don't
like you, either, but it would have been about ten against
one. It wouldn't have ever worked, so I just smiled. She
must be down with Kim, but that team has sunk because
I'm wifey.

I had my marriage license, so I went to the DMV and
changed my identification. I was still deciding if I
wanted to become Shonda Robinson Moore or just
Shonda Moore. Malik wanted me to be Mrs. Moore, so
that's what I'm going to change it to. I got him and me
a life insurance policy.

* * *

Since we were husband and wife now, I was going to do everything humanly possible to make my man happy. After work I ran home and put a load of clothes in. Then I started on dinner. I made turkey meat loaf, Rice-a-Roni, green beans, and cornbread. When Malik came in I gave him a long kiss, sat him down, and placed a napkin in his lap. I began serving him his food. He kissed me between servings. Then he said, "Baby, stop. I have something to tell you."

I playfully extended my body back. He grabbed me before I leaned too far back. "What do you have to tell me, that you love me?" I said.

"Yes, I love you, but that's not it," Malik said, looking very serious.

I sat up and said, "What is it, Malik?"

"My brother is going to move in with us."

"What?" I said as I removed myself from his lap. I stood up and said, "You didn't even ask me."

"I didn't have time. He needed a place to stay."

"Okay, what is wrong with your mom's house?" I asked as I looked him straight in his eye.

"My mom got section-eight. Felons can't stay in federal-funded properties. There was no room at my sister's. So he is going to come stay with us."

"I don't think so," I said.

"If he doesn't stay here, he is going to have to live in a halfway house. He can't stay there—he will be back in the same environment and run back into the same crowd."

"What about my daughter? I don't want her around an ex-criminal."

"My brother's not like that. You work with convicts."

"That is different. And speaking about my job, I could

get fired. I'm about to graduate. I can't have an inmate living with me."

"You can change your address to your dad's address. Shonda, please do this for me, okay? I need this."

"Okay, Malik, whatever." I didn't want Malik's brother living with us, but what was I going to do? When I came home, Malik and his brother were on my sofa.

"What's up—how you?" he said. He was thick, borderline fat, and light with freckles and reddish brown hair with a blue do-rag on his head. I tried to smile. He thanked me for letting him stay and said he wouldn't be a problem. I faked another smile and said he could stay as long as he needed. Malik and him were catching up on everything. I went upstairs and washed. Then I came back downstairs and decided I was going to be a good wifey and sister-in-law. I was Malik's wife, so I had to play my position.

"Are you hungry?" I asked.

"Yes, I haven't had a home-cooked meal in years." Malik looked at me and said, "Baby, you don't have to cook—I was about to take him to get something."

"I don't mind. I'll fry some chicken real quick." Malik smiled, got off the sofa, gave me a kiss, and whispered that he loved me.

It didn't take me any time to fry the chicken, and I baked the potatoes in the microwave, then poured a ready-made salad onto their plates. Dinner was served in forty-five minutes.

"Yo—this is so good," Omar said as he gulped the food down like a starving dog.

"Thank you," I said.

We were in the middle of eating when unexpectedly there was a knock at the door. Malik got up and answered it. It was their mother, Ms. Gloria, and sister Nadia, stopping by. They walked in and half spoke to me. I started cleaning up the dishes.

"It smells good," Ms. Gloria said.

"Would you like some?" I offered.

"Yeah, I'll take a little," she said as she took off her coat and made herself comfortable. Nadia gave her a look like, *What are you doing?* I guess the ice was breaking.

I cleaned and then excused myself and I went upstairs and let Malik and his family catch up on old times. After they left, I called Tae to see what she was up to. A man answered, so I hung up. I dialed the phone back. I looked down at my screen on my cell phone to make sure I had dialed the right number.

"Hello—may I speak to Tae?"

"Oh, she's in the house. I have her phone."

"And who are you?" I asked. He laughed, then said, "This is Ken—who is this?"

I didn't answer his question, I just hung up the phone. Okay, what's going on with my girl? She getting dumb or something? I called Tae on her house phone.

"Tae, what's going on with you, girl?"

"Nothing—getting dressed."

"Who has your phone?"

"Oh, that is my new boyfriend I was telling you about. Hold on—that's my other line." Tae clicked back over to me and laughed.

"Were you getting smart with my baby?"

"What? No, I just asked him who he was. Why you got some nut-ass dude answering your phone, anyway?"

"It was in my car."

"He got your car, too? Oh I'm hanging up—what is wrong with you?"

"Nothing, girl. Don't worry—everything is cool."

"Well, Malik's brother has moved in."

"The one from jail?"

"Yes, the one from jail."

"Oh my, you going to have to give me a report on that situation. But I got to go—my boo at the door." Tae is moving way too fast, I thought.

Chapter 17

Nadine

Mrs. Dorsey was walking down the hall. Time was good to her face but not to her body. She was one hamburger away from being a super-sized meal. Her ass was as wide as a backseat of a car. When she walked, it bounced from side to side. The sad thing for her is that she is probably going to get fatter. Her mom was a hippo. I remembered her coming up to the school. Well, at least she is already married, because she will not be attracting anyone new. She had four kids, I heard—courtesy of Mrs. Meyers—but her marriage is on the rocks. That's probably stressful, but I still hate the bitch. But for some reason she keeps trying to be my friend, smiling when she sees me and making small talk. Bitch, I'm not your friend, I wanted to tell her. She tried to apologize to me one day. I looked at her like she was stupid. I had better things to worry about than Mrs. Dorsey. Before my kids came back from Art I had to clean my room—there were pencil shavings and paper balls all over the place. I straightened the desk back up and began writing my lesson on the board.

* * *

I was waiting for the students to complete their assignment.

"Ms. Clark, can I go to the bathroom?" Natasha Byrd asked.

"No, not till the end of the day."

"We have an assembly today," she said. I checked the schedule—she was right. Big as day in red marker was "fire assembly." I looked down at my watch—we had about ten minutes before the assembly.

"So, can I go to the bathroom, Ms. Clark?"

"You just asked me and I said no."

"I know, Ms. Clark, but my period is on," she whispered.

"Go ahead—meet us in the auditorium."

I escorted my class to the assembly. I heard a friendly voice say in the crowded auditorium, "Good morning, Ms. Clark." I was about to return the greeting until I realized who was giving it. It was Mrs. Dorsey waving at me. She really didn't get it. I wasn't her friend. She waved again. I looked behind me, like you must be waving to somebody else. I didn't even feel like seeing her face, and the fact that the other teachers were jocking her every movement made me mad. Even the principal was in on it. Before she came, I was the young, cool teacher with bright ideas. Now this bitch comes in and sets up a damn school newspaper and drama club in a few short weeks.

As soon as the assembly was over, I dismissed my students and called my aunt.

"Aunt Connie, I need to talk to you."

"What's going on with you?"

"Auntie, one of the girls that I used to hate from high school now works at my job. She makes me want to quit."

"What?"

"I hate her. Remember the whole school year no one spoke to me?"

"Yes, I remember, but that was so long ago, and you're not worried about that, are you?"

"I still hate her for making my senior year miserable."

"Niecy, please forget her—she's probably fat now with a bunch of kids."

"She is."

"Well, see? She got her punishment and look at you. You have it going on with no kids. I got to call you later."

Talking to my aunt did make me feel better. But I still didn't have any dates, no prospects, and was very lonely. I was spending my Friday night all alone in the house by myself. I'm not depressed. I don't know what I am. I want to get back with Erick. Every man I have met since him, there has been something wrong with them. Quentin has not called since our conversation. I have come to the conclusion I don't understand men and they don't understand me. I don't like being single—it is no fun. I thought all those men that made passes at me when I was in a relationship would be knocking at my door. The ones who said, if you didn't have a man. The ones who pulled up at the stoplight and I turned, trying to act like I didn't see them. Where are they now? Home with their women, probably.

I want a family—I want to have a baby and get married and just be happy. Maybe Brandy coming to my school is a sign. The more I thought about it, the more obvious it seemed—I have to get my man back. I haven't spoken to him since we broke up in January, and the few times he has called I've told him I needed him to give me some more time. I want my man back—I should call him, I thought. But what would I say? Hey, baby, what are you doing? I haven't called him, I've ignored his calls and told him to stop sending me flowers. I don't know how well he will take hearing from me. My cell phone vibrated—I picked up.

"What's up, Aunt Connie?"

"Stop by," Aunt Connie said.

"Why, what's going on?"

"We're having a card party. I cooked. Toya is coming with her friend Lynn. Come get a plate."

"Okay, I will stop."

They were playing poker. My extent of gambling and cards were, I Declare War or Pitty-pat. I learned to play that in camp for candy. Toya wasn't here yet—I didn't know if she was still coming. Uncle Chuck's friend, Mr. Sonny, who was with his wife, kept finding reasons to brush up on me. The first time, he said he was sorry. Then the second time, he smiled. There is not going to be a third time. Fresh old man—I'm going to find his wife and ask her, is he clumsy with his played out hoop earring and kangol to the side? I grabbed a kiwi-strawberry cooler and sat back and waited for Toya. She and her friend Lynn arrived a half an hour later. Toya's stomach was now poking through her belly shirt. Most people would look and think, she needs to work out and just has a gut.

"Look at your little stomach."

"I know—I'm trying to get my last go-out before I get too big. Why don't you go out with us?"

"Where y'all going?"

"We was going to ride to New York, but the clubs be

acting funny. Last week she rode all the way up there and couldn't get in the 40/40—isn't that a fuck-up?"

"Well, I'm not riding to New York."

"Me neither, I think we should just stay here because I'm tired. Rodney called me and said he was coming over, and Lynn about to make some martinis."

Lynn made us apple martinis. She took sliced green apples out of a yellow plastic bag, ice, and a mixer.

"You better not drink one," I said to Toya.

"I'm not," Toya said. After I drank my first apple martini, I suggested to Lynn she should go to bartending school.

"I was thinking about it," she said. Me, Toya, and Lynn sat in the kitchen and joked, and sipped on apple martinis. By the time my step-cousin Rodney arrived, I had two more apple martinis. And Rodney was looking good. So good, I started coming on to him. When Toya and Lynn walked out of the kitchen, I blew a kiss at him. He looked at me, confused. I didn't care that he was supposed to be my cousin. I walked over to him and did something I wanted to do since I was seventeen—I kissed his lips with my tongue. He didn't move. As soon as I pulled away from him, Toya walked back in. I touched his face and stumbled into the living room. My Uncle Chuck was complaining about his friend, Mr. Sonny, because he had slipped cards under the table, and beat him for a hundred dollars.

"Damn, that niggah was cheating," Uncle Chuck said.

"Chuck, I told you he was cheating—you should have been listening," Aunt Connie said. Then she turned to me and said, "You want to stay? You sure you can drive home?"

"I'm fine. I will call you when I get in." I didn't feel drunk. I felt fine to drive home. I slid my seat belt on and began my drive home. I switched stations—there was nothing on but commercials. Then the perfect song was playing while I'm coming home, all alone. I was forced to listen to Usher sing, "Let It Burn." "Shut up, Usher—you let it burn," I yelled at the radio. The lyrics hit too close to home. I started thinking about Erick. So I decided to give Erick a phone call. My daddy used to always say, a drunk man is an honest man. That saying is very true. The liquor gave me the heart I didn't have when I was sober. I called Erick at 3:30 in the morning. The phone rang, then it rang again. I was nervous. He answered and I said, "Erick, I love you."

"Who is this?"

"Baby, it's me. I love you so much. I miss you. I wish I would have never broke up with you. I wished we never broken up."

"Nadine, I'll talk to you later—I'm asleep."

"Can I come sleep with you?"

"No!"

"Why not?" I slurred.

"Because you can't. Call me tomorrow."

"We were meant for each other, Erick. We belong together," I sang. He didn't say anything—he was not moved at all by my confession. Erick simply laughed at me and told me to carry my drunk ass to sleep. It was my fault we weren't together. I had to correct my wrong. I decided since Erick didn't get the intensity of my message on the phone, I had to tell him in person. I drove over to his house. His bedroom light was on and his car was parked at the corner. In a perfect world, he would open up the door and say *I love you* and make beautiful love to me and hold me until I went to sleep. I knocked on the door—he came to the door in his boxers.

"Hey, baby," I said as I went to hug him. He had a puzzled expression.

"What are you doing here?" he said, annoyed.

"I wanted to see you."

"Didn't I tell you I was 'sleep and to call me tomorrow?"

"Yes, but I wanted to see you, baby," I said, still trying to hold him. He was resisting my hug.

"Can I come in?"

"No, I have company."

"You have what?" I asked as I sobered up temporarily.

"I'm a single man and I have company," he restated.

"Who is over here this time of night?"

"A friend—good night." He shut the door in my face. I felt like trash. My ex-boyfriend had dissed me and I kissed my cousin.

Chapter 18

Kim

Kevin's dad never called back, but I guess that is for the better. I have been talking about the entire incident with Dr. Weltz. She was even afraid for me to meet him.

"Do you think you are ready? He raped you."

"I know, but you know, I am over it—he doesn't think he raped me. He thinks it was consensual since we both were drinking and high."

"There is no excuse."

"I know, I know, but I got to let go of the way I feel and give Kevin his family."

"Well, I would suggest that you take it slow."

"I will—thank you, Dr. Weltz."

After my session I went back to the office. I had a bunch of messages from various people, but the one that stood out was the one from Darius Miller, Kevin's father. I immediately returned the call.

"Hello—may I speak to Darius Miller?"

"Hello, Kimberly, this is him. I'm sorry it took so long to contact you back, but I'll be in the Maryland area at a church. Can you meet me down there? We can meet, talk, and schedule the paternity test."

"Not a problem—just call me with the exact address so I can get directions," I said. I was so happy Darius had called, I told Nicole everything that was going on.

The day was moving slowly—it was raining hard. I hoped the rain would calm down by the time it was time for me to go home. My phone kept ringing and I kept sending it to voice mail.

"Who is that that keeps calling you? Are you still ducking Malik?" Nicole asked.

"No, this isn't Malik. It's this guy I met at the restaurant the other night with my sister."

"So, why aren't you answering the telephone?" she asked.

"Because I gave him my number just to be nice. He's white, but he was cute," I said.

"You're not going to date him because he is not black."

"I don't date outside of my race," I said as a matter of fact.

"And why not?"

"Because I just don't. I mean, it won't work out, anyway. I prefer a brother."

"What's wrong with you? What have the brothers done for you lately?"

"And what is that supposed to mean?"

"I'm not trying to be in your business, but look at both of your kids' fathers. Sorry I have to be the one to tell you, but all our good black men is already taken."

"No, they are not—I'm not falling for that myth," I said.

"That is not a myth—they are all married already. The rest is in jail, gay, or broke players. Shit, let a white man come my way—I'm taking him up on his offer. I'm not growing old waiting for a black man in shining armor. Because they don't wait for us," Nicole said.

"Well, I am," I snapped.

"Please—I'm not waiting for a brother. We give these damn black men too much coddling. We commend them for having a job or taking care of their kids. Don't know another race of men do so much fuck-up shit to their children. I went down to child support court because this motherfucker thinks since we broke up he don't have to pay child support, and I have to say it was about ninety percent black."

"That's not everybody," I said.

"Well, it's a large percentage of them. Plus, I want a man on the same level as me. We're buying houses and having degrees," Nicole said.

"I don't care what you say. I'm not interested in a white man."

"I will answer your phone for you—ask him if he wants to date me."

"I can't."

"Why?"

"Because I do everything the same; nothing out of the ordinary. I eat the same things and I just like what I like."

"But you did say he was cute."

"Yeah, he is but I definitely can't go out with him. We will have nothing in common."

"How do you know?"

"Because I know," I said as I forwarded his call to voice mail.

"How about we do some work?" I said, changing the subject.

"Kim, let me ask you something. When was the last time you had your eyebrows waxed."

"Why?" I asked, pulling a small compact mirror out

of my desk. I tried to shape my brows. But they were bushy and out of place.

"You need them professionally waxed."

"Well, thank you. Nicole, do some work."

I took Nicole's advice and stopped by the nail salon to get my eyebrows waxed. I sat down in the chair and the woman wiped hot wax across my brow. Then, she ripped off the strip of wax material. My eyebrow felt like it was on fire. My cell phone was ringing, I answered.

"Hello, hello," I said as I was still absorbing the pain from having hair removed.

"Hey, how are you? You are hard to get in touch with."

"I'm fine—who is this."

"This is Andrew. You're a busy woman."

"Not really. Listen, can I call you back?" *He finally caught me,* I thought.

"No, because I don't think you will." I laughed at his assumption. He was right—I had no intention of calling him back.

"You're laughing because you know I'm telling the truth. I don't know how much longer I can chase you, Kimberly," he said as I paid the cashier and walked out of the nail salon.

"Huh? You haven't been chasing me. It's not like that. I just . . ." before I completed my sentence he interrupted me and said, "I do believe I at least deserve an opportunity to prove myself."

"You're right—go ahead," I said, getting in my car.

"How is your day going so far?" he asked.

"Okay, I guess. How about you?"

"I'm okay. I'm in Detroit and it is so cold."

"Detroit—why are you there?"

"I'm here on business."

"Oh, okay, what do you do?"

"I have my own consultant firm. So when are we going to be able to talk in person?"

"Real soon. Call me when you get back into town."

"You promise you are going to answer the phone?"

"I promise I will."

"Okay, Kim, I will. Have a nice evening."

Chapter 19

Shonda

Graduation was in two weeks. We had a big final exam, and I had to be able to do two hundred crunches in three minutes. And run two miles in fifteen minutes. I have been training and studying—I feel pretty good about everything. As long as I study, I should be good. I didn't want to let Brianna go back over Brian's house, but she is a distraction. Every other minute coming to tell me she is bored or hungry or tired when she is at the house. I started talking to one of the girls in the young-girl clique—her name was Angie. She was a cute, dark-brown chick with blond micro-braids and an enormous forehead. She really needed bangs to cover it up. She wanted to get together and have a study session.

I met her at her house, prepared to study. She was twenty-two and still lived at home with her mother, father, and three sisters. It was really noisy at her house. Her baby sister was crying, her mother was cussing her thirteen-year-old sister out for having a boy come to the door. And then there was the dad, watching basketball highlights on ESPN like he was deaf. I don't know why she suggested we study at her house.

"There is nobody at my house. We can go there," I suggested.

"It is usually not this noisy. My sister usually be at work and my dad at his other job."

We packed up and drove to my house, and suddenly I wished we would have stayed at hers. Omar had been staying with us for a while now, and I notice he wasn't fond of bathing or cleaning. He was just so messy and funky. I asked Malik a couple of times to have a conversation with him, but I don't think he has. Omar was there and so was his corn-chip aroma.

"Omar, I'm about to study in here."

"Okay," he said as he lowered the television.

"No, I'm going to need total silence."

"Oh, all right then, I'm out." He went and put on a jean jacket and his dusty, ten-lifetimes timbs, and headed for the door.

"Tell Malik I'll be at Mom's."

"Uh-huh." Call him yourself, I thought.

"Who is that?" Angie asked.

"My brother-in-law."

"He is cute."

"No, he is not. You don't want him." I said, curling my lip.

"He got a car?" she asked.

"No."

"A job?"

"No, and he lives in my basement."

"Okay, you right—I don't want him. But I can't wait until we graduate because I already been to the car dealership. Then I'm getting my own place." Angie was acting like when we graduated we were going to be making a lot of money. It was okay money but not great—we started at thirty-two thousand and could get all the overtime we wanted. I guess she planned on getting a bunch of overtime. She wrote down key terms on the back of flash cards and kept going through them over and over again. We had almost one hundred terms and procedures. I'm sure we won't be using all these once we actually get in the prison.

"Let's try to make sure we pass first before you plan your future," I said.

"You know we going to pass—it's going to be easy."

I hope so.

Angie stayed until two in the morning. Malik was still not home. I called him.

"Malik, where are you?"

"Dropping Jarrod off."

"I don't believe you," I said.

"You don't believe me? Do you want me to put him on the phone?"

"Yeah, put him on the phone." I heard Jarrod in the background, saying, "What, man? No, I'm not getting on the phone—I'm not with that dumb shit."

The next morning I was tired and running late. I walked in the testing room. I just sat down and reread each question two times before I answered them. After the test, I met up with Angie.

"How do you think you did?"

"I know I passed."

"Me, too. Let's go celebrate that this is over."

"No, I have to go home and see my husband."

We both passed with an eighty-four—you needed an eighty to make it. And out of our thirty, only sixteen made it. I really felt like I accomplished something. I was married and I had a good job that I could retire from with benefits. All I got to do is buy my house, and I'll be on the same level as Brian. Me and Malik will probably be doing better in a few years.

They assigned me to Salter Correction, a county prison. I had to report to my job on Monday. Malik took me out to dinner. My dad, Marjorie, and Brianna all came—we all got a big table. I was happy.

Chapter 20

Shonda

Salter Correctional Facility was a women and men's prison. The jail was on State Road in Northeast Philadelphia, the outer part of the city. A row of prisons lined the road. There was barbed wire around the gray, high, stone walls. I parked my car in the crowded parking lot. I didn't wear my uniform to work—I took it out of my trunk and was going to change inside.

"Excuse me, you know which way to Salter?"

"That's the building over there." The woman thanked me and continued to pull her two small children toward the prison.

There was a long, pebbled road to the jail. I walked toward the prison. I saw a truck being inspected. The driver had to get out and open the back of the truck to make sure there weren't any escapees. A little further down the road, inmates tapped the window and were holding a sign. The sign read, SHOW TITS SHOW ASS. I turned my head the other way.

I reported to C/O Riddick. She walked up and said, "You'll be with me tonight—let me show you around." She was a mean, big girl, like five-ten. She had a big gap in her two front teeth and her hair in corn rows going back with a part in the middle.

"There are five units, A through E."

"How many people in each unit?" I asked, looking around the prison.

"Each unit holds, like, 115. We are so overcrowded, it's more like 125 in each unit. You'll probably be put on unit B on the second floor—they need help down there. Units D and E are the women's units."

"When will I get assigned to a unit?" I asked.

"They probably will be moving you around for the next couple of months. You can report to me to find out where they need you. We keep everybody apart. There is a little gang situation going on, but mostly we got North Philly at war with South Philly," she said as she opened the cell for me to look at. The bed was a dark gray, steel flat bed with a thin mattress. We walked into the rec room—about fifty inmates in orange jumpsuits were watching a big television. Other inmates were in line to use the telephone.

"They get ten minutes free direct phone time and unlimited calling card calls. They have codes—do not give any of them their codes, they know them." A few inmates were huddled around, playing cards. Riddick picked out one guy that was hiding from her and said, "Yo, Riley, if I see you again, you going to be sorry." The inmate said, "I'm sorry Ms. Riddick. I got you."

"Don't play with me, Riley," she said, then took me to meet our supervisor, Sergeant Wilson. We walked in his office—he was short with some kind of curly process in his hair. He looked up from his computer.

"Nice to meet you," he said. "Riddick, what do you have her doing?"

"I was walking her around, then I was about to go to lunch."

"Take her down there on Unit A until you come back from lunch."

"Okay, sir." We walked out of his office, and Riddick said, "I'm about to take my lunch. Do you want me to get you something while I'm out?"

"No, I will just order something. Do you have menus?"

"Menus. No, I don't know why they didn't tell you that in training there is no ordering food to the jail. Now, if you want to you can go and pick food up, but you can't bring it back in."

"Oh—well, I'll just eat something when I get home," I said.

"All right—let me introduce you to Hicks."

"Hey, this is Robinson—she is new. Show her around. I'm going to lunch."

Riddick left me, and I trained with Hicks until my break. He was a tall, thin, young guy, about twenty-six with light facial hair and a low 'fro. He just showed me how to operate the cameras that monitored the different areas of the prison until it was time for me to go on break.

At my break, I walked back to my car and tried to call Malik. He didn't answer, so I just sat in the car and listened to the radio. The rest of the evening, C/O Riddick showed me how to fill out paperwork.

When I came home, it was 12:30. I looked in the refrigerator to see if Malik had ordered me something. There was an iced tea and cheeseburgers and fries. I warmed my food, then sat at the kitchen table. Malik walked into the kitchen.

"How was your day?" he said as he put dishes in the sink.

"It was okay," I said sadly.

"So what shift are you going to work?" he asked as he pulled out a chair and took a seat.

"I have to work all three shifts for the first six months. I'm still considered a trainee."

"You're not going to change your name at work, Mrs. Moore," he played.

"No, I'm going to stay Ms. Robinson at work." I yawned.

"What's wrong, baby? You like it? You think you're going to be able to last?" he asked.

"I think so, baby. I'm tired. I'm going to go upstairs and take a bath and get in the bed." I put what was left of my food in the refrigerator, then I dragged up the steps to the bathroom. I pulled out my facial cleanser and body wash, then pulled the shower curtain back and saw a big, brown ring of dirt in the tub.

"Malik," I screamed.

He came racing up the steps to see what was wrong. "You okay?"

"No, I am not. Look at this nasty shit," I said pointing at the ring in the tub.

"You called me up here to show me that?"

"I want to take a bath."

Malik shoved me and said, "Shonda, move. I'll clean it up."

"You act like it is no big deal. That is nasty—I don't want to have to clean up after no grown man." *If you want this to work, you better tell him something,* I thought. Malik cleaned the tub out and I took my postponed bath.

They have been placing me somewhere different each shift. Today it was the visiting room with Angie, aka C/O Sheppard. She was still silly—she made me laugh, talking about everybody. She had a nickname for everybody at the job. Kids were crying, screaming for their daddies when the visits were over. It was actually kind of sad. I saw guys in the visiting room with different visits from several women, each thinking she was the one. My job was just to make sure they didn't get too close and to tell them to leave when it was time. I tried to be nice about telling them their visit was over. I mean, that is the least I could do. They were locked up. I would go and tell them to leave before they got in any trouble. They understood. But Riddick was just mean as shit. If you looked funny at her or didn't get up soon enough, she took your name off the visiting list for a week. A lot of these correction officers are just some mean, spiteful bitches. It's like their first time having a real job and some control. Most of them are power freaks and get pleasure from disrespecting and abusing inmates.

Maybe Malik is right—I don't know if I am built for this. I think Malik *is* right. Maybe I can't stomach this every day. It is depressing. I know that people do wrong shit—that's how they got here. I don't cosign with no murderers or child molesters, or rapists. But being at the job, I see how hard it is. I go home every day and they are still here. Some of them going to still be here until their trial dates come. Some people are sitting for a two-hundred-dollar bail. Nobody cares enough about you to get you out of jail and pay the two-hundred-dollar bail. I'm seeing guys that are young as hell, and I know they just got a body. My job is to keep them inside of the high-stoned barbed-wired walls, but I felt sorry for them. A lot of them didn't do it or refused to snitch on each other. They'd rather do a possible five-year bid and still be able to come home and be the man on their block. I don't know, I wasn't expecting this. It is crazy. They say, leave your job at work. But it is hard—I have been coming home thinking about it.

Chapter 21

Nadine

Tonight I will go in the house, turn on the E Channel, and call it a night. A rerun of *E! True Hollywood Story* was on. Between VH-1 and E Channel, I have my dose of celebrity news. I knew who was too thin and whose marriage was about to end. I don't care about them, but when you don't have a life, hearing about somebody else's drama is comforting.

I thought about trying to call somebody, but then I would have to ask them what they are doing in the house or alone on a Saturday night. Then they would wonder the same thing about me. This is so, so sad—I wish I could call Erick. I dialed his number, and before the call connected I closed my phone. I want my baby back. It hurts so bad—*I shouldn't have never left him.* I want to call him. I know he got to feel the same way—he couldn't have turned his feelings off just like that. He was just leaving me messages, telling me he loved me. I know I did tell him I didn't want to be with him. And when he did try to get with me I did ignore him, but so what? I made a mistake. My baby got the right to be mad at me for leaving him. But I got the right to try to get back with him. I miss my man—I miss him so much. I want to call Erick and tell him that I was wrong. But I was upset with him. Who was in his house that he couldn't let me in? Who is in my baby's ear, turning him against me? Somebody is making him into a monster. Somebody must have told him he was a good catch or cute, because he sure is fronting. Who is this bitch that can garner so much respect that he could tell me, his woman, that he was asleep? My missing him and loving him turned to anger. I was not going to plead my case to him, I was just going to let him know what he was missing. I was going to ruin his Saturday night. I called his voice mail and purposely put the phone away from my mouth and began to speak to my imaginary boyfriend. "Yes, I'm dressed. No, baby, I'm waiting on you. As soon as you get here, we can be out. Don't worry about what I have on—hurry up, okay? I miss you." My conversation was getting so good, I was starting to believe I was really on the phone with someone and that I had a date. I made noises like I was walking around in the house—I turned the television on, and then the water in the sink.

"Hold on, okay? Hey, girl—u-huh, me and Tyreek—yup, him—we are going out for dinner. Plus, I bought a bottle of champagne—we going to pop that. Erick? Please, nobody ain't thinking about him. I know, that's right—fuck him. All right—well, hold on. Matter of fact, let me call you back before he hang up. Hello? Yeah, um, sorry about that—that was my cousin, Toya. I'll see you when you get here." I then walked around a little, made some noise, and then hung up the phone. I know Erick nosey-ass would listen to it all. Well, at least he won't think I'm home all by myself on a Saturday night, depressed about him. Even though I am.

* * *

Right now I needed to speak to somebody that knew about relationships. Somebody that has been through all of this and has seen the light. I called my Aunt Connie.

"Aunt Connie, what you think I should do? I miss him. I told him I love him and he told me to take my drunk ass back to sleep. Then he didn't let me in when I showed up at his house. He acted like I was somebody off the street."

"Didn't I tell you not to let go of that good man?"

"Yes, I know."

"Well, now you're going to have to wait. Nobody wants a crying pathetic telling them they love them. You have to be strong and wait for him to come back to you. Time will tell."

Okay, I thought my aunt would give me an inspirational, motivational speech. That mess she was talking might have worked back in the day, but it doesn't work now. I have to take matters into my own hands. I have to go claim my man one way or the other. I'm going to track his ass down. I dialed Toya.

"Toya, you think you can go with me to Roy's Lounge?"

"For what? Isn't that the bar where your ex hangs out at?"

"Yeah."

"So why are you trying to go there?"

"I just want to see if he is with anyone else."

"Didn't you go to his door and he wouldn't let you in?"

"Yeah. I just want to see if . . . she looks better than me and see if he's happy."

"No, girl, you are crazy. Plus I got the kids."

"I'll pay you. Ask your mom can she watch the kids and ask her can we hold her car, too!"

"You ask her for the car, and I'll just meet you over there."

I arrived in all black to my aunt's house. Toya and the girls were watching TV and Ariel was on her cell phone. I walked in the kitchen and took a seat. I was trying to think of a reason to ask for her car. I didn't have one, so I just asked.

"Aunt Connie, can I hold your car?" I pleaded with my hands held together.

"Why do you need my car?" she asked.

"Because we are about to go stalk Erick, and he knows what Nadine looks like," Toya butted in.

"I wouldn't even bother if I was you. But if you feel like you have to chase after a man, you can hold my car." Aunt Connie grabbed her bag and said, "Here are my keys. Fill my tank up, too." I went to grab them from her when she said, "Slow down—I'm trying to get the key off this ring. Don't get my windows broke out, 'cause if you do, you're paying for them."

We rode up to Roy's Lounge, and just as I suspected, his car was out there. That meant he was inside. I didn't know if that meant his new girl was with him. I didn't really care. I wanted to go in and confront him, but I didn't have the heart. We waited in the car.

"So, are you going to go in there?"

"No."

"We just going to wait here?" Toya asked.

"Yeah," I said as I pulled out binoculars. Toya snatched them out of my hand and said, "Where did you get that spy nightvision thing from?"

"One of the kids at my school."

"You are crazy, Nae. I can't believe you got me out here like this," she said, pulling out a cigarette.

"I know you not about to smoke."

"I smoked with the other two and they came out fine."

I didn't say anything. I just wanted her to stay with me.

One hour into our stakeout, my partner decided she was hungry. I took her to the drive-thru at McDonald's as fast as I could and she was happy. Then her man called and she had to explain our mission to him. All I heard was Nate screaming at Toya to put on the speakerphone. She did.

"Yo Nadine!" Nate yelled.

"Yeah?"

"You can't be having my woman out in the street chasing after your man."

Sighing, I said, "Nate, we will be there." Toya giggled and hung up the call as I peeped back in my binoculars. "Oh my God, oh my God. There he goes," I said as I ducked down and continued to peep in my binoculars.

He looked over at the car—he wasn't with a girl, he was with his cousin Tommy. He looked so nice. Damn— I wanted to get out and say, "Hey baby, I miss you," but he might diss me in front of my cousin, and I'm a grown woman and I can't have that happen. He got in his car and left.

"So, you not going to say anything to him?"

"No."

"You mean to tell me we sat here for all this time and you are not going to say anything?"

"No."

"You are going crazy, Nadine. Take me home."

"I'm about to," I said as I pulled out of the parking space. I couldn't wait for Toya to get out of my car so I could call Erick and try to talk to him.

I switched cars and dropped off Toya. I decided to try my luck again with Erick. Maybe he was ready to talk to me. I drove to his house to make sure he was alone. I wondered if his new woman might have went out with her friends and was meeting him at his house. Or was he meeting her at her house.

I parked down the street from his house. Lights from cars riding past kept me from nodding off. He wasn't home yet. He had to drop Tommy off. Then I saw him pull up—he was alone and went into the house. I started to get out and tell him how much I loved him and missed him, but I couldn't. I would look like a stalker. I stayed until 5:47. I was then convinced that the booty call-time limit was over. It was early Sunday morning. It was time for me to go home, go to sleep, and sulk. Lights out.

I got to get over Erick—I have been thinking about him. I need to see him while I'm sober. With a clear head. That would make him remember how good we are together. So, the next morning, I knew Erick was home alone so I decided to go and spill my heart out to him. I dressed, then dialed his number as quickly as I could. He didn't answer. My stomach filled with anxiety. I have to talk to my baby. I'm going to tell him how I feel. I was going over what I was going to say in my head. I called him again—he didn't pick up. I went to his house and knocked on the door, then rang the bell. I didn't know how he was going to react to me. Here it was—we had been broke up all of this time.

"Good morning." I said, with Krispy Kremes in my hand and a smile on my face.

I tried to walk around him but he stopped me. "I brought you breakfast," I said.

"I have breakfast," he said as I noticed the plate in his hand.

"What, do you have company?" I said, noticing that something wasn't right.

"Yes, I do," he said.

"This early? What?" I said in disbelief. I know there wasn't anyone there when I left here a few hours ago.

"We are single, right?"

I didn't care if he had company or not, I had to tell him how I feel. "Baby, I miss you so much. I need you. I don't care who is here with you. I need you to tell them to leave. We need to talk—I want to get you back, baby. I miss you. We shouldn't have broke up," I cried.

"That's not going to happen, Nadine."

"Why not? I want you to talk to me now. We need to talk, Erick."

"Listen, Nadine. We can't have this conversation right now."

"Why not, Erick? Why can't you talk to me now? Who is more important than me, Erick? Huh? Who?" I yelled.

"Because I can't," he said, attempting to close the door.

"You're going to talk to me right now," I said, blocking the door with my foot.

"It's not a good time. I'll talk to you later."

"No—now, Erick, now. Talk to me about it now."

"No, Nadine, I have company."

"How could you do this to me?" I said, backing away from the door. I wanted to speak, but the tears that were forming in my eyes didn't let me. I didn't care if his visitor heard my cries—I wanted her to hear it. I wanted her to know who I was.

"Do what? We broke up. Nadine, I have to talk to you later."

"You're wrong. Erick, you're wrong," I said, shaking my head and crying.

"I'm wrong, Nadine? Please. Shit does not happen when you say so, Nadine. You just can't clap your hands and our relationship is back on. I have to go." Erick closed the door right in my face. After he did that I realized two things. One, Erick was over me, and two, I had to get over him. *Absence makes the heart grow fonder—* who said that dumb shit? Whatever, because Erick is not thinking about me. He is thinking, out of sight, out of mind, and whoever he has in his house is probably sleeping in my space on my side of the bed. Hugged up under my man, watching one of my DVDs that I bought, eating Sunday breakfast.

Chapter 22

Kim

Andrew said he wasn't going to call me anymore because I didn't return his calls. He said he wasn't, but he called and called. He is very persistent. I have to give him credit for that. Actually, I'm rewarding him with a date. I'm going out with him tonight—it was either go out with him or change my phone number. He left me a cute message every morning, telling me why I should date him. If I didn't think he was a little cute, it would have been creepy.

We were going to meet in Manayunk on Main Street at 9:00. My sister Karen had the boys. Everybody has still been helping me out with them, and it feels good to have time alone to myself.

Main Street was a narrow, hilly street with restaurants, clothing boutiques, and night life. I drove around the block and finally found a parking space. My Altima was crammed into a compact-only parking space. The owner I parked next to is going to curse me out when they see how close my bumper is to theirs. I set the alarm and walked down the dark street. The air and wind was tapering off. People were bustling up and down the street. I looked for the restaurant, Lagos. I went in and had a seat. The restaurant was very small—little candles sat on each table. I was about to take a seat at the bar when I saw a man wearing an oxford-blue, button-down shirt. He held a Yuengling beer in one hand.

"Hey, beautiful—you made it," he said as he directed me to our table.

"You thought I wasn't going to show up?"

"It was a possibility," he said as he pulled my chair out for me. I sat and took off my coat. The waitress came over and asked me what I was having. I looked at the menu, and she said she would give me a few moments and went to service another table.

"What are you having?"

"I don't know yet."

"How was your friends' wedding?" I asked.

"It was good. Remember—he was so upset at his brother for getting married that he decided to protest and they had to escort him out of the wedding."

"That is funny. So, what do you like to do?"

"I try to get my daughter, Cianni, on the weekends. Her mother keeps her so busy with soccer and her tap class, she barely has time for me. But for the most part, me and her hang out. I take her on little day dates. I try to show her how a man is supposed to treat her. So when a little boy comes up and he doesn't have himself together, my daughter will laugh at him."

"That's cute—I want my boys to grow up to be good guys," I said, looking around and out the window.

"Kimberly, you look nervous—are you waiting for someone to walk through the door?" he asked.

"No." I was mad at myself for him being able to read me.

"Well, why do you keep staring at the door and the window?" he asked. "Are you expecting someone?"

"No. So have you always dated black women?" I asked, changing the subject.

"No, I have always dated all women. I went to a mixed school—growing up I was attracted to all women. I like who I like."

"Really?"

"Yeah, really. Why do you say *really* like that?"

"I don't know—white guys don't usually approach me."

"So you never dated outside of your race?"

"No."

"Why not?"

"I didn't really have an opportunity. I was in college with my first son, and I had him and I didn't really date. Then I met my second son's father, and we were together for five years. We were at our wedding when he decided he wasn't ready."

"I thought you were divorced."

"No, I have never been married."

"It must have hurt you when he left the wedding."

"Yeah, it did, but I'm over it now. I just hate being stereotyped, like, in that single-mom category that the media sends out."

"My mother and stepfather raised me. My mother is a very strong woman. What about your parents?"

"They are still together."

"You seem pretty strong—two children, and boys at that."

"Yeah, they keep me going," I said, looking for the waitress. I was ready to order. He was getting too intrusive.

"So where do you go to school?"

"I originally went to Lincoln University, then I transferred to Community and finished up at Drexel."

"My sister went to Drexel. I did my ungrad at Indiana

University of Pennsylvania and got my MBA from U Penn."

"That's great."

"I want to go back and get my master's one day."

"What's stopping you?"

"Timing—I would have to make arrangements for my children, and then I haven't even looked into any programs yet. But I definitely want to do it. I was looking online at Holy Family College. They have a pretty good accelerated program."

"So how old are you?"

"Twenty-eight, and you?"

"I'll be thirty-two in April," he said as the waitress came over and took our order. I ordered a seafood gumbo and Andrew had a turkey club sandwich. The rest of dinner went well. I was impressed with Andrew— he had a great personality. We talked a little more and the waitress came over and gave us our bill. Andrew pulled out his wallet and then said, "Kimberly, where's your half?" I looked up at him. I couldn't believe that he was asking me to pay for my half. I pulled out a credit card—I didn't have any cash on me. I placed my card on the table.

"Kim, I was only playing with you," he said as he handed the waitress the bill.

"Oh," I said, relieved. He put his brown leather jacket on and pushed his chair in.

"Where are you parked?"

"Around the corner."

"I'll walk you to your car."

"Okay," I said as I looked around the table to make sure I wasn't forgetting anything. Andrew held the door open for me and we walked toward my car. The wind began to whip hard, almost knocking me down. I tried to walk sideways to avoid it. When we reached my car, I hit my car remote and said good night. I took my coat off and set it in the passenger seat. Andrew was still standing there as I rolled my window down.

"Are you going to go out with me again?" Andrew asked.

"Yes. I'll call you."

He said good night again and then left. Our date was not different—it was the same as any guy I ever dated. He was just a regular guy and really sweet.

Andrew e-mailed me a few times throughout the week. He asked me what I was doing after work, and did I have time to meet up with him briefly. I told him I would, and he asked me to meet him at a coffeehouse on Walnut Street. I entered the coffeehouse and saw Andrew sitting at a table, typing something on his laptop and talking into his cell phone earpiece. He saw me, smiled, and motioned for me to have a seat. Andrew ended his conversation and we exchanged a brief hug.

"Do you want some coffee?" he asked.

"Sure, I'll have an espresso."

Andrew walked to the counter and ordered me a large espresso and brought it over to me and said, "So what's going on?"

"Not much," I said, sprinkling sugar into my drink.

"I wanted to see you again, Kim, before I went out of town. I'm flying out tonight."

"Where are you going?"

"I have a meeting with a prospective client in Minneapolis, but I wanted to see you, plus I wanted to give you this," he said as he pulled a large white envelope out of his bag. He handed it to me. I opened the envelope and it was an application for the master's program at Holy Family College.

"Thank you," I said, surprised.

"I wanted to get you an application because the deadline to apply is in a few weeks."

"I'm going to fill this out tonight," I said as a call came in for Andrew. I looked at my watch—it was getting late, and I had to pick up the boys from Karen's house. I told Andrew to have a safe trip and that I would see him when he got back.

Andrew was nice. He would be perfect if he was a few shades darker. Damn. I knew we could not take it any further. He is a nice person, but I need a black man. I don't want to give up on the hope of finding my black king. I don't care what Nicole said, there isn't a shortage of them. I turned the radio on in my car, I inserted my earpiece in my ear, and dialed Karen.

"I'll be right there—have them ready, please."

"All right."

I beeped the horn outside Karen's house. I told her to have them ready—of course, they weren't. I got out of the car and walked inside Karen's house. She had just bought the house less than six months ago and was still making repairs. There were sheets draped over everything to cover her furniture. She kept the kids upstairs so they wouldn't get in the way. Lonnie, Karen's husband, comes home every day after work and tries to make repairs.

I yelled up the steps, "Karen I'm here!"

"Hey—I'm about to tear your nephew up."

"Why, what's wrong?"

"Ryan's teacher just called my damn cell phone, saying he was acting up." As she was talking to me, she caught Ryan off guard and popped him right in his face. Kevin jumped and Kayden started crying.

"Karen" I said as I grabbed Ryan. He was crying and his lip was bleeding.

"Ryan, I told you not to let that teacher call my damn

phone again—she is not my damn friend using my damn minutes. I don't want to hear her mouth telling me why my child can't control himself. Do you hear me?"

"Yes," he stuttered.

"Damn, Karen, did you have to hit him like that?"

"You don't even know what he did."

"I don't care, Karen, you don't have to hit him. Get him some tissue, Kevin." Kevin ran to the bathroom.

Karen tried to see Ryan, to see how hard her blow was. Then she said, "His teacher was talking to him, and he said 'Get out of my face—your breath stink,' and the whole class laughed at her. Now, is that right?"

"Well, it probably did smell," I said, taking up for my nephew. Karen looked at me and began to laugh. She tried to hide her smile from Ryan.

"You can't talk to your teacher like that. You can come home with us. Okay?" I said.

"Okay," he said.

"Go get your stuff," I told him.

"Thanks for taking him. It's just, I'm under a lot of stress right now."

"You should have told me—I would have let Mommy watch the boys."

"No, they were fine. I just have to get some things in order."

"Get your clothes, Ryan, and come on." I put Kayden and Kevin in the car and waited for Ryan. Ryan ran out of the house with his clothes in a plastic bag like he was escaping a madhouse. He was breathing heavy and got in the car. I turned the radio on loud so they couldn't hear my conversation. I called Karen, "Karen, what's going on?"

"Nothing—everything is okay."

"You said you had to get things in order—what is that all about?"

"Okay, okay. You know we have been in this house not even six months, and we are about to lose it."

"What are you talking about?" I asked, confused.

"Kim, people are riding past my house, knocking on my door, asking me to take a look in my house."

"I don't understand," I said.

"My house is in the newspaper, up for sheriff sale."

"What?"

"Yeah, Lonnie hasn't paid the mortgage. He was waiting on hurrying making the improvements and refinancing. It's just been so hard."

"Why didn't you tell anyone?" I asked.

"You have been going through your thing, and I didn't want to worry Mommy. I thought I could catch up."

"What are the people saying?"

"That my house is going to be sold on Tuesday, March ninth."

"That's less than two weeks away. We have to do something."

"I mean, who do you call for this type of thing? It might be too late, and I can't afford an attorney."

"It's never too late. I'll call Malik—he has to know somebody."

"No, you hate him."

"I do hate him, but he will be able to tell us something."

Kevin, Ryan, and Kayden ran all over the house. I loved my nephew, but when he was over he brought out the devilish side of Kevin. If they weren't busy breaking something like a glass or a plate, they were arguing over who is the fastest or tallest. They ran in my bedroom, Kayden trailing behind them. Kevin yelled, "Mom, tell Ryan I'm taller than him." He stood his shoulders up as high as he could.

"No, you not—your head come to my neck. I'm the tallest—right, Aunt Kim?" I had to disappoint Kevin and tell him he was the shortest. Ryan said *Told you*, and they both ran back into Kevin's room.

I got up in the middle of the night to go to the bathroom and check on the boys. I couldn't sleep, thinking about my sister. I couldn't imagine her losing that house—she just bought it. I don't care if she wants Malik's help or not, I'm going to call him tomorrow. I walked into Kevin's room—he had left his television on again. I pushed the remote to turn it off when I seen two girls dancing seductively with each other. I checked to see what station it was. I know my baby didn't fall asleep watching this. I know I had programmed Kevin's television to block any inappropriate things. But it was BET. I checked the guide channel. It was a show called *UnCut*. I shook my head in disbelief. I wanted to write them a letter. Before I could begin to think about how I was going to title the letter, I saw a woman that looked like my sister Kianna, with pink pasties and a pink-and-white thong. I wanted to pause the television, but I couldn't. I stared intently, waiting to see if this woman that looked like my sister would appear in another scene, and she did. And this scene confirmed that my sister was being a freak in a video. She was in the video with chocolate syrup running down the crack of her ass. The only thing she had covering her butt was a thin thong; another girl was slapping her with an oversized white feather. They were also gliding their bodies on the guy that was rapping. I held my hand over my mouth—I could not believe it. *Kianna, my sister, a video ho. Oh my God,* I thought. I found her number in my cell phone and called her. She answered sleepily.

"Kianna?"

"Yeah, what's wrong? Why you calling me so late? Is everything okay?"

"I just saw your video. Give it up girl, right now."

"Really? What channel?" she said, excited. I heard her tell her boyfriend to wake up.

"Thanks for telling me," she said, like it was nothing wrong with being naked in a video.

"Kianna, what are you thinking about? Why are you making pornographic videos?"

"It's not pornography. I got all my clothes on."

"Barely—how about if Mommy see this? Do you know how disappointed she would be?"

"I'm not killing or stealing. I'm dancing, having fun meeting a lot of interesting people."

"Kianna, those girls are bisexuals and probably prostitutes waiting to turn your naive ass out."

"That's not true. Most of the girls I met are in college or they're actresses. They aren't like that, either. It is all for the camera—trust me."

"Kianna, you are not doing anything else, are you?"

"Like what?"

"Movies? Internet porn? Drugs? Exotic dancing?"

"No, I told you—it's all fun. I get paid—there is plenty of camera people there."

"Well, I think you should tell Mommy before someone tells her or she stumbles across it."

"All right, I will tell her. Please don't say anything to Karen. I don't want her in my biz."

"I won't say anything."

My life was coming together, and now I had to help my sister. I called Malik. I knew he would tell me I had a lot of nerve calling him, since I haven't been letting him see Kayden.

"Hello, Malik."

"Kim, what's wrong with little Malik?"

"Nothing—I was thinking if you want, you can come and get Kayden."

"When?"

"We will talk about that, but listen, I have a question for you."

"Go ahead."

"What do you do when your house is up for sheriff sale."

"Sheriff sale? You haven't been paying your mortgage?"

"No, it's not me. It's Karen—her house is in the newspaper. Is there any way to stop a sheriff sale?"

"Yes and no."

"Do you know anything or anybody that can help her?"

"Let me make a few calls. I'm going to call you back."

I opened the yellow pages and started looking for attorneys. The first attorney I called said he couldn't help, the second needed a thousand dollars. I was on the phone with my bank, checking my balance, when Malik called and said he knew what to do.

"Kim, get a pen. Listen, you are going to need her social security and docket number. I know somebody that will represent them. He can stop the sheriff sale. Everything will be okay."

Malik saved the day. He knew this cheap attorney whose specialty was foreclosures and sheriff sale. I was so grateful to him. We were talking and communicating like regular people. I even let Malik pick Kayden up from day care. My life was making progress. At my next visit with Dr. Weltz, I will tell her how good everything is going. I even mailed off my graduate school application.

Chapter 23

Shonda

Tae called to ask me how it was going. I think she got over not getting the job. I told her my job was going okay, and she said, "Girl, you got to meet my boyfriend."

"What boyfriend?"

"I met him outside of the gym a few weeks ago. That's why you haven't heard from me. He is so good to me, girl. The one who answered my phone. He asked me to move in with him. And I'm going to."

"Tae, you just met him."

"I know, but he is the best thing I ran across in a long time."

"Girl, slow down. Where was he living at before?" I said, amazed that she was falling for another man so soon.

"With his mother."

"With his mother—a momma's boy."

"No, trust me—he's no momma's boy. He is a good dude. You know when it is right. We are signing our lease today. And I have a new job. He got me a job at FedEx."

"Tae, you just got the car, and Pop-Pop didn't work out. I just don't want you to get hurt or get in over your head."

"Shonda, you are not going to be the only one happily married. I got to go," she said. My friend is falling for anyone that pays attention to her.

Me and Riddick were walking the floor. We were supposed to walk the floor every hour, just to make sure inmates were where they belonged. There was a prisoner Jones peeing in his cell. He didn't bother to turn or hide his dick when we walked by. He exposed himself to us. I turned my head and kept walking.

"Um, you got a fat ass," he said as he shook his dick dry a few times while looking at us.

"Niggah, please. Don't disrespect me," Riddick said as she stopped in front of the cell.

"Ain't nobody talking about *your* fat ass, Riddick," Jones said as he fondled and held his dick at her while still looking at me.

"I'm talking to her," he said with a dirty smirk. I continued to walk, but Riddick stopped. I got three cells away when I heard her scream and she was wiping something gooey from her face. Inmate Jones had ejaculated right in her face. I called for backup, and all these guards came and opened the cell and began to beat his ass. They dragged him out of his cell and took clubs out and began to hit, kick and punch him. Riddick was more embarrassed than anything. But thinking on her feet, she said he was stroking his dick at me.

"Wasn't he, Robinson?" I stuttered yes. After they beat him viciously, the inmate couldn't open his eyes—they were sealed shut. He had big lumps on his cheek. Then they dragged him out of the cell and a bloody trail followed him down the hall. They put him in the hole. We had to file a report. I was a little disturbed after that—I never seen anybody get beat that bad.

When it was time to go, I was so happy to get in my car and leave. I started my car. I was letting it warm up when it cut off, so I put my foot on the gas and tried to start it again. It started right up. I revved the engine a little and went to pull off. My car shut off the second I put it in drive. This time it went a little further, then cut off again. I saw lights coming toward me.

"What's wrong?" Hicks said.

"I don't know—my car won't start." He pulled over, his car still running.

"Do you have gas?" he asked.

"Yes," I said as I checked my gas gauge. He popped the hood and then walked over to his car and got a flashlight.

"When's the last time you had your plugs changed?" he asked. I got out of the car and walked toward him.

"I don't know." I said as I peeked under the hood with him.

"I think your plugs are done. They are getting a little juice. You're not going to make it home, though. I can give you a ride."

"That's okay—I'll call my husband," I said. He closed my hood and said okay. He was getting back in his car. I called Malik twice—his answering machine came on. Instead of being stranded, I took Hicks up on his offer and got in his car. He must spend all his money on tricking his car out. He had a television and big speakers and his car sounded like a truck purposely so it could go faster.

"Thank you—I appreciate this. I don't know where

my husband is," I said so he can know it wasn't nothing jumping off.

"So how you like the job so far?" he asked.

"So far, it's cool. It is just a little more intense than I thought it would be. A lot more."

"Yeah, this job is not for the weak-hearted. You just got to keep your cool and just remember the inmates are human. I mean, of course, you get the talkers and the mentals. Everybody wants to blame something on their mother or their momma's boyfriend that fucked them while they was little. I have seen some shit, trust me. Niggs talking through toilets, gay dudes being the most popular dude on the unit, and then you got dudes that just made a mistake and you have to treat them all right."

"Yeah, I noticed that a lot of people don't be doing that."

"Yes and no. I just know I do what I got to do for me and mine. And it's a lot of perks to the job. It's a lot of ways to make money. You just got to know how."

"Yeah, I heard you can get all the overtime you want."

"Overtime is not as sweet as it used to be. A lot has changed."

"Why?"

"Something about budget cuts when the new warden came in. I don't really know, but like I say, it's other ways to make money."

We pulled up to my door. I was glad Malik didn't come home yet. It would have been hard to explain why a guy was bringing me home.

"If you ever need anything, and you need to make some money, let me know." I said okay, not knowing exactly what he meant.

"Well, I'll talk to you, but you can make an extra five hundred a week—trust me."

"Okay, I will. Thank you for the ride."

Omar was chilling on my sofa. Doing what bums do, absolutely nothing. An empty McDonald's French fry container and split-open bag was spread across the table. Salt, pepper, and a ketchup packet. I was tired of him leaving shit around, so I said something.

"You think you can clean up after yourself?" I said as I opened my mail. I walked into the kitchen and popped some popcorn.

"I'm going to do it," he said.

"Could you do it now?" I asked. Omar didn't budge. I looked in the refrigerator and he had put a ginger ale container with just a swallow in it. Ooh, I was so tired of his ass. I threw it in the trash. *Wait to Malik comes home,* I said under my breath. *This bruh got to go.*

Malik came in the door and went straight up the steps. He didn't say hi, baby, or nothing. I walked behind him. I didn't know what was going on with him. I went upstairs to find out. When I reached the top of the steps, I heard the door slam closed. Okay, I thought. I opened the door. He was sitting on the edge of the bed, taking his shoes off. And then he fell back on the bed.

"Malik, what's going on?" I asked.

"I got fired."

"What?"

"Yes, fired."

"Why?"

"All they said was that Mr. Rhome was retiring. So that's it—no severance package, no benefits."

"Baby, you will get a new job," I said as I tried to console him.

"I hope so." he said.

"You will."

Malik was in such a funk. He didn't see this coming. His job hardly gave him any notice, and he was a loyal employee. That just doesn't make any sense. I decided I wasn't going to mention Omar's dirtiness. Right now it seemed petty, and I didn't want to put any more pressure on Malik. Maybe I could deal with Omar for a little while. It will go by fast. I got to be there for my man.

Chapter 24

Nadine

I have been advised not to mention or reminisce about Erick. Nobody wants to hear anything about him—if I say "Er," before I get the "ick" out, they stop me. Everybody hates him now. But for some reason I still got love for this stupid motherfucker. I don't know why love is not fair. I'm flip-flopping every other minute. I love him, I love him not. He wasn't doing everything right—that's why I left him, is what I try to tell myself. I wasn't sure about him. Because I have been talking about him all the time, telling anybody that would listen to all of our problems. I even been talking to Mrs. Meyers, and I can see it in her eyes—she wants me to shut up. But I can't let go. It's, like, me knowing he has someone else makes me want him back even more. I don't know why. I thought I could always count on my family to cosign with me. But even Aunt Connie said, you can't be playing with people's emotions. I wasn't playing with him. It was just, when I was with him I didn't know what I wanted. I'm lost—one day I want him and the next day I don't.

I went to pick up my class from lunch. I had got a

movie for them to watch, and after that I had copied three packets of work. That would keep them busy. I didn't feel like teaching a lesson. The kids ran when I said walk down the hall. I heard over the loudspeaker that Mark Coleman had an early dismissal—he ran toward the room and got his books.

"Ms. Clark, you have flowers on your desk."

"I do?" I said as I walked into the classroom. Maybe they were from my baby. The flowers were azaleas, lilies, and roses. I told the students to get in their seats. I snatched the small note card off the flowers. It read:

> *You deserve better! He is not worth your time. You need to go out and find someone better.*
> *Love,*
> *Someone who cares*

I didn't have any idea who could have sent the flowers. I guess somebody cares about me and knows how hurt I am. It definitely wasn't Toya or Aunt Connie. Neither of them would have sent flowers. I balled the card up and turned on the movie. While the students watched, I plotted out how I was going to get my man back.

I just dismissed my students. As soon as I got in my car, I called him. I hung up each time. I'm just an idiot when it comes to love. I have to stop calling him. He's not stupid—I know he probably suspects it's me. Calling from block numbers so I can hear his voice is getting old. But I love him—I have to get him back, I have to. He is so much better at this than me. It's like he doesn't care, or maybe that's the problem—he never cared. I try not to care, but it is so hard.

*   *   *

I'm going to call him just one more time and say, listen, we need to talk. I called—the phone rang once, then it rang again. Then someone picked up the phone and it wasn't Erick. It was a woman's voice. "Hello. Hello," she repeated. She then took a deep breath and said hello again. I hung up before she could say hello one more time. My heart dropped to my ankles. Who was answering his telephone? Erick had crossed the line. So what if we were broke up—he had someone answering his telephone already. Who is this girl staying over, spending the night, and she gets to answer the telephone, too? Oh hell, to the no. What is wrong with you? I said to Erick, as if he was standing near me. You know he barely let me answer the phone. Now he's going to let this woman he knew a month or two answer the phone like she's his woman? I can't believe this. Who is she? What does she have that I don't have? I don't know. Maybe he was always dealing with her all along. That's it—no more. Fuck him—he has a girlfriend, it is apparent he is doing what he wants, and he must be happy, because he hasn't called me. He hasn't called me one time to ask how I was doing or how my day went. He wants to act like I don't exist, then he won't exist to me, either. I took every picture we had together and put them in a shredder.

Last night I cried myself to sleep. I really still love Erick, but I'm going to get over him. I need to go shopping and in order to do that, I need money. I'm going to get my taxes done. Shopping will definitely take my mind off Erick Alton King. I will buy new clothes, makeup, and I'm going to meet someone new.

* * *

I called my Aunt Connie to ask her what was the place she used to do her taxes. I then called Toya. She picked up the phone, cussing Nate out. Then she said, "Hello," like she was mad someone was calling.

"What's wrong with you?"

"Nothing. What's up?"

"Can I use your Monet for my taxes?"

"Tony using Monet. I'll let you use Destiny. How much you going to give me?"

"I'll give you three hundred."

"Tony said he going to give me six hundred."

"I'm not giving you six hundred. I would only be making an extra five hundred. In that case it would not be worth it. I can only give you three-fifty, okay?"

"All right. Come get her social security card."

"I'll be there—are you going to be home tomorrow?"

"I have to go to the doctor tomorrow to get my ultrasound—they goin' to tell me how many months I am."

"How come you don't know?"

"Easy—I think I'm, like, six months."

"That far?"

"Yeah, I'll tell you what they say."

Chapter 25

Kim

I was so scared to meet up with Darius—I don't know why I was nervous. I changed my clothes three times. I wanted to be completely covered. I didn't want his wife to get the wrong impression. I didn't need her thinking I was trying to get with Darius. All I wanted him to do was take care of his child and possibly be a part of his life.

We dropped Kayden off with my mother. She questioned what I was doing. I told her I was just spending a few hours with Kevin alone. I didn't want her to try to talk me out of meeting up with Darius. We drove down Interstate 95 to Silver Spring, Maryland. The trees were green and the ride was taking forever. We were meeting him after a church service at a Chinese buffet near the church where he was the visiting pastor. I had tried to block all of the memories of him out of my head. I explained everything to Kevin as best I could. He was excited to meet his father, and full of questions.

I had forgotten what he looked like, and every black

EX-GIRL TO THE NEXT GIRL   189

man I saw with a suit on, I wondered if it was him. Darius approached us. He looked different—his waist had expanded a few inches. I hadn't seen Darius since that night, but I could see the resemblance with him and Kevin. His wife was an older woman with gold-framed glasses and short hair.

"Hello, Kim," he said.

"Hi."

"Let me introduce you to my wife, Jocelyn."

"Nice to meet you," she said.

"This is your father, Kevin," I said as I nudged him toward Darius.

"My father," he said, confused and creeping back toward me.

"Yes, your father." He gave him a hug.

"Are you ready to eat?" We all went to the buffet and then came back to a table and sat down.

"So what sports do you like?" Darius asked Kevin.

"I like all kinds of sports. I like baseball and I really like basketball. My mom said I have to go to college first, but when I finish college then I can get drafted by the NBA." Darius's wife laughed and joined in the conversation.

"So, Kevin, do you like school?" she asked while nibbling on General Tso's chicken.

"Yeah, it's okay. I hate my teacher, though—she is mean. She is not like my teacher before, Ms. Ellerbe. She was nice. She used to let us color, but this teacher makes us read all this reading." They listened intently as Kevin chattered on about school, his dog I won't let him have, and his baby brother, Kayden.

"So, are you married, Kim?" Jocelyn asked.

"No, never married," I said, smiling slightly uncomfortably. I still didn't want the woman to think I was after her man.

After dinner they walked us to the car so we all could

finish talking. When it was time to leave, Darius said that he was moving to Maryland and that he would like to start a relationship with Kevin. "When can we get him?"

"Let's move slow—this is all so new to us. I want you to be able to bond, but I want to be able to talk to him about what's going on."

"I understand," he said. "When you are ready, let us know."

"I will."

"Well, it was a pleasure," Jocelyn said as I went to shake her hand, but she hugged me.

"Oh, what about the paternity test?" I asked as they walked away.

"It's not necessary—he looks just like his sisters. I can't wait to introduce them," Jocelyn said. "Again, it was a pleasure meeting you. Darius, I'll be in the ladies' room."

Darius said okay, and when she walked away, he looked at Kevin, then at me, and said, "Kimberly, we didn't know each other back then. I used to do so many drugs. I have been clean for about seven years. I found God, and I just changed my life. What I'm saying is, if I hurt you, I am so sorry."

"Apology accepted," I said as I grabbed Kevin's hand and walked away. "I'll call you." On the way home, Kevin dozed off from the ride. I cried one more time. I was relieved Kevin had his father.

It was Sunday, and Andrew wanted to take me to the movies. We had been e-mailing and talking on the phone. He was constantly out of town. I told him I would try to call him back and let him know. Kevin would be staying with Ryan, and I did want to get out of the house. So I called Malik's sister, Nadia, because she said she would watch Kayden for me. I scrolled through my cell phone phonebook and dialed her number. She picked the phone up.

"Hey, how are you, Nadia? It's me Kim."

"Hey, girl. How are you? How's my little nephew?"

"He's fine. I'm fine. Um, I was wondering if you could watch him for a few hours."

"Sure, I can. Come to my mother's house. That's where I'll be."

"All right—see you around four."

I dropped Kevin off at Karen's house—he was happy to see Ryan.

"What time are you coming to get him?"

"Early—before noon. Why?"

"Because I got somewhere to go in the morning."

"Where?" I asked.

"None of your business."

"Since it is none of my business, I might come back tonight. I'm only going to the movies. I'll be back."

"Just make sure you pick him up."

"I will," I said. I had just saved Karen's ass—now she was back to getting smart. She is one of those people who are only nice when she needs you.

"Just call me and let me know what you're going to do."

I pulled up to Ms. Gloria's apartment. I saw Nadia's Oldsmobile station wagon.

"Hey, baby, you look great," she said as she came out and grabbed Kayden out of my arms. Nadia came over with a green t-shirt that read "Free Pedro," blue Diesel jeans, and long braids. I sat on the brown tweed sofa. Nadia's daughters were screaming and chasing each other around the living room.

"So how are you taking everything?" Nadia asked as she sat next to me, reaching for my hand to hold.

"Taking what?" I asked, confused and snatching my hand away from her.

"Malik getting married to that skank? I know you was mad. I would have been, because I was mad for you," she said, standing and putting her hand on her hip.

"What are you talking about?" I asked, staring at her.

"You don't know, do you?" she asked, realizing she gave up a little too much information. She looked over at me and said, "I thought you knew. Oh, I'm so, so sorry."

"Nadia, you talk too much," Ms. Gloria yelled at her.

Thinking fast, I said, "Ms. Gloria, I know about Malik getting married. I heard all about that."

"You did?" Ms. Gloria asked, surprised that I knew.

"Mmm. Yeah, and I feel okay as long as he's happy," I said as I cracked a smile.

"Whew, for a moment there I thought you didn't know," Nadia said, flicking her braids off her shoulder.

"We aren't together anymore, and I'm not thinking about your brother."

"I know that's right. I wouldn't be thinking about him, either."

"Well, I have to go. Here is Kayden's stuff," I said as I got up to leave.

I walked out of the apartment. I made it right to the front door before I starting bawling. My whole chest became tight. I couldn't breathe. Tears streamed fast down my face. I thought I was over Malik, but I guess I'm not. I guess I still love Malik. I don't want to love him, but I love him—we had our family and we made a life together. I got in my car and drove off. My nose was dripping just as fast as my eyes. I could taste the salty taste in my mouth. I looked in my rearview mirror and saw my eyes were becoming red. I didn't know what to think. I tried to wipe my eyes dry. It wasn't working. I needed a tissue. I checked the glove box and under the seats. I had none. In the backseat was a box of diaper wipes. I took a few out and wiped my nose and eyes. I blew my nose into the soft, wet wipe. *It was okay when he was just dating that bitch, but he married her. He fucking married that bitch. She is his wife now. I was supposed to be his wife. I put all those years in with him, I gave him a son, and he went and married her. I just can't believe it. I wanted to call him, but I couldn't—he might be with her.* He had been helping me with Karen, and I thought we were getting along. I thought we were working on being friends. I was letting my son go with him and everything. He could have told me he got married. I would have still let him get the baby. I wanted him to be honest with me. I know he lived with her and had started a new life. But somewhere in the back of my mind, I thought Malik would come back to me. I thought he might get tired of her and just come running back. At first I would have made him beg, and then, after several months of trying to persuade me, I would have accepted his apology, but now that is not going to happen. He is married and that bitch probably thinks she won. But she didn't win shit. I looked back in the mirror—my eyes were officially red. My time alone had been ruined. Instead of meeting up with Andrew, I found myself in front of my mother's door. I ran in the front door, my neckline soaked with tears.

"What's the matter? Calm down!"

"Mommy, he married her. Malik is married!" I sobbed as my mother took me in her arms and guided me to the sofa. My mother couldn't say anything—she continued to hold me. Her hugging made me let everything out. Then she tried to wipe my face for me. I felt embarrassed. My mother wiping my face like I was a little girl, but I couldn't stop crying.

"Mom, he left me, then he married her. He was supposed to marry me."

"It's going to be okay," she said, patting my back.

"Mom, no, it's not okay. I feel awful," I said as I tried to get myself together and sniffled through the stream of tears.

"Don't you do it, Kim. Don't you let that lowlife son of a bitch take your glory. Let that bitch have him. He's not worth it."

"He was supposed to marry me, Mom. Not her. I am supposed to be his wife," I cried.

"So what? He married her, but one thing is true—a leopard don't change its spots. What he did to you, he will do to her. You do dirt, you get dirt."

"I know. I know. He's going to get his," I said.

My mother got off the sofa and got me a paper towel from the kitchen. I felt so empty. I just sat there, frozen, on my mother's sofa. I was oblivious to the loud ringing of my cell phone. I looked at the phone—it was Andrew. I didn't answer. A few seconds later, my phone beeped, letting me know I had a message.

"Is that Malik?" my mother asked.

"No, my date," I said, trying to regain my composure.

"Why didn't you answer?"

"Because I don't feel like talking to anyone or going anywhere."

"I think you should go out. Your life does not end or begin with Malik. You don't have the children. You look nice—go out and have a good time. Kim, you will feel so much better. If you stay here, you are going to feel bad."

"You're right, Mom. But I can't—I look and feel a mess. Look at my clothes."

"All you have to do is go upstairs and wash your face with some cold water, and when you go outside, the air will make your eyes clear up."

I took a deep breath and went upstairs to the bathroom and washed my face. Andrew called again and again. I pushed his calls to voice mail each time. My phone rang again. This time I answered.

"Where are you?" Andrew asked.

"I'm sorry—something came up," I lied.

"So, do you still want to meet up?"

"Yes, I do. I could be there in, like, ten minutes. I looked down at my watch and corrected myself and said thirty minutes.

I met Andrew at the Loews Theater in Cherry Hill, New Jersey. It was just across the Benjamin Franklin Bridge, fifteen minutes away from Philly. It was easy to get to and nobody would see us. There was a mixed crowd—neither of us would feel out of place. When I arrived he was already there. I thought being with Andrew would make me feel better, but it didn't; I was questioning everything about him, my life, Malik, my kids. For some reason, Andrew looked like an extra-white boy today. And that upset me. He had on khakis and a red polo shirt with the collar semi-up. His brown curls looked lighter, close to blond and his complexion looked paler. I wanted him to be able to pass for at least a light Puerto Rican man. But he was who he was. It might have been all in my mind. He greeted me with a warm hug. I pulled back, because people would see us and think we were a couple. I turned around to see if anyone was watching. Nobody paid us any mind. He handed me my ticket and we walked toward the concession stand.

"Do you want any popcorn or anything? Their Nachos are really good," he said.

"No."

"You sure?" he asked.

"I'll take something to drink. I'll take a Sprite."

"They have Sierra Mist. What about some candy?"

"If they have Skittles, I'll take them. I'll be right back—I'm going to go to the ladies' room."

I walked into the crowed bathroom. I didn't really have to go. I just needed an exit. I had to get my thoughts together. I checked my hair and face. My eyes were still a little puffy, but I looked way better. I glanced at my reflection in the mirror. For a moment, I wanted to cry again, but I stopped myself. I had to admit that Malik is gone forever. Move on, girl, you have to, I told myself. I took a deep breath. Okay, you're on a date. Andrew is a nice person. You don't have the kids. You're out, you should be having fun. Enjoying yourself, not thinking about Malik. I took another deep breath and walked out of the bathroom. I saw Andrew holding two sodas and a large thing of Twizzlers.

"They didn't have any Skittles so I got you Twizzlers."

"Thank you," I said taking the Twizzlers out of his hand.

After the movie we met up with his friends at a karaoke bar in Deptford, New Jersey. All his friends from the night we met were there. Even the guy Rick was with a date and having fun. I guess he got over his brother getting married. We had a lot of fun watching them get on stage and make fools of themselves. I was having so much fun I didn't notice people were staring at me, but I felt eyes burning a hole in my back. I turned around and I looked over at a couple to the right of us. Every time I would turn around, the man was in my face. As the couple left, the man said, "You need to find yourself a good black man and leave that cracker alone." I couldn't believe the boldness of the couple.

"Do you know them? Are you okay?" Andrew asked.

"No, I'm fine," I said, realizing he didn't hear what the couple had said about him.

He walked me to my car. He gave me a kiss on the cheek and told me to be careful. Once I was in my car, he called me on my cell.

"Are you sure you're okay?"

"Yes, I'm fine."

"I had a nice time with you this evening—maybe we can get together sometime this weekend. I'll call you," he said.

"Okay."

I don't know if I can deal with Andrew. Most people just do a double take and then they smirk and look away. We get mixed looks. It was weird—I felt like we were back in the day. What was surprising is I got stares from white women, just as angry and just as hard as the stares a black man would receive from a sister if he was dating a white woman.

Chapter 26

Shonda

It's been a month since Malik gave me any money. I had to pay everything myself. I just put our rent money in the bank so that can be paid on time—at least we will have somewhere to live. Malik has been looking for a job, but he hasn't had an interviews yet. Law firms would rather pay a recent grad less money to do the same job as someone with experience. In the meantime, I don't mind holding Malik down. It's just that that niggah named Omar is downstairs. I don't like the fact Omar is in my basement at all. He is not contributing to anything. The other day I went into the basement to wash clothes and there were Olde English 40 bottles lined up against the wall. There was something yellow in one of the containers and it wasn't beer. I looked at it closer—it was pee. *Oh, his ass got to go,* I thought. Cigarette butts, Blunt wrappers, and weed particles and Baggies. I don't know why I'm putting up with this bullshit. His brother ain't bringing no money into our household. As a matter fact, Malik ain't good for nothing. He better hurry up and get a job for real—this is serious. I spent my whole check on bills. I didn't even have enough left to get my hair done. I got a man—fuck that, I got a husband, and I'm struggling. As soon as Malik walked in, I told him how unhappy I was with the present situation.

"Malik, I want to talk to you about Omar."

"What about him?"

"He has to go! One, he funks up the basement. Two, he don't do nothing all day—he uses dishes and don't clean up. Then he's pissing in bottles in my damn basement."

"I'm going to talk to him," he said as he went up the steps.

"You going to talk to him? What can you possibly say to him! 'Omar, stop being a nasty bastard.' He is nasty—I don't like him."

"Listen, I'm all he has. What do you want me to do?"

"You are not all he has. He can go live with your mother."

"I really don't have time for this shit. Shonda, sit down—I want to talk to you about something. I'm going to start getting my son more. Kim called and said I can have him for the weekend."

My mouth dropped. My idea of a relaxing weekend was not watching her son. I don't feel like babysitting—my daughter is gone. *Why would I want to watch somebody else's child,* I thought.

"I don't care, but I'm going to be busy this weekend," I said.

"So that's okay with you?" he asked.

"Sure, bring him over. I don't care—I'm not watching him," I murmured. *And I'm not changing any funky diapers,* I thought.

I went to work, mad as hell. How was I supposed to keep functioning when I wasn't happy at home? I'm broke as shit, my man's derelict brother is in my basement. These bills are kicking my butt.

After work I was going to finish my conversation with Malik. I was thinking about it the whole day. I walked in the living room and he was watching basketball. I turned the television off and said, "Malik, we need to finish our conversation."

"About what, Shonda? I'm tired of talking," he said as he turned his back to me.

"What are you tired from? You ain't do shit all day."

"I'm looking for a job. I'm on the computer every day."

"Well, you need to look a little harder, 'cause I can't keep holding everything together by myself and I'm not taking care of your brother."

"My brother ain't even been here that long."

"He's got to go," I said.

"He is not going anywhere. If he goes, I'm going."

"Well," I said, looking him directly in the eye.

"Well, what?"

"Well, maybe you need to leave, too. 'Cause I'm not taking care of two grown men," I said as I left Malik and his funky-ass brother in the house.

I drove to my father's house. I used my key to open the door. I startled him as I walked through the door. He was sitting reading a newspaper.

"Dad I need to talk to you."

"You okay?"

"No, Malik moved his brother into the house and everything has been going wrong ever since."

"Well did you talk to Malik about it?"

"Yes, and he won't do anything but take up for his brother and he told me if he leave I leave."

"I don't know what man would choose his brother over his wife. But if you think it's not going to work out, you might as well get you marriage annulled because it doesn't make any sense wasting time with somebody who isn't working. You get to be my age and it will be too late and you will have wasted your life. Either make it work or leave. I thought about what my dad said and decided to make it work. I went home and made up with Malik.

Malik was out with Kayden. He has been getting him more often. I didn't care as long as he didn't spend time with Kim, because I know how she is all hyped on trying to get her family back, but that's a big not-going-to-happen.

The next day I walked into the office. I heard Sergeant Wilson tell Riddick, "I'll send Robinson with you." Wilson turned to me and said to come on. I had no idea where we were going. We turned the corner and I saw a female inmate frantically shaking. They ordered me to hold her head so she wouldn't hit it again. There was blood flowing from a gash on her head. I took out my plastic gloves and placed my hands behind her head. She stared mindlessly in the air. I had never seen anybody go into a seizure before. It was like she was a zombie in a trance.

We escorted her to the nearest local hospital and waited with her while they treated her. The hospital was extremely busy. They ran out of examination rooms, so patients were waiting on gurneys in the hallway. In the emergency room every seat was taken. "Can we wait outside?" I asked as I looked around at all the sick people.

"No, if something happens to her, we both are responsible. We have to wait. You want a stick of gum?" I said yes and she passed me the gum. I popped the gum in my mouth and she continued to talk. "She could come out of that seizure and be out. And then we both would be out of a job. I remember one time, we had an inmate that was in labor handcuffed to the bed. Freedom is a beautiful thing and they lost theirs," she laughed.

I guess she was right, but I still didn't feel comfortable having a sick person restrained to a bed.

After work, I went to Tae's new apartment. I had to meet Tae's new Mr. Wonderful, Kenneth. I was in no rush to go to my own home. My house is so miserable, I can't even move around in my own space. Me and Malik have been arguing every day. Omar has put a definite strain on our marriage. So it will be nice to see somebody else happy. And Tae must be happy, because every time I talk to her, all she talks about is her man. I had to see if he really existed. After Poppa Smurf, any man is going to be good for her. Tae and her new boyfriend were moving so fast. Already they were living together. If she was happy, I guess I was happy.

I had to walk up three flights of steep steps to get to her apartment. I was out of breath. I knocked on her apartment door and Tae answered.

"You made it. Come in and take a look around," she said while pulling me into the apartment. Her kitchen was on the left and the living room was on the right of the kitchen. A few steps away from the living room was the bedroom, and beside that was the bathroom. Her apartment was small, but just right for two people.

"You want something to eat?" Tae asked.

"Yeah, it smells good. So what are you cooking?"

"He's cooking fried tilapia, corn, and rice."

"He cooks, too?" I asked as I opened my mouth in disbelief and thought, he is perfect.

"Does he cook? He is going to get me fat. He has been cooking almost every day since we moved in. He even went with me to get my nails done and just sat there and waited with me," she said.

"Okay, he sprung. What did you put on him?" I asked.

"Nothing—I swear. He put something on me," she whispered, leaning closer to me.

"Damn, I need a man like that. Malik and his brother don't do shit, but leave dishes in my sink and dirty up. I'm the only one that cleans the house. Did I tell you what I found in my basement?"

"No, let me guess—a gun?"

"No, pee in a damn bottle."

"Oh hell, no. His ass got to go," she said as she got up.

"I know—I told Malik, he just isn't listening," I said as I sampled some of the talapia he had made.

"So, are you in love?" I asked.

"I think so."

"Either you are, or you're going to play with him. You have anything to drink?" I said. Tae got up and poured me a glass of pink lemonade.

"I think I like him. He makes me feel special. We went to the mall the other day and there were all these other women around, and he didn't look around at them. The entire time, he just kept his eyes on me. I think I'm giving up on my rich-man dream. I'm just trying to build with my husband and get money together. He wants to get married—he has a pretty good job and is just a good guy."

I couldn't take it anymore. Okay, he wants to settle down, cooks, knows how to put it down, and pays bills. Something is wrong. I had to see what this man looked like. He had to be a frog. Got to be.

"So where is he?" I asked.

"In the bedroom."

"Call him out here—I want to see him. I mean, meet him."

Tae screamed "Boo," and out walked a tall, creamy

brown muscular man with baggy pants and a large red t-shirt. He was so gorgeous.

"Hi," I said, looking up at him.

"It's nice to finally meet you. We all have to get together and do something." I agreed and then he turned to Tae and said, "Boo, did you start eating?"

"No, I gave Shonda some."

"Well, I'm about to leave," I said as I stood up and told Tae I had to get home. She walked me to my car. I congratulated her on her new place and new man.

When I arrived home, Malik was not there yet. He has been staying out a lot lately like it is my fault he doesn't have a job. He claims he's out drinking with Jarrod. Whatever.

Chapter 27

Shonda

Tae and her boyfriend Kenneth had invited us out to dinner. Malik didn't want to go—he said he was tired.

"Baby, please go," I begged.

"I don't feel like being in nobody's face. Your girl-friend's okay, but I don't know her man like that. I don't feel like it."

I screamed at him, "I want you to go! Damn, Malik, you can't do nothing I ask you to do!"

"Fuck it, Shonda, if it is going to make you happy, I will go with you," he said as he threw his shoe at the wall. The shoe almost hit me. I looked at him, then just grabbed the rest of my clothes and went into the bathroom to get ready. I started doing my hair and tried to concentrate on getting dressed. When I came out of the bathroom, Malik was sitting on the edge of the bed, looking unenthused. A tear began to roll out of my eye, landing on my shirt. Malik ignored my tears. He smirked at me and then asked me was I ready, and brushed his hair. He had slopped together an outfit. I wanted to tell him stay home, don't make me miserable with you.

I wiped my tears away and said, "Look, if you don't want to go, you don't have to."

"I'm dressed now."

You can get undressed, I thought.

We arrived at Spiley's Restaurant and Bar. I walked in—it was new and had a modern look to it. Instead of regular booths, they had circular velvet booths with hanging, triangle-shape lights. It was very chic. My immediate thought was, I hope nobody notices my eyes were red. Tae and Kenneth were sitting at a table. We walked up to them. They were smiling and laughing, all coupled up, drinking champagne out of each other's glasses.

"I'm so glad you could make it," Tae said.

"Yeah, we made it," I said. I introduced Malik to Kenneth—they gave each other a firm handshake.

"What y'all drinking?" Kenneth asked.

"I'll have a Cosmopolitan," I said.

"All right—I'll be right back, and you?" he asked Malik. Malik shook his head and said, "I'm cool—I'll get my own drink."

As soon as Kenneth left the table, Malik said he was going to the restroom. When he got up, Tae said, "Look at this, girl."

"What is that?" I asked, looking down at what appeared to be an engagement band on her hand.

"A promise ring."

"Congratulations—that is a nice promise ring."

"Girl, it's not real, but he said we were going to buy me one just like this."

Kenneth came back with my Cosmopolitan—it was raspberry-colored and delicious. The entire night we sipped drinks and ate appetizers. Malik started to come around, joining in on our jokes and laughs. We had ordered another bottle of champagne and were tore up and having a good time. Every ten minutes, Tae and Kenneth complimented each other, and then kissed—they were so cute. They were dancing near the bar. I was thinking, *They are so happy together and such a cute couple. So perfect.*

Instead, I said it aloud, and Malik's response was "Everybody have problems. You never know what's going on behind closed doors. There is no such thing as perfect—you know that." I looked over at him as he swished ice around in his mouth. He was being real hateful. A big, fucking hater, and I was beginning to hate him.

"Well, they're perfect to me," I said as I watched them dance. Tae had the perfect ring, the perfect man, and she was so happy. I was so miserable. I was paying all of our bills and Kenneth paid all of their bills. I looked at the dance floor at Tae and Kenneth and then back at Malik. Till death do us part? I'm not so sure. I was so upset with Malik—so much potential going to waste. I looked over at him in disgust. I swallowed the last of my third Cosmopolitan, then walked away from Malik and hatingness and went to the bathroom.

When I came from the bathroom, I heard the bartender say, "Last call for alcohol." It was almost time to leave. Malik ordered another bottle of champagne while I was gone. He must have money in his pocket.

"You ready?" he asked as he reached in his pocket and placed a few twenties on the table.

"Yeah, I'm ready—let me just say good-bye," I said as I searched for Tae. "It's getting late, so we are going to leave. See y'all." I said.

"All right—call me," Tae said.

I reached Malik and the lights came on in the club. I

was squinting my eyes and trying to walk straight enough to get out of the club. If the light hadn't awakened me, the cool April air got my attention. "Malik, pick me up," I said drunkenly. He laughed and then he took my hand and led me to the car. Malik unlocked the car with the remote. Tae ran up behind us and scared me. Malik got inside the car and started it.

"What's up, girl?" I asked.

"Malik didn't leave enough for y'all tab."

"Oh, he's drunk—he must have forgot. How much more do we owe?" I asked as I pulled out my debit card like it was no big thing.

"It is three-seventy-nine."

"Huh? How much did he leave?"

"He left eighty. The bottles of champagne was two-fifty by itself, then appetizers and other drinks. Then they added on gratuity," she said as we walked back into the club. I handed her my debit card. I was about to spend my rent money. When the waitress came back, I signed the slip and she gave me a copy.

"Sorry about that, Tae."

"No problem," she said as she gave me a hug. Malik was still waiting in the car. I stormed to the car.

"Malik, what the fuck is wrong with you? Why didn't you find out how much the champagne was before you ordered it? Those bottles were two-hundred-fifty. I just had to spend our rent money to pay the bill."

"You spent the rent money?"

"Yeah, I had to. What was I supposed to do?" I asked as I shook my head. I'd already wrote our rent check out. When our landlord deposits that shit, it is going to bounce so hard it is going to break out a window. I have to figure out how to get another three hundred dollars.

"Malik, do you have any money?"

"No, that was it. I'm not working. Where am I supposed to get money from?"

"Ask your brother, ask somebody. Do something, Malik. Do fucking something."

"Man, I told you I didn't want to go in the first place," he said. I didn't look at him or say anything. I just wanted to get home and out of the car before I killed him.

I had successfully hustled up the rent money again. That was one less worry on my mind. I was going to go to the bank in the morning before the check cleared. My dad loaned me a hundred. I got fifty dollars from Brian—I said Brianna needed it for Girl Scouts. Then my grandmother gave me a hundred and fifty dollars. I felt bad for borrowing rent money when I just got married and was a newlywed. But nobody knew actually what was going on.

I wasn't speaking to Malik because he was slowly but surely becoming an idiot. I walked right past him. He was on the bed, watching television. I undressed and put my nightclothes on and placed the money I had collected on the dresser. I took my wig off and wrapped my hair up—it was trying to grow back.

I got in the bed and turned my back to Malik and snuggled under the covers. I heard the television go off. And then Malik asked me was I asleep. I ignored him. He got under the covers with me and pulled me in closer to him. I didn't fight it. I just listened as he spoke. He said, "Baby, I'm trying my best to get a job. I know it has been hard on you. It's been just as hard on me. I'm sorry I've been down. I'm sorry I haven't been a good husband to you. I promise I will make all of this up to you. I have an interview tomorrow." A single tear ran down my face. Malik's reassurance made me feel confident that everything was going to be okay. He held me the entire night.

The next morning he rushed and took a shower for his interview. After he was dressed, he gave me a kiss and I rolled over and went back to sleep. I awoke around nine. I was going to sleep a little longer until I realized I had to deposit the money in the bank. I took my shower and then threw on my jeans and a t-shirt. I put on a pair of silver dangling earrings. I grabbed my cell phone and handbag. I reached for the money, but it was not there. I immediately called Malik.

"Malik, did you see some money on the dresser?"

"No, I didn't see any money."

"I can't find the money. I put the money on the dresser last night," I said as I lifted my jewelry box and searched around my dresser.

"Shonda, look for your money. You're always misplacing things."

"Malik, I know where I left the money. I just hope nobody stole that money. It was for the rent."

"Who could have possibly stole your money?" he asked.

"I don't know, but I know I'm not crazy. What am I supposed to tell the landlord? He is going to evict us."

"No, he won't. I'm in my interview—I'll call you back." I searched the room some more. Lifted and overturned everything around and near the dresser. I know where I left my money and I know if I didn't have it and Malik didn't have it, then Omar had my money.

Malik called back about ten minutes later and said, "I asked Omar, did he see the money? He said he didn't." I didn't believe this shit—I was trying to hold my composure. Malik was stupid.

"Malik, listen, he got my money. It was right here."

"He said he doesn't have it. Did you see him take it?"

"No, but wake the fuck up, Malik—your brother is a thief."

"Shonda, he is not a thief. If he said he doesn't have it, then he doesn't have it."

"What comes out of your brother's mouth is not the Bible, Malik. Who said he is always telling the truth? That's the problem—you give that niggah too much credit." I banged on Malik and went downstairs to Omar—I knew he had my money. He was sitting, smacking on some bacon and eggs. He had a huge breakfast platter.

"Omar, I'm missing some money," I said calmly.

"I know—Malik was telling me. If I see it, I'll put it up for you," he said between smacks. He was really playing me. Ain't this some bullshit. I need my money. I'm not playing any games with his ass. So I stepped right in front of him and said, "I know you got my money and I want it now or your ass is out."

"Shonda, I didn't take your money," he said.

"I know you got it. You better give me my money before it get ugly in here."

"Yo, I ain't my brother," he said, standing up like he was about to swing on me.

"And what's that supposed to mean? You better give me my money."

He dialed Malik on his cell phone and said like I was standing right in front of him, "Yo Malik—come handle your chick!"

"He don't got to handle me," I said. "Just give me my money. How about that?"

"I don't want to." Hurt, he stopped mid-sentence, closed his phone, and left the house. I closed the Styrofoam container and threw his food in the trash.

Hours later, I was still flipping everything over in the house. I knew that money was gone, but just so there would be no doubt in my mind, I searched and I searched and found nothing. My searching was interrupted by a private number coming up on my cell phone.

I answered "Hello." Then this ghetto voice said, "Do you have a fucking problem?"

"What—who is this?" I didn't exactly recognize the voice at first.

"You know who the fuck it is, bitch. My brother didn't steal your money. Let me just tell you, if you got a problem with my brother, then you have a problem with me."

It was Nadia—I had to put her in her place before I stomped a mud hole into her ass. I tried to reason with her and said, "Listen, Nadia, I don't think you want to call me like this. I'm not trying to argue with you. So I would appreciate it if you don't call back and don't call me no bitch."

"What you going to do if I do?"

"I'm not going to do anything."

"I know you ain't going to do nothing, bitch!"

Okay, now that bitch was pushing my buttons. I wanted to cuss her out. I was trying not to cuss her out—*please don't make me cuss you out,* I said to myself. I had to hold back. She called back.

"Hello," I answered.

"Yeah, and I can call you whatever the fuck I want to, bitch. You don't running anything, bitch. I know my brother sorry he married your ass. Bitch. You don't even cook, you dirty, nasty bitch. And my brother can stay there as long as he wants because that's my brother Malik's house, too!"

"Your brother is out. He can come and live with you. You fucking broke-ass. Your broke-ass just called Malik and asked him to get fifty dollars to buy food. And he got the money from me. So keep talking shit, bitch. I put food in your kids' mouth." She was silent—what else could she say? I had pulled her card. But she still wanted to talk shit.

"Shonda, don't nobody like your home-wrecking ass. He should have stayed with Kim. She is a real woman."

"Real woman this. If you call back again, I will tell your caseworker you got an under-the-table job."

"What?"

"You get welfare, and I'll tell your worker you working at that restaurant on the weekends." She was speechless and hung up. His entire family could go to hell—I wanted my money.

Malik came home, still dressed from his interview, trying to yell at me. "My sister is crying—what did you say to her?"

"I didn't say anything to her, Malik. She called me a home-wrecker."

"Please don't argue with her, because she tells my mom stuff and then it's this big thing."

"It was your sister's fault."

"Forget it. I got the job," he said, taking off his dress shirt.

"Congratulations. Where at?"

"A tax place down on Market Street—I'm going to do taxes."

"How is the pay?"

"It is pretty good. I'm going to file tax returns. I will be super busy. The owner could barely step away from his desk to interview me." I was happy Malik had a job— okay, maybe now everything might work out. Get Omar up and out of here and I would have hit the jackpot.

"They need me ASAP. I'm going to start tomorrow."

I wanted to ask him when was he going to get his first paycheck so he can pay me back. Instead I gave him a kiss and said, "I love you. I'm glad you have the job—I knew you would get one."

The next day I was still heated about my money. I had called the bank to try to stop payment on the check. It was too late—it had bounced twice. I feel like in my mind I was hoping that Malik may somehow get the money back from his brother, but that didn't happen.

"Shonda, he doesn't have your money."

"Malik, your brother is a thief and y'all sugar coat everything for him. He is no different from any other person I see at my job every day." Omar was right there, listening to me. I didn't care because it was the truth.

"He is trying to come up off of somebody else." Omar went downstairs and started packing. He ran downstairs after Omar's punk ass.

"Shonda, if his probation officer comes here or finds out he doesn't live here, he can get sent back."

"I don't care," I said, crossing my arms.

"I know—that's the problem," he said.

"I don't care, Malik. He stole our rent money."

"You don't have any proof."

"I got plenty of proof—it's gone. And I have an overdrawn bank account."

I called Tae after Malik left and explained the whole situation to her. "So that's messed up, right? I can't even leave money down in my own home."

"Yo, that's so foul. Malik is not going to do anything about it?"

"No, he believes everything the niggah say. I cannot take this. I can't even pay my rent."

"I can loan you the money. It is my car note money,

but I can wait to pay them by the fifteenth, before it is really late."

"Tae, oh my God—that would be so nice. I will give it back to you the minute I cash my check."

"It's cool. It's fuck-up that you got to go through some bullshit like that."

"I know—I'll be over as soon as I get dressed."

"My uncle used to be like that, steal everything. He was so good he could take your money from under your mattress while you were sleeping. And the mess-up thing about it is that he wasn't even on drugs. He just liked to steal, like a klepto. He would come home with perfume tester bottles from the department stores and give them to my mom and aunt. One day he stole all these tickets for us to go to the carnival."

"Well, Omar's stealing doesn't help me."

I went to pick up the money from Tae and went straight to put it in my account. I then picked up Bree and stopped and got Boston Market. That was fast food, but it wasn't. I was not in the mood to cook anything. Malik could fend for himself. We came in the house, and Bree turned on the television.

"Mom, something is wrong with the cable!" she screamed. I went to check Bree's television. The cable had a dark blue screen and said, *please contact customer service.* I called the cable company. They informed me that my service had been disrupted. My rent was paid, but now the cable was off. If it wasn't one thing, it was another. There was nothing to watch on regular television, plus the stations didn't come in clear.

Chapter 28

Nadine

I walked into the tax office. A bunch of people were sitting around, waiting to be called. There was an older woman receptionist with blotted, glued, fake eyelashes all over her eyelids. Her face was painted all different colors of the rainbow. Her cheeks were rosy red. The same color covered her lips and she used bright blue eye shadow.

"Hi, yes, I'm looking for Mr. Rollins."

"You can take a seat," she said as she answered the telephone. She fluttered her eyelashes nervously. "Uh, Mr. Rollins no longer works here, but this is Mr. Vaughn—he can help you." The man she introduced me to was tall—he had to be about six-six with a brown pinstriped suit. He looked like he was going to pimp in Detroit or go give a sermon somewhere in the South. His suit was too loud for an office environment. When he looked over at me, he looked at me like he had just won the lottery.

"How you doing, miss? I'm Mr. Vaughn, and I'm going to get your taxes done," he said with a sexual overtone as he touched my hand. I snatched my hand back. I didn't want him to do my taxes. I didn't want him to know how much I made, have my phone number or address. He looked, as my aunt would say, *slick*. He could be one of those people that steal identities. I had enough debt by myself. I didn't need anybody else to run anything up for me. I already had my return planned out—I was going to pay all my bills up for a few months. Then I could take my paycheck and try to start paying on my credit cards. Or maybe I'll do it the other way around.

"That's okay," I said, as I turned back to the receptionist. "Is there anybody else that can help me?"

"Well, there is Mr. Moore, but he is with a client right now."

"Will I be his next client?"

"Yes."

"I'll wait for him," I said as I sat down and started reading a *Time* magazine. Mr. Vaughn took the next client, another woman who had two children with her. One was in a stroller, the other following behind her. He looked at her two times, rubbed his hands together, and took her into his cubicle area.

"Nadine Clark."

I looked up from the magazine and the exact opposite of Mr. Vaughn was calling my name. He introduced himself as Mr. Moore. He was so handsome, brown, and muscular. He came up and said, "Follow me."

I sat down and asked, "Where is Mr. Rollins? My aunt told me to use him."

"Mr. Rollins is not here, but I will do the best I can for you, I assure you."

"My aunt said he was good."

"Well, he doesn't work here anymore because he was so good. So tell whoever used him to beware," he said, looking at me while grabbing some documents.

"Are you serious?" I asked.

"Yeah, he was taking deductions that he shouldn't have." He looked over at his computer screen and asked me did I have all my paperwork. I pulled out Destiny's social security card and all my documents. He asked a few questions and then printed a few sheets for me to sign. He made me laugh a few times and kept good conversation.

"My sister's name is Nadia. I like that name. She is beautiful. I guess all women with the name beginning with N-A-D are."

I smiled. I looked around his desk—he didn't have a wedding ring on and any pictures of children. I had to ask to see if I was right. I said something. "I know you are busy all night long?" I asked, sitting up.

"Yeah, sometimes we don't get out of here until, like, ten," he said as he grabbed another paper off the printer for me to sign.

"Well, what does your wife say about that?" I asked.

"Wife? I'm divorced. I'm going through something now with my ex over my son."

"Aw that's a shame," I said.

"Yeah, it is. Here is a picture of him," he said, taking a picture out of his desk. He was the most adorable little boy. He told me my check would be ready for pickup in a few days.

I walked out of the tax office. Mr. Moore was so attractive—I should have given him my number. I should have said something. *If he wanted to say something to me, he would have. No, but, I should go back and ask him out,* I thought. I went back in the crowded office. Mr. Moore was in his cubicle with another client. I walked past the receptionist, who didn't notice. I said very boldly, "Here is my number. Call me if you get a chance—maybe we can get together when you get off." I felt his eyes watching my hips and butt as they swayed side to side out of the office.

My return check was for three thousand—Malik Moore called and left a message. I could come and pick it up after 3:00 P.M. on Thursday. I couldn't wait. Already in my mind I was thinking about not paying my credit cards off or bills and just going shopping. I wanted to just go on a shopping spree. I was happy I didn't run into Mr. Moore when I picked up my check, because he never called. Right now I'm getting dissed by everyone. I stared at the check. I knew I was supposed to pay bills, but I think half will go to bills and the other half needs to go to me because I deserve it. I have been having a rough time and a nice bag might help me cope. With that thought, I had raced to Franklin Mills, an outlet mall, and spent twenty-one hundred dollars on what you ask. I don't know. I had lots of bags and a gift for everyone but I didn't buy anything that I really needed except for Prada boots and a bag on sale at Last Call at Nieman Marcus. That came to sixteen hundred. I thought if I went to an outlet mall, I wouldn't spend as much money but that was a joke. I'll pay down my credit card bills next income tax. I came home and my phone was ringing.

"Hello."

"This is Malik."

"Hey, how you doing?"

"Good."

"I missed you at the office today."

"Yeah, you did?" *And you about three days late*, I wanted to say.

"So what are you doing tonight?"

"Grading papers and resting."

"I was going to ask if you wanted to meet up."

"When?"

"In, like, an hour," he said.

I paused. *Tell him no. Tell him no*, a voice said in the back of my mind. *He waited too many days to call you.* But

the desperate woman answered for me, and said,
"Okay—where do you want to meet at?"

"Let's meet at Circa Re."

"Okay, I'll meet you in about an hour."

When I reached the Circa Re, he was waiting by the
bar. He stood up and said, "You look nice." He grabbed
my hand and guided me to the bar.

"Thanks."

"No, really—wow," he said.

I sat at the bar with him. His phone rang once, then
it rang again. His phone kept ringing. I finally said,
"Dag, who keeps calling you like that?"

"My ex. She is so crazy—you have no idea," he said,
shaking his head.

"Why is she calling you?" I asked, nonchalant.

"Just to harass me. I do everything for my son. But
enough about her—let's talk about us."

Malik made me blush several times throughout the
evening. He told me about how he already had an associate's degree in criminal justice and was going to take
classes to get his bachelor's this summer. A man with a
plan—that's what I'm talking about. I already was liking
Malik Moore—better yet, loving him.

I have been talking to Malik regularly. He is so smart
and funny. I was in the middle of class when I got a text
message from him. He asked me what I was doing—I
told him I was in class and to call me at lunch. At lunch
I waited for Malik to call. I let the phone ring three
times, then I picked up.

"Hey."

"How are you?"

"I'm fine."

"I'm glad the day is almost over."

"Me too! What are you doing tonight?"

"Nothing."

"I wanted to see if you wanted to come to my house for dinner."

"Oh, you going to make me dinner?"

"Yeah."

"Give me your address."

I bought a bottle of wine, but then I decided I didn't want to drink with him. I'll just bring a pie—I don't want to send the wrong message. I'll pick one up on my way home. It is a school night. I'll eat and then leave.

Malik's house looked halfway lived-in. It was sparsely furnished. He had dinner already on a plate, waiting for me. He had a salad, garlic bread, and turkey lasagna. He was a great cook.

"You have a very nice place."

"Thanks—I'm still getting things together. It's hard starting over."

"I can imagine."

"I have a lot of stuff still in storage. My ex is real crazy—she tried to burn my belongings."

"Really?"

"Yeah, she is a real mental case. We never really talked about his ex—he just said that it was a chapter in his life he'd like to close. So I left it at that. I ate a small piece of the pie for dessert.

"Thank you for dinner. Good night," I said as I left his house. I was full, happy, and excited. Full from the meal, excited about the possibilities, and happy I had someone to take my mind off of Erick.

Me and Malik had been on three dates—technically, four. We went to the movies, dinner at his house, met at a restaurant, and now tonight at the bar. Malik was all over me with his hands and mouth. I was waiting for someone to tell us to get a room. While he was grabbing on my breast, his tongue was all the way down my throat. Nobody had to tell us—we got a room at the Hilton in New Jersey. I was ready for Malik. I had made him wait a month—that was good enough. I got his home and cell phone number—I know where he works and I know where he lives. He has a good job. A nice person—he has been spending time with me. It was time to take our relationship further. The room had a steamy, hot Jacuzzi, one large king bed, and a mini wet bar. We opened the little bottle of liquor like teenagers. He undressed me and I stood over him. He just kept playing with the cherry shape outside that sheltered my walls. I begged him to stop, but he didn't. Then he started slowly slurping while gliding his finger up and down the surface. The water splashed and my head was up against the tile, hitting it. I tried to control my balance. He was thrusting upon me. He sat me in the water and entered me. The water made my pussy feel a little dry, but the rough friction was a different kind of good sensation. I massaged his dick—it grew every time I went up and down in a cyclone twist. He was firm and stout and a decent length. I gave him my all. I wasn't supposed to, but I did. Malik begged me to stop. He couldn't take the constant clenching of my walls back and forth on him. He buckled and asked for water.

I was thinking about him every day, but I refused to call him. I like Malik, but not like that. I was debating if I even was going to call him again. Maybe I'm just using him to get over Erick. He was okay, I guess. I'm not in a rush to settle down again. Everything has to be fifty-fifty. I would like to be in a forty-sixty relationship. I want the man to love me a little bit more than I love him. I didn't have to call Malik because he called me.

* * *

"So what, you wasn't going to call me?" Malik snapped from the other end of my phone.

"Yeah, I was going to call you—I just have been busy," I said.

"I thought something happened to you. What are you doing later?"

"I don't know. Why, what's up?" I asked.

"I want to see you right now."

"Malik, I like you, but—"

"What, you think I'm getting too serious?" he asked.

"No, I don't think that. That's not how I feel. I really like you, Malik, but I just came out of a relationship."

"We can take our time, but I can't lie. I am falling for you."

"You falling for me?" I asked.

"Yeah, I think so. Can I see you tonight?"

"Yes, I'll call you when I get off of work."

Malik has been taking up a lot of my time. But I still miss my baby, Erick. I can't move on with Malik unless I see that I'm really over Erick. I know I still have feelings for Erick. I can say Malik has been keeping my mind off of him, but not totally. I turned on the television and watched Dr. Phil. I wished I could have a conversation with him.

I was in the classroom, going over a test review.

"Does anyone know what the age of reason or en-lightenment was? Raise your hand if you know the answer." I turned my back to write the answer on the board. When I turned back around, the desks were being pushed across the floor, making a shrieking noise as they scraped against the floor.

Natasha Byrd stood up with her hands balled up and said, "Somebody better tell her," she shouted as she pushed Sharaya.

"Sit down, both of y'all," I yelled. Before I knew it, there was a big bang against the wall. I ran over to try to stop the two girls from fighting. Sharaya was kicking Natasha in the face, and Natasha had Sharaya by the hair and they wouldn't separate. I tried my best to tear them apart. Sharaya's grip on Natasha's hair was unyielding. The kids were cheering them on. Mrs. Dorsey and Mrs. Meyers ran in and tried to help me. I finally got Sharaya off of Natasha. Mrs. Dorsey and Mrs. Meyers tried to contain Natasha. She had a handful of Sharaya's hair in her hands and her face had scratches all over it. I was out of breath, and Natasha somehow got away from them and tried to hit Sharaya. Instead, she hit me. I literally saw stars, and then fell to the ground.

"Oooh, y'all hit Ms. Clark," I heard the students yell. I was on the ground, holding my eye. "Call the office, call security," Mrs. Meyers said, and picked me up from the ground as I held my eye.

"Are you okay, Ms. Clark?" I regained my composure. "What is wrong with you two?" I said as I held my eye. We pulled them out of the classroom.

"Nothing, Ms. Clark. I'm sorry—are you okay? She likes Mannie and he was talking to me and she got in my face asking about him—he is *my* boyfriend," Sharaya said.

"No, he's not. He likes *me*," Natasha said.

Security came and they escorted me to the bathroom. I looked in the mirror. I was a little dizzy and my face hurt.

Mrs. Meyers took over my class. I walked to the

nurse's office. My head was ringing a little, but I felt okay.

The nurse saw my eye and she gasped and said, "Let me get an ice packet." I had to get a look at my eye. "Did you get attacked?" she asked as she handed me the ice pack.

"No, they were fighting."

"Miss Clark, are you okay?" Mr. Mitchell asked, running into the nurse's office.

"Yes, I'm fine."

"No, you're not. Look at your eye. It is closed shut."

I got off the nurse's table and looked at myself in the mirror. My right eye was sealed shut, like a boxer's after losing a match.

"I cannot have one of my teachers assaulted. I'm calling the police. They both will be arrested."

"No, no, just suspend them. They didn't mean it. It was an accident. They were fighting over a boy."

"What boy?"

"Mannie Turner."

"He is getting suspended, too! Ms. Clark, take the rest of the day off. Call us tomorrow and tell us how you feel."

I called Malik to see if he could come and get me. "Malik, can you pick me up from school?"

"Are you okay?"

"Yes, it is a long story. If you can't do it, I will call my aunt."

"No, I'll be right there."

I retrieved my things from the classroom. "I want you guys to finish reading chapter twenty-four and answer the study questions."

Malik called my cell phone to let me know he was outside. As soon as he saw me, he said, "What happened to you?"

"I was trying to stop a fight."

"You should have told me to bring you a piece of steak. You are still beautiful," he said as he kissed my forehead and carried my belongings to the car. "Who popped you in your eye?"

"Two students fighting over a boy."

"He must be something special," he said.

"No, not really." I didn't want to laugh. I just wanted to get home and try to stop my eye from swelling or blackening. Malik took me home and ran my bath water for me. I soaked and went to the pharmacy to get me some Tylenol. When I came out of the tub, he dried me off and held a cold compress on my head until I fell asleep.

Chapter 29

Kim

Malik asked if he could he watch Kayden. I was allowing Kayden to go because it was only overnight. If I was over him, I would let Kayden go, I told myself. And I was over Malik—I was going on with my life. I overpacked Kayden's baby bag. Malik told me to have him ready by three. When Malik rang my bell, Kayden would be ready to go. That way there would be no awkwardness, or long conversations. No *how's it going?* No time to stare and wonder *what if.* Just, *here is the baby, have a nice day.*

Malik showed up exactly at three. He had on jeans and an olive green shirt and dark blue faded jeans. He actually looked handsome.

He smiled and I said, "Here is his milk, diapers, and snacks, and you need his car seat."

I walked to my car and got the car seat. He put it in his car and I looked down at the shiny gold band on Malik's hand. It was official. I saw it with my own eyes—Malik was married. He was forever gone from my life. I had to be a big person and let it go. My life with Malik was over.

I had the entire house to myself for twenty-four hours. Kevin was with Karen for Ryan's sleepover for his birthday. The house was so quiet without the boys. I missed them, but I needed to be taking the opportunity to relax. I called and left a message for Andrew to see if he wanted to get together. Maybe we could do another movie. I sat around, doing nothing, finding things to do around the house. I couldn't stop wondering if my baby was okay. I called Malik's phone to check on Kayden, but he didn't answer. So I left him a message. "Malik, this is Kim. Make sure he eats and make sure he has enough to drink." I tried to take a nap. I lay in the bed and pulled the covers over my head. I couldn't fall asleep, so I left Andrew another message. Then I went into the basement and put a load of laundry in. After that I decided I would drive to Wal-Mart to see if I needed anything. I know I didn't, but I was bored. I always have the boys—now that I didn't have them, I didn't know what to do. In Wal-Mart they were having a sale on towels. And they had name-brand cereal for $2.50 a box. That was a good deal. I was twenty-eight years old, becoming excited about sales at Wal-Mart. This is so sad, I thought. I unloaded all my bags into my trunk and the phone rang.

"Hey, Kim—what's going on? I didn't check my messages." I was so happy he called me.

"Andrew, I wanted to see if you wanted to hook up and go out."

"I would love to, but I have Cee with me, but how about you come over? I can order us something to eat."

"Oh, no. I don't want to intrude. You have your

daughter. We'll get together some other time," I said, disappointed.

"You won't be intruding—she is taking her bath, about to go to bed. She will be asleep."

"Okay, I'll come over for a little while," I said. He just didn't know he was about to save me from a night of boredom. Andrew gave me his address and I drove to his house. I was a little nervous. He opened the door and he gave me a hug. He took my jacket and we sat on the sofa.

"Where's your bathroom?" I asked.

"Straight up the steps." I walked into the bathroom, passing his bedroom. His daughter, Cianni, was lying across the pillow. Her ponytails were longer and thicker than in her picture—she was a slightly tanner version of her father.

When I came down the steps, Andrew hugged me and said, "I missed you." It took me by surprise, but I missed him a little, too, so I hugged back.

We watched a movie on HBO and Andrew brought me closer to him. He then began kneading my shoulders and back. His touch was so relaxing, it was sending me to sleep. I felt so at ease and safe in his arms that I closed my eyes for a little while but just as I got too comfortable I awoke and said, "What time is it? I'm going to get ready to get out of here." I jumped up.

"Why? It's dark—just stay the night."

"No, I can't—your daughter is here," I protested.

"She won't be up until around nine. Stay until the morning."

"I can't."

"Kim, you can't leave—it is one in the morning. You fell asleep. You might as well finish sleeping—you need the rest. I promise you, I will have you out of here first thing in the morning," he said. Andrew began to kiss me. His tongue went in and out of my mouth. His kisses were sweet, and tickled. He just held me and told me if I wanted to go home, he would drive me, because he didn't want me out late at night.

"Please stay," he said as he kissed me.

"Okay," I said as I kissed him back. He turned the television off, and then held me until I went to sleep. I woke up to fluffy yellow eggs and cinnamon pancakes, and a crook in my neck from sleeping on the sofa. Cianni was already eating her breakfast at the table. She stared at me. I felt nervous. I didn't want to meet her yet—it was too soon. If he introduced me to her, he would think I would introduce him to my children, and that was not happening. I smiled at her, told Andrew I had to go, and left.

Nicole ran into my office. "It's Andrew," she said.

"What are you doing when you get off work?" he asked.

"Picking the kids up."

"Can I see you later?"

"I have to find a sitter," I said.

"I'll come to your house," he said.

"I have a lot of work." I like Andrew, but I couldn't let him come to the house, at least not yet.

"Kim, are you afraid one of your neighbors might see you with a white man? Kim, you know what? I'm having a lot of fun with you. I enjoy your company, but I'm starting to think me and you are not on the same page. We have been going out, doing a lot of talking, and you still haven't opened up to me. Why are you still holding back?"

"I'm not holding back. It's just—my oldest son, Kevin—my boys will be there."

"I'll come over when they are asleep."

"How about if they wake up? I don't want to confuse them."

Before I could finish, Andrew stopped me and said, "Listen, Kim, when you decide what exactly it is you want, call me. Until then, have a nice life."

Was Andrew right? Was I treating him like there was something wrong with him? There was nothing wrong with him. There was something wrong with me. I was acting very foolish. I liked him, but I was trying to find reasons not to like him. I'm going to let him come over and whatever happens will happen. He is who he is. I came home, fed the boys, let them play for a little while.

"Kevin, come get ready for bed," I yelled.

"Mom, it's Friday!"

"You heard what I said—get ready for bed." He turned off his PlayStation, and got in the bed. I put Kayden down, then took a shower. I kept constantly thinking about what Andrew said. He is white, and so what. He is nice, he treats me good, and he is very attentive. I mean, he isn't trying to be hip, and I'm not trying to be anything other than what I am. I mean, we really just connect. I don't care if he is white, I don't care what anyone else will say. I like him, and I called Andrew back. His phone rang four times before he answered.

"Hello."

"Andrew, um I wanted to say I'm sorry for the way I have been treating you. So why don't you come over so we can talk." Andrew coming over meant that we were really dating, but I didn't care. I couldn't deny him any-more.

Andrew called to tell me he was outside. I went to open the door.

"Where are your boys?"

"Asleep."

"You know what you want now?" he asked.

"Yes."

"Good, because I know I want you," he said as he kissed me and squeezed my shoulders.

"You are so tense. You need a massage."

"Okay—we can go upstairs," I said. I walked him to my room and lay on my bed. He took off his shoes. I pulled out baby oil. His smooth hands were soft as he rubbed oil in between my toes and poured a few drops of oil down the center of my back—then he took his index finger and slid it up and down my vertebrae and began massaging my shoulder caps and arms. After my massage was over, he began kissing my back; he then flipped me over and kissed my ears, neck, and shoul-ders. He lifted my shirt and pulled my bra up and took the oil and massaged my breasts. My nipples rose and melted at the touch of his hand. He placed himself on top of me and kissed my neck, then my ear again. He unfastened his pants and then mine. I didn't move. I was curious, scared and anxious. He pulled a condom out of his wallet and placed it on his member. He en-tered me and spread my legs so far apart that I thought they were going to break. He entered a region in my pelvis that had never been touched. It was so over-whelming, so beautiful. I hadn't had sex in over a year, and somehow I don't remember it ever feeling like this. It was pleasure and pain. I tried to muffle my screams into the pillows. The last thing I wanted was Kevin knocking on my door, saying, *Mommy, what's wrong?* Andrew's lovemaking skills were incredible. I didn't want to let him go. I looked at him a little differently when it was over.

Chapter 30

Shonda

Malik's new job was such a blessing. He stays at work real late but I don't care. I am so happy he is working. But now we are playing catch-up with our bills. So until then, I am so broke. I have learned that you can ride up to thirty miles on an empty gas tank. I am so tempted to ask Hicks what I needed to do to make five hundred extra a week. I really could use that money. I was so hungry—I had left my lunch at home, and the aroma from his food was creeping into my nose.

"Hey, Robinson—you okay?" Hicks asked.

"Yeah, I'm fine."

"Did you eat?" His spaghetti smelled so good. My stomach was doing somersaults.

"No, not yet," I said.

"You want something to eat?"

"No," I said. I was so hungry, but I didn't want to let him know it.

"You sure?" he asked.

"Okay, I'll try a little." I got a plate and ate a little. I felt more comfortable. I complimented him on his spaghetti and he told me he made it himself.

"You can have some more—I have a whole pot full."

I grabbed a plate and took him up on his offer. "So tell me what you were talking about, when you said I can make money."

"I'll talk to you about that later," he said, a little agitated.

"Okay."

The rest of the day was just like every day. The same people leaving jail. People coming in and out like a revolving door. Hicks told me he was going out for cigarettes, and asked me, did I want to take the ride with him? I took the ride, and he closed the door and said, "First, let me tell you—you have to watch what you say and how you say it."

"Sorry."

"Naw, it's okay. So, here is how you make the money. It's like you have to see how you feel about things, right? All you have to do is go to the Wawa on Cottman Avenue and order hoagies. Come back up here, and I'm going to leave a box by the door. Just sit the hoagies in the boxes, and you can get fifty dollars."

"That's it?"

"Yeah, that's it. And if you do that right, we will get into the other things with you. We are going to try it tomorrow."

Before I came in to work, I went to buy the hoagies. I placed the sandwiches in the box and walked into the building. Hicks got ten dollars for two dollar hoagies. He gave me my fifty and told me he would let me know about other things.

It was sweet as hell, bringing in the sandwiches three times a week. At night, before the end of my shift, I would help Hicks collect the trash. He would mix in some real trash and he would take it out to the Dumpster himself. Hicks told me if I see a prisoner with food to turn my head and just do what I had to do to keep from looking suspicious unless there was a superior around. Next, Hicks wanted me to bring in cigarettes. They went for twenty dollars a pack. Loosie went for five. I brought in a carton and sold it for two hundred.

I was walking the floor, doing my rounds, when Riddick approached me and said, "Robinson, where is Hicks?"

"Up on Unit E."

"What is he doing over there again? Tell Hicks to get his ass over here. Hicks been spending a lot of time in the women's unit."

"Okay," I said. I'd noticed it, too, but I didn't say anything. He always has me bring snacks and cigarettes to this one big, bone-white girl. Oh well, that was on him. I was making enough money to catch up on bills and treat myself.

Malik brought the baby over to spend the night. That little boy was full of energy, running around. I was so upset because I didn't have anywhere for that little boy to sleep.

"Malik, why didn't you ask me?"

"I have to ask you to bring my son over?"

"No, I didn't mean it like that. Why didn't you just let me know so I can have things ready for him? Like, where is he going to sleep?"

"With us."

"He might fall out of the bed."

"No, he won't—we will just put him between us." Malik said, going up the steps. The phone rang—I thought it was Brian, saying he was outside, dropping Bree off. Instead it was Jarrod. "Malik there?" he asked.

"Hold on a minute. Malik, pick up the phone," I yelled. "So, where you trying to get my husband to go?" I asked him, prying.

"I don't know yet," he said. I knew he was covering for Malik. Before the conversation went any further, Malik picked up the cordless phone. I wished I could stay on the line and see what they were talking about.

Malik screamed, "Shonda, hang up—I got it."

Bree ran through the door. She saw Kayden and dropped her bags and ran over to him. "Hi, Kayden," she said, hugging him. "My dad said he'll bring the rest of my clothes home tomorrow, Mom."

"I'll be right back," Malik said, putting on his coat as he came down the stairs.

"All right, how long you going to be?" I asked.

"Not long."

An hour and a half had passed by and Malik wasn't back yet. Kayden was playing with Bree and still just getting into everything. I couldn't wait for Malik to get back to put his little ass to sleep. When he started getting whiny, I couldn't wait any more for Malik.

"Mom, can I help you give him a bath?"

"No, Bree, you have school tomorrow—go get ready for bed." Bree brushed her teeth and washed her face and changed into her nightclothes.

"Good night, Mom."

"Good night," I said as I gave her a kiss good night and took Kayden's clothes off and ran his bathwater. He became instantly tired when the warm water touched him. He splashed the water and smiled at me. In his smile I saw glimpses of Malik. I dried him off and patted "Lil' Malik" to sleep and fell asleep with him.

Malik came in and me and the baby were asleep.

"Thank you for putting him down. Look at you, being a good stepmom."

Umm, I'm asleep," I said drowsily. "Where were you?" I asked as Malik got in the bed with us.

"With Heather and Jarrod—they getting married, and he is trying to sell his place. I'm going to be helping him move."

"That's nice," I said as I went back to sleep.

Kayden began kicking me. I moved over to the right, and so did that little boy. He kicked me again. He was such a wild sleeper. Malik was knocked out and wasn't bothered by Kayden's tossing and turning at all. I, on the other hand, could not go to sleep. I finally got frustrated and decided to go downstairs to get some rest on the sofa. At least, I *thought* I was going to sleep on my sofa. Instead I saw Omar had some dirty young girl, watching television with the lights out. I made eye contact with him, rolled my eyes, and went to lie in Bree's bed with her.

Chapter 31

Kim

"What are you doing?" Karen asked.

"Sitting back, about to eat and watch that movie, *Woman, Thou Are Loosed*."

"Why don't you bring the boys over?"

"I only have Kevin," I said.

"Where is my baby boy?" Karen asked.

"I let him go with Malik."

"You what? I would have watched him. You don't have to let Kayden go over there. I am grateful that Malik got me out of this jam, but just because he helped me doesn't mean you have to be his friend."

"I know, but I think it is time to let him see his father. Malik is married now, and I'm moving on. He has changed—he seems a lot more mature."

"Don't let him weasel his way back into your life."

"I'm not. Never."

"You better than me. I wouldn't have a sympathetic ear for him. He dogged you. Fuck him. I'll send him something for helping me out, but I still don't like him. I'll never forgive him after what he did to you. Just because you forgave him doesn't mean God has. He has something coming to him. Mark my words."

"I know—he has changed a lot, though."

"His ass still not to be trusted."

I guess you can say that Andrew was my man, boyfriend, or something like that. We've been to a winery, Salsa classes and a live jazz show. He even took my car to get serviced. Meeting Andrew after work for happy hours had become our little routine. Kevin had signed up for baseball, and Lonnie dropped him off after practice. I didn't have to get Kayden because Malik was getting him on Wednesday and Thursday. I was slowly falling in love with Andrew.

"So, what you having?" the bartender said as I took a seat.

"I'm not ready to order yet."

"Are you waiting for someone?" he asked, wiping a glass clean.

"Yes, I am," I said, opening my compact and applying new lip gloss. I waited for Andrew, and then he showed up. He came and had a seat.

I went to the bathroom, and when I came back, the bartender said, "Ma'am, are you going to order?"

"One moment," I said.

"Is your party here?" he asked as he looked around.

"Yes, he is," I said as I turned toward Andrew. This was getting real old—look who's coming to dinner.

He looked at Andrew and said, "Oh, I see." He didn't even apologize to me. He looked me over and then asked Andrew what he was having.

"What does he mean, *Oh, I see?*"

"Don't worry about him—tell me about your day."

"No, forget that." I went and found a manager.

"What's the problem?"

"Your waiter is rude."

"Oh, that guy—he is a prick. Listen here, your drinks are on the house. Don't take it personal."

"No, I'll pay for my own drink—I wasn't looking for a freebie."

"I don't know how much of this I can take, Andrew. I really like you, but I'm not used to this kind of discrimination. This has happened twice in the last week. People being rude or saying something disrespectful." I didn't have much time to dwell on that because my son's father, Malik, had just walked through the door. Oh my God, I didn't want Malik to see me with Andrew. Would he think I was desperate? I know he wouldn't understand. But then it dawned on me that I should not be worried about Malik seeing me on a date, but where the hell was my son? If he is here on a date with this young girl, where is my child? Is he home with that woman? What is she doing with my child all alone? They were about to leave. I should tell the woman he was with that Malik was married. I really thought Malik was getting himself together, but I guess that is impossible. Here he is, canoodling and kissing a woman that wasn't his wife. I didn't want to cause a scene. I just excused myself and went into the ladies' room and called him.

"Malik, you are out. Who has my son? And don't say your mom, because I already called there and she is not home."

"Nadia has him—call her."

I hung up on him and dialed her number. Coincidentally, Nadia's phone was off. I called Malik's mom and got no answer. I was worried about my baby. By the time I came out of the bathroom, Malik and his date were gone. He was not allowed to watch him anymore. I called Malik for three hours straight, but he never answered.

Chapter 32

Nadine

My Aunt Connie was having her fiftieth birthday party. I had invited Malik—he said he would meet me here. I walked in and had a seat. Betty Wright's "Tonight is the Night" was blasting from the speakers. The entire bar was decorated with silver and black streamers. My aunt had a whole pamphlet dedicated to her life. There were pictures of her sweet sixteen, graduation, and wedding day. I spoke to a few of her friends and people that I didn't remember, but that remembered me and told me how nice I looked. I saw all my aunt's friends with their men or alone. Some looked my aunt's age and others looked like they could use a facial rejuvenation (face-lift). They looked twice as old as she was. I wonder how I will be in another twenty-five years—with my husband and kids, or by myself. Rodney was walking in my directon. I hadn't seen him since the card party. I hoped he didn't see me. I wanted to crawl in the corner. But here he was walking up to me. I was so embarrassed, I didn't want to face him. "Nadine, I think we need to talk," he said "Okay." I said, like make it quick.

"Listen, I'm sorry Nadine. I always felt attracted to

you too! But you know we can't ever be. One, we are family. Two, I have a girlfriend and she is here. Are you okay with that?"

"Yes. Rody, I was drunk, it was a mistake."

"Oh, I thought you really had a thing for me."

"No!"

"Well that's a relief because we would have been kissing cousins," he said as he gave me a non-threatening hug. Even though I would love to tear Rodney apart, I knew I had to leave well enough alone. I had to call Malik to see where he was.

Toya came over to me with her big stomach, interrupting my thoughts, and said, "Why is Rodney's girlfriend here? She is fat, ugly, and trying to be down. Look at her," she said pointing. "There she goes."

"Oh, she is ugly," I said, turning my lips up.

"I told you. What Rody see in her?"

"I don't know, but if that's what he likes, that is on him," I said. Her eyes were cocked. Her left eye was looking in a whole other direction from her right. She had on a thin wifebeater that thinly veiled the rolls of fat that was her stomach.

"Why she trying to be in the family, calling me sis and my mother mom? My mom was like 'girl, I'm not your mom.'"

I thought Toya was lying—then the girl came over to me and screamed, "You must be Nadine. Nice to finally meet you."

"And you are," I said, intentionally trying to play her.

"I'm Rody's girlfriend, Ayinde."

"Oh, okay. Nice to meet you," I said as I walked away. Toya followed and said under her breath, "She must have money. Why would my brother bring this chimpanzee home?"

"I don't know. I have to find your mom," I said as I walked away from Toya. Aunt Connie had a long, black dress with hanging sleeves and a diamond tiara and unbelievable diamond earrings and necklace. I had to find her and give her my card.

I gave her the card—she ripped it open and took the money out, fanning it. "You gave me my favorite gift. Thanks, niecey."

I went upstairs to where the food was. There were big silver aluminum containers of buffalo chicken, honey wings, spinach garlic salad, a spaghetti pasta salad, and crab casserole. There were little silver plates. I got a little of everything and I came back down the steps and waited for Malik to show up. I can't wait for everybody to meet him. I checked my cell phone to see if he had called and I missed it. I called Malik and got his voice mail. It was starting to get late. I hoped he could make it.

Uncle Chuck told everyone to get on the dance floor. Everybody joined him middle of the floor. One of the bartenders rolled out a huge cake in the shape of a high heel. The cake read HAPPY BIRTHDAY CONNIE AKA HIGH MAINTENANCE. My aunt laughed and asked, "Am I high maintenance, Chuck?" He didn't say anything, so she asked him again.

"I'm high maintenance, Chuck?"

Somebody said, "Think about that before you answer, Chuck."

"Yes, but I still love you," he said. We all laughed and they kissed and he said, "Happy fiftieth, baby." Then we all sang Stevie Wonder's version of "Happy Birthday." *Hap-py Birth-day, Happy Birthday.* Everybody was singing in unison. I called Malik to see if he was still coming.

"Malik, are you on your way?"

"Nah—sorry, I won't be able to make it."

"Are you serious?" I asked.

"Yeah, something came up."

"Okay, well, I'll talk to you later." I sat down at the

bar, a little sad. I guess I will be alone all night. I thought me and Malik were headed somewhere. I ordered a double apple martini and started thinking about Erick. I walked to the bathroom and wanted to cry, but I didn't. Men are so damn unpredictable. I couldn't let anyone see me cry, so I wiped my tears away. The moment the first tear runs, your eyes get a little pink; then you wipe and they become red, then the bottom under your eyes puffs and people start asking you if you're okay. I don't need that. I pulled a towel from the towel holder, wet it, and wiped my face. I opened my eyes to keep the tears back. I had got myself together and walked out of the bathroom. I saw Toya and went and had a seat next to her.

"What's going on, girl?"

"Nothing. You know, everybody all in my business, talking about when I'm going to get married. I told them to mind their business." She then stopped and said, "You didn't tell me you was bringing your replacement."

"Who?" I asked, looking to see who she was talking about.

"Malik."

"How'd you know what he looks like? He's not here. He couldn't make it," I said, turning around.

"Yes, he is—I know that's not one of my mom's friend. He's right over there," she said, pointing Malik out.

I fixed my clothes and hair and he was walking towards us. "Malik, I thought something came up."

"I was playing with you. I was looking for somewhere to park," he said as he pulled me closer to him and gave me a hug.

"Don't play like that. You lucky you look and smell good," I said as I inhaled his cologne.

"Thank you," he said, and I asked him if he wanted

something to eat. He said he was a little hungry. We walked through the party and upstairs—nobody was upstairs but us. I began fixing his plate and he came up from behind and hugged me.

"Ooh, you feel so good," he said. I turned around and nudged him away. I felt a little spark shoot through my breast to my pelvic bone. I shook it off.

"So, what do you want to eat?" I asked.

"You."

"Stop playing, Malik." He told me what he wanted on his plate. I wanted to introduce everybody to Malik. He was looking so good.

"Aunt Connie, this is Malik."

She said "nice to meet you" and winked at me. I needed my family to see that I was so over Erick. Me and Malik danced to the oldies and at the end of the night I went into the bathroom and took my thong off. When I went back to the dance floor, I handed it to Malik.

"What's this?" he said as he opened his fist up. Once he realized they were my panties, he then began massaging my waist and butt because he knew I didn't have any underwear on.

"You're a freak and I love it," he whispered in my ear.

"Let's go back to my house." I was so hot all over and my body was excited. I couldn't wait to have him in me. I thought about how I was going to mount his dick and rub every inch of my walls over him.

Once we reached my house, we started kissing. We went into my house. I turned on a movie from Erick's collection. He didn't say anything; he just kissed me. I kissed him back. His body felt so warm and firm. We stood there; just tongues swirling each other back and forth. There was a woman getting her breast licked by another woman on the screen and the man was fucking her. "You ever had a threesome?" he playfully asked as he nibbled on my ears and eyed the movie.

"Absolutely not," I said.

"You ever think about one?"

"No, I think a man can only handle me. He wouldn't have enough energy for another woman."

"Really?"

"Yeah, really." I said. Malik came closer and unleashed my breast. They began to jiggle as he massaged my breasts, and he played with them until they grew in size and color from a deep brown to dark burgundy. He took every inch of them into his mouth. His suckling hurt, but was pleasurable at the same time. I went into my drawer and grabbed my purple vibrator.

"What are you going to do with that?" he asked.

"I'm going to use it," I said as I opened my legs and let the thick wand of pulsation enter me. Malik watched in silence as I pleasured myself. I gave the toy to him. He inserted it deep into my cervix. He was enjoying sticking and twisting the toy in me. He used it until I couldn't take it anymore. I grabbed his pants and pulled them down. He stood up, and I bent down and reached for motion lotion. I poured some on him, rubbing it up and down the shaft of his penis. Then I blew on him. The lotion became warm when you blew on it. I then placed him into my mouth and pulled so tightly with my jaws and mouth that I almost gagged. Malik's facial expressions let me know I was satisfying him in more ways than one. I think he is going to be my baby. I know I am his because he told me.

Chapter 33

Shonda

Me and Malik have not been spending a lot of time together. We have been working so much I wanted to spend quality time with my husband. I cooked a nice, big dinner, for him: I put it in the microwave so he could have it when he came home. Malik entered the house, took his coat off, and gave me a kiss on the cheek.

"Malik, your plate is in the microwave."

"I already ate," he said.

"You ate what? Where are you coming from?" I asked, upset.

"Nowhere—I'll eat it later," he said as he covered and wrapped the plate with foil.

"I cooked all this food for you. You could at least eat some of it."

"I'm not hungry right now. I'll eat it."

"You ungrateful thing," I said under my breath as I rolled my eyes. "Malik, I want us to spend some time together." I went behind him and gave him a kiss.

"All right, let me get something out of the car."

I went upstairs to wait for him. I undressed and

waited for him to get in the bed. He turned off the light and placed a little bag by the side of the bed.

"What you got, Malik?"

"Nothing—sit back," he said as he began to kiss me. I sat up and grabbed the back of his head and kissed him. He pulled out a purple object and rubbed it up against my leg, then he began winding it in and out of me. I climaxed intensely. I never used a dildo, vibrator, or anything like that.

"What would make you buy me a vibrator?"

"I just thought you would want one," he said.

"Thank you, baby," I said as I pulled him on top of me. I didn't want to think too much about it. I wanted to enjoy this moment under the covers with my husband.

"Surprise me like that more often." I said.

"I will," he said as he took off his clothes and got in the bed. He held me and made love to me like he missed me.

I have been bringing in sandwiches and cigarettes, and now Hicks asked me to bring in weed. I was scared at first, but I agreed to. All I had to do was stuff the weed in a plastic wrap, then stick it in my coochie and come in the building. Then I would go into the bathroom and leave it behind the toilet and walk out. Hicks would have someone in maintenance come around and pick it up. She would drop it off to the inmates, and then he would collect the money. Another time I took some coke out of a baby's Pamper in the visiting room, wrapped it up, and stuck it in my bra. Everything was real planned-out. I didn't feel bad about bringing anything into the jails because they don't treat the prisoners right, anyway. And really, they don't give them a chance on the streets in the first place. Sometimes I hate this job and I do hate the way some men gawk at me. But then, sometimes I like it. I don't mind being admired. All these men wanting me, writing me letters, and telling me how pretty I was. The compliments made me feel special. I was the only good-looking thing they got to look at all day. Riddick was a man in a woman's body, and she wore her clothes so loose nobody could figure out where her butt begins and her back ends. And Sheppard has the body and is young, but ditzy. By now I was used to the inmates flirting, playing, and being crazy, reading books, cracking jokes. It made their time go by faster—they had nothing else to do. Inmates are so damn funny like that. I walked past one named Ocho. He was medium built, with smooth, dark chocolate complexion and wavy black hair.

"How you doing, Ms. Robinson?" he said confidently.

"I'm fine."

"You look real nice—you married?" he asked.

"Yeah, I'm married."

"Why your man not taking proper care of you?"

"Why you say that?" I questioned.

"Because if you was my woman, you wouldn't be working at all."

"Is that right?"

"Yeah, take this," he said as he passed me a note. It read:

Ms. Robinson,
You don't know me, my name is Ocho. I see u got that ring on your finger, but not a smile on your face. U the kind of lady that should have everything. I'm not going to keep writing. I'm just say real niggahs do real things, and I'ma real niggah. I like what I see and I get what I want and I want you. Don't think I'm one of these dudes that is just talking shit. The truth is I really want to be

able to holla at you on some real shit. So let me know
what's up. My case is minor and I'll be out of here in a
matter of months.

I'm worth the wait.
Ocho

I balled the letter up and stashed it in my pocket. I
finished my walk around and found Sheppard to see
what she was up to at her post.

"What's that inmate, Ocho's, charges?" I asked.

"Ocho—oh, that's Edward Johnson. He has attempted-
murder charges. I read about him in the paper. He's in
here for trying to kill some dude that tried to rape his
sister. But he's going to get off. Because the guy he shot
had a loaded gun in his hand and he is claiming self-defense. He is paid like a motherfucker. He got a picture
with everybody famous in his cell. He is even refusing
visits."

"Why?"

"Well, chicks was coming up here, fighting to visit
him. He don't just mess with anything. These was nice-
looking women."

"Why? Who is he?" I asked.

"Because that niggah is, like, a millionaire on the
streets."

"Well, now all that doesn't matter because he is behind bars."

"Yes it do 'cause he about to come home," she laughed.

Malik has been cutting up lately. We have been growing apart. I'm working nights and him in the daytime.
We really have to set some time alone to be together. I
came in from work and the smell of soap was lingering
in the air. I peeked in the basement—I knew it wasn't
Omar's funky-ass. He didn't believe in bathing. There

was tags on the bed off of new clothes, the smell of Irish Spring deodorant soap, and the bathroom mirror was still foggy. I wondered where Malik went. Let him tell it, he's been with Jarrod all this week at the gym. I don't believe him, but if he thinks I'm stupid then that's on him. I know Jarrod has a woman now and doesn't seem like he goes out as much. Malik might be cheating, but I doubt it, though. He doesn't have any money to cheat. How can he afford to take somebody out? I just gave him money to fill up his gas tank and we're catching up on bills. Plus, why would he marry me and still cheat? That does not make sense. When men get married, that means they are ready to settle down. I don't have time to worry about him. I have to get some rest. Malik loves me and I love him, and now I'm wifey, so even if he did have someone else, she is not his top priority. She would be just a piece of ass.

I saw Ocho a few times this week—he winked at me and licked out his tongue. If he wasn't so cute, I would have got him in trouble. I smiled and turned away. He had someone slip me a note asking for my telephone number. Everybody talking about him made me really interested to see who he was and what he was about and why he was interested in me. At first I was scared to tell him anything about me. It could be a setup—I didn't know. But I did give him my number.

"How you going to call me?" I asked.

"How you think? On my phone." All inmates that had money had someone bring them in a cell phone, and then he said, "I'm going to call you tonight after lights out."

I was so nervous when I got his first call.

"Hey, how you doing?"

"Hi—I'm surprised you called."

"So what's up, Ma?"

"What's up with you?" I asked.

"Nothing—trying to get to the other side of these walls with you. My lawyer's working on making that happen."

"Really?" I asked.

"Yeah, man, he's trying to get my bail reduced or get me on house arrest. My gun charge got thrown out already. Then I got an attempted-murder charge, but I'm going to beat that case. Then I got one more assault charge."

"How'd you get the attempted-murder case?" I asked, looking out the window. I kept looking to see if Malik was coming home.

"See, this guy was fucking with my sister. He tried to rape her. I went to try to talk to the niggah, and he tried to pull fire on me. So I pulled mine out first. It was self-defense."

"Did he die?"

"No, but he did suffer, though. He lost an eye. I shot him in the head. But that was a dummy move. I got a real bad attitude. I need somebody to keep me at peace so I won't be acting all wild. My temper is a motherfucker."

"Uh-huh," I said. "Where is your sister at now?"

"My sister, she is cut. She don't be looking out for me or my son. She ain't sent me no kites, flicks, or put money on my books."

"That's messed up," I said.

"Yeah, I know. I got people in here and on the streets holding me down, though."

"So that's the only charge you have?"

"Naw, I got this stupid other assault case. Because I went to court on the gun charge and the bailiff kept being smart. Every time I signed my name on my papers, he snatched the pen and said, 'sign here.' So I finally said, 'yo man, don't keep snatching the pen from me.' He did it again, so I flipped over the papers and pen and they gave me another charge. It's about to be count—I'll see you tomorrow," he said, hanging up the call.

I spoke to Ocho all this week on the phone. He filled me in on his struggle growing up. His mom wasn't around much, his parents were doing them, he said— drugs, drinking, selling drugs. He lived with his grand- mother, but when she died, he had to step up and take care of his sister. His conversation was good and he seemed all right. He sent me flowers somehow to the job and passed me an envelope filled with money the other day. He told me to buy myself something. It was only two hundred dollars, but it meant a lot to me.

Malik was asleep in the bed. He had been running the street so much, I guess he was tired. I snuck down- stairs to wait for Ocho's call—I wanted to thank him for the money. As soon as he called, I picked up.

"Thanks for the money."

"It's cool—that ain't nothing. You can get whatever when I get out. Shonda, my old girl, I used to give her, like, five thousand just because—and now that bitch ain't never come and see me. I mean, I'm used to peo- ple forgetting about you when they think you're down. But that's okay—I'm doing things differently this time when I get out. I mean that shit. My goal is to open a seafood restaurant. I was stupid with my money, helping everybody out. Not this time—I'm just worrying about me and mine. You feel me. I just want to take care of my son and my woman. Hopefully, that will be you," he said, rambling on.

"How you think that is going to happen? I'm married," I said, reminding him we could just be friends.

"I don't care. Dude not making you happy," he said. "I'm going to make you happy."

"How you going to do that?" I asked.

"You'll see."

Chapter 34

Kim

Andrew wanted to take all the kids out so Cianni could meet the boys. We met at the Chuck E. Cheese. I introduced them, and at first Kevin was nice to Cianni, but by the end of the day they were arguing. They argued about any and everything, from who could run the fastest to what cartoon was the best. Andrew talked to both of them, letting them know both of their favorites were the best. They agreed and went to play.

"Andrew, Andrew, come see this," Kevin yelled as he challenged him in the arcade basketball game. I chased Kayden around—he cried every time he saw a character walking and dancing around. The next weekend we took the children to the Please Touch Museum and The New Jersey Adventure Aquarium.

Andrew had been staying over a lot and we were really a couple. It is so amazing that this man I wanted nothing to do with is now a man I think I love. I was nestled in his arms. Then I heard a knock at my door.

"Mom, can I come in?" Kevin was up early. I tapped

Andrew to tell him. His response was, "Just act like I just came over this morning," he said.

"Kevin, good morning—you ready to eat?" I said as I tried to fix my clothes and close my door behind me.

"Yes," he said as he wiped his eye.

"Kayden still asleep, Mom?"

"Yes," I answered nervously. Kevin sat at the table as I poured the Sugar Smacks. Andrew came walking down the steps, playing along with my charade.

"Good morning, Kev."

"What's up, Andrew? Did you spend the night again?" Kevin asked.

"No. I never spent the night before," Andrew said.

"Oh, 'cause I was going to say if you are going to keep spending the night you should bring some new clothes over."

Andrew said, "Well, if I ever do, I will, okay?"

I had to tell my family about Andrew. He had introduced me to his parents, and they were very nice and accepting. Me and his mother, Julia, hit it off right away—she was a retired secretary and his stepdad, Joe, was a retired banker. My mother was making a Sunday dinner. I could talk to my mom, Karen, and Kianna all at once. That would be the perfect opportunity to discuss my relationship with Andrew.

During dinner I was going to say something, but I didn't have the nerve. So I waited until my mom pulled out dessert. I cleared my throat and said, "Mommy, you know I have been dating someone," as I took a hunk of pineapple upside down cake. Kianna and Karen focused their attention on me.

"Do tell," she said, as she sat down and grabbed her own cake.

"Well, his name is Andrew, and I want you to meet him."

"Does he have any children?" she asked.

"Yes, one from his first marriage."

"How many times has he been married?"

"Once."

"That is so nice," my mom said.

"When do we get to meet him?" Kianna asked.

"You two have already met him," I said.

"We did? When?" Karen asked as they looked at one another.

"That night we went to Glam."

"I don't remember you meeting anybody," Kianna said.

"I did meet somebody—the guy at the table."

"You mean that white guy? You're dating that white guy, Kim?" Karen shouted.

"Yes," I said, "and I don't care what y'all think."

"You're dating a white man!" my mother said shocked, like I just announced I was gay or pregnant again.

"His name is Andrew, Mother. He is a great person and we are getting serious."

"Listen to his name, *Andrew*," Kianna said in her nerdy white-man impression. Then they started laughing.

"So, when do we get to meet whitey again?" Kianna asked.

"Kianna, I didn't raise you like that," my mother said.

"Okay, Mom. I'm just having some fun." Kianna laughed.

"You don't joke like that—your sister will learn," my mom said, shaking her head.

"Learn what, Mom?" I asked.

"You will learn that all he is doing is living out his fantasy," my mother said.

"What fantasy, Mom?"

"The one all white men have about bedding a black woman. It has existed since slavery time. They like our butts. If you think any differently, you are crazy."

"That's not true, Mom. It just what he prefers. Some men like dark-skinned women, others prefer light-skinned."

"Well, it will never work," she said.

"Why won't it work, Mom? We are getting serious," I said.

"Because it just ain't right. There are good black men out here and you need to find one."

"Whatever, Mom. You haven't even met Andrew. Won't you meet him first, then say what he is not? So what if he is not black? He is a good man and treats me a lot better than most of the black men I have dealt with in my life. He has treated me like a queen. And he hasn't tried to dog me or cheat on me."

"Kim, are you saying all black men are dogs and cheat? Your daddy ain't cheat on me. You need to go try to find a good brother. Just because you got one bad egg, you can't jump ship and get a white man."

Karen butted in the conversation. "You said you're getting serious, but what if this leads to marriage or even moving in together? How is a white man going to help you raise your black boys? Did you think about that? He don't know anything about our struggle or even where to take them to get a haircut."

"Andrew is a good person—we are still dating, so I don't even have to worry about that yet. But if it did happen, then I'm sure he would be up for the challenge."

"You sure about that? Because my nephews need a man in their life to show them the way. And a white man can't do that for them, unfortunately."

"Why not?"

"Kim, don't get me wrong. I think it is great you met someone, but just don't build yourself up for failure. Where is he from?" Karen asked.

"He's from New Jersey, but his parents live in Paoli. He was raised by his stepfather. He is a good person. They are very nice people," I said.

"I'm happy if you are happy," Kianna said.

"I'm going to be happy for me and my children. Be happy for me. Mom, I'm going to bring him over to meet you and take you out."

"Okay—when y'all going to take me out? I'll meet him."

I wanted Andrew to look good when he met my mom and sisters. I bought him an outfit. He was upset because he thought I was implying that he didn't know how to dress. I wasn't. I just wanted him to look his very best. I didn't want my mom to be able to find a reason not to like him. Everybody was already seated at the table when we arrived at Hibachi Restaurant. It was a Japanese restaurant where they cooked your food in front of you. I introduced him to everybody. My mom looked the other way, like she had lost something.

"How is your crazy friend doing?" Karen asked to make conversation as we sat.

"He is doing okay." Andrew said.

"So you like brown sugar," my mother asked when she finally turned around.

"No, actually I prefer Equal." We all started laughing. My mom even had to laugh.

I thought she was done with her investigation about his motives. But then she asked unapologetically, "What do you want with my daughter?" Andrew said that the first thing he noticed was my beauty, and since we've been dating he has learned what an intelligent, articulate, motivated and caring person I was. I was blushing and my sisters were hanging on to his every word. By the end of the night Andrew had won my mother over. He answered all her questions and Karen's inquiries. He paid for the entire dinner and held my mother's door and walked them to their car. By the time we reached my car my mother had called on my cellphone and said she liked him.

Chapter 35

Nadine

I stayed at Malik's house twice this week. I didn't want to be too intrusive, but when I stayed there, I noticed he needed a lot of things in his house. His living room was empty and his bedroom only had a bed in it. I went to Target and bought him a new tan-and-gold paisley bed-in-a-bag for his bedroom. I got him a pot-and-pan set and dishes. His ex-wife had taken everything from the house. Poor baby. I hoped he wouldn't take it as me trying to move in on him, but wherever I'm at, I like to feel comfortable. I was going to surprise him with all the stuff. When I arrived at his house, his friend Jarrod looked at me and just began shaking his head.

"Why are you shaking your head?" I asked.

"Because he wishes he had a girl like you," Malik said as he looked over at him.

"That's what it is?" Jarrod said as Malik pushed him toward the door. I began to take everything out of the bags. I overheard him say, "Man, you don't deserve her." Malik then said, "Go home to your woman and leave us alone." He said good-bye as he grabbed his jacket. Malik was so happy that I had bought that little bit of stuff for his place. He thanked me over and over again.

He put everything up and did his dishes. I went home to get ready for the next school day, but before I left him I wrote a note and placed it in his jacket.

Malik,
     You are a special man. I am enjoying our time to-gether.

Nadine Clark

I went home and thought about Malik and our possible future. I was wondering if I was putting too much into him too fast, because I was trying to get over Erick. I wasn't sure. I did still think about Erick from time to time. I hadn't talked to him since that day he didn't let me in.

More than likely, if someone rings my phone in the middle of the night, someone has news for me. Hopefully, it was good news. The last time it wasn't. The last time my phone rang in the middle of the night, it was my aunt informing me that my grandfather died. That thought crossed my mind as I scoped my room in the darkness, looking for the cordless phone. I saw the red light blinking. The phone was on my dresser. I extended my arm over and grabbed the telephone.

"Hello, Nadine—wake up."

"Aunt Connie? What's going on? Is something wrong? Is everything okay? Why are you calling me at three-thirty in the morning?"

"Toya is having the baby, and that sorry-ass man of hers has not shown up yet. I have to go to work at six and I don't want to leave her alone. I can't take a day off."

"What hospital are you at?"

"Pennsylvania."

"Okay, I'll be right there," I said, and hit the OFF button on the phone. I so did not feel like going to a hospital. I wanted to lie right in my bed. I'd wish I never answered the phone. I don't know why everybody always wanted to call me when they needed something—be it money or a ride, call Nadine. Nadine is fucking tired. I wanted to say fuck Toya so bad, but I couldn't. She was supposed to have this baby for the last three weeks, but they kept sending her home. False alarm after false alarm. I didn't want to go, but I decided I would just lie back in the bed for about ten minutes. When I awoke, then I'd go to the hospital.

My ten-minute rest turned into an hour-and-a-half catnap. I almost went back to sleep, but I remembered I had to be there for Toya. I put my clothes on and drove to the hospital. I made my way to the labor and delivery floor. Nate's ass was laid up on the sofa, snuggled with a blanket. Toya was in pain and this niggah was asleep. I kindly woke him up.

"What's up—she have the baby?" he said, sitting up, startled.

"No, but you ass should be up, holding her hand, not asleep," I said.

"Man, she cool," he said as he pulled the cover back over his head. I waited a few seconds, and then I snatched the cover off of him but he still remained asleep. So I cut on all the lights and turned the television on and the volume up.

"Get up and go over there with my cousin."

Nate looked at me with his scruffy beard and weed-smelling ass. "She knows I'm here for her. I love her. I started a new job. I got three kids—I'm sleepy."

"You still have to get up with her. Where you working at, anyway?" I asked.

"I'm got two jobs. I have three kids and a soon-to-be wife to take care of," he said, yawning, realizing that I was not going to allow him to sleep. I wanted to apogize but, work or not, he needed to be up.

Toya gave birth to an eight-pound, seven-ounce baby boy. By the time she completed her twelve hours of labor, my Aunt Connie was back to greet her new grand-child.

"He is so handsome," I said as I entered the room filled with balloons and flowers.

"I know—I got me a handsome grandbaby," Aunt Connie said as Uncle Chuck was holding him.

"You need anything?" I asked Toya as I touched her legs.

"No, I'm good if you can get me some water. My body is aching—tell them to bring me a Percocet. I'm not going through this anymore. I'm twenty-four with three kids. I know I'm a good mom. But the nurses know me here. They said, "See you next year," Toya said.

"You kidding, right?" I laughed.

"That shit is not funny, but the laugh is on them because I got my tubes tied. I can't do the pain anymore. I got my boy—that's all I need."

A powder-blue-and-white banner that read HEAVEN SENT US A BOY extended across the porch of Aunt Connie's house. Even though she said she wasn't going to spoil this grandbaby, I think she takes that back already. She had bought the baby tons of everything blue. Aunt Connie was hanging up decorations in the living room.

"My little boopie-boop is coming home," she ex-claimed.

"You see all this stuff I bought him?" she asked as she pulled out blankets, toys, and clothes.

"Yes, I do," I said, amazed.

"What's going on with you? How is Malik?"

"Malik is fine. I really like him."

"Does he have any children?"

"Yeah, by his crazy ex-wife."

"Well, you don't need that, because that baby is going to be in his life forever."

"I know. I mean, she hasn't caused any problems yet, and he is so sweet."

"He is very nice-looking, too!"

"I know, and he knows how to treat me."

I went to the store and bought my new little cousin a bassinet. It was lily-white and so pretty. All the baby clothes and furniture was so adorable. Walking around the Babies 'R' Us made me want a baby. I wonder if Malik wanted any more kids.

Chapter 36

Shonda

Me and Malik's relationship has gone from bad to worse. We don't spend any time together. He does not come home—he stays out with Jarrod all the time, and I'm just plain tired of it. Things have been awful. He keeps saying he is helping him move and pack. But I'm not stupid—it doesn't take anyone weeks to move.

"Nae—I mean, Shonda."

"What did you call me?" I asked. I swore he called me Nae.

"I called you Shonda."

"Who is Nae?"

"I didn't say anything about Nae—I said hey."

"Hey *what*, Malik?"

"I was asking you to get me a towel."

I handed him a towel out of the closet. "Who the hell is Nae, and where are you going?" I asked as he dried off.

"Nowhere—can't I take a shower and get clean? I'm just in the house. I'm not a prisoner."

"Why are you trying to get cute if you're staying in the house?"

"You sound stupid. I'm about to go downstairs and watch television." Ten minutes later he came up the steps and said, "Shonda, me and Omar about to go out for a minute."

"Where y'all going?" I asked.

"I have to take him somewhere so he can handle some of his business."

"How long are you going to be?" I asked.

"I don't know—I'll call you," he said as he slid a navy blue hooded sweatshirt over his head.

While Malik was gone, Ocho called me and we talked for two hours. When I hung up, Malik's ass still wasn't home. One side of me thought, I need to look good for my man when he came in. The other side was ready for bed and didn't care about Malik anymore. I had to be at work in the morning and I was tired. I wrapped my hair around, put a scarf on it, and took my ass to bed. I figure if he didn't know I looked good by now, oh well. Destiny's Child "Cater to You"—yeah, fucking right. All I know is when he comes in here, he better not touch me—he better stay on his side of the bed. I decided to call his phone to see what he was doing.

"Malik, when you coming home?"

"I'll be there," he said, irritated.

"When?"

"I'll be there. I met up with Jarrod—we all having a few beers real quick."

"Niggah, what—you fucking Jarrod on the down low?"

"Shonda, that's some real ignorant shit to say," he said.

"I don't care—come home, stop staying out with Jarrod, and I won't have anything to say."

"I'll be there when I get there."

Malik came in the room smelling like beer. My eyes

were burning, and I felt pressure over them. His beer smell made me sick. I hate him. I hate him. I hate him.

Working overnight was the pits. I came home tired as hell—I wanted to lie down. Malik was not in the house—his car was already gone. I looked over at our bed. It didn't look like anyone had slept in it. I opened up my phone and dialed Malik.

"Malik, where are you?" I asked.

"I already left out for work. You just got in? How was work?" he asked.

"Malik, you be leaving out mighty earlier in the morning," I said suspiciously.

"Yeah, I have been trying to get a jump-start on my day."

"That's funny, because the tub is not cleaned out and there aren't any damp wash cloths in the bathroom," I said as I closed my phone and the conversation with Malik.

Talking to Ocho was good for my self-esteem. He always complimented me and told me how beautiful I was.

"You look good today, and you smell even better. You know what they say, right?" Ocho asked as we talked on the telephone.

"No, what do they say?" I asked.

"The first piece of ass you get when you come home, you going to sprung. You going to have me breaking out of this, bitch," I laughed. "You just don't know how your ass be moving in the tight-ass uniform pants. My dick be standing straight up every time you pass me."

"Next time I'm going to have to come and sit on it," I teased.

"Your pussy be looking fat. Damn, girl, just thinking about you."

"What you doing?" I asked.

"Stroking my man—he needs some attention."

"When you get out, I'm going to give you all the attention you need," I said.

"That's in another six weeks—I can't wait that long."

"You going to have to. I got to get ready for bed. I'll see you tomorrow."

I couldn't wait to hold Ocho. We have been talking, but I do want to feel him. I played every scene in my mind. How I would pick him up from the jail. We would go get a room. I would take off his clothes and lick his whole body. I won't leave Malik for him—he will just be a side dude with money.

I wish I could afford to pay for a private detective—I want to see if Malik is really cheating on me. He has been working and still hasn't given me a dime for any of the bills. I had to stop thinking about Malik—it felt like he wasn't mine anymore. I couldn't keep worrying about him. I did everything in my power to keep him here. I am doing everything right by him. If it's something else out there, I'm going to let him have it. Where is he? What is he doing? I'm getting a headache from worrying. I don't want to worry about Malik. I just want peace of mind. I wonder what great excuse he will have now. He was doing whatever it was he wanted to do, so I'm going to show him that two can play that game. I'm going to go up to work and give Ocho what he wants.

I took Ocho into the ladies' bathroom. I had Hicks cover for me. We went into the closet. I was so nervous to see if anyone saw us go in together. We had to hurry, so nobody would walk in on us. I would lose my job and everything. Ocho stood me up next to the wall. He stroked my back and it felt a little like spiders were crawling all over my body. He slid his jumpsuit down to his boots. He pulled his erect, thick tool out and rubbed it up and down my leg, then entered me. He was not able to withstand the wetness and tightness of my interior. He was finished quickly, and I rushed him back to his cell. I went back to my post and freshened up in the bathroom. His smell was still all over me. That was our routine for the next couple of nights, each time longer and harder.

I spent time with Ocho when I could. I snuck into his cell. His celly had court that morning. He had already left on the bus and was about to go to court. I knew I might get caught, but that made the sex better and more exciting. It made my senses tingle. Nobody was looking, so I left the door open. He sat on the bed and I grinded my ass on his dick. If I could have, I would have screamed and woke everybody in that prison up. I squeezed my pussy hard, bringing my muscles in and out to wrap around him like a suction cup. He held me up and said, "You are mine now—you have to leave him."

"I can't leave him."

"Yes, you can. I didn't want to tell you until it was finalized, but I'm coming home on house arrest." I looked at him—I couldn't believe what he was telling me. Then he said, "So, you won't have to worry about anything. Shonda, you are the kind of female that a man needs to take care of. I don't want you bringing anything else in this jail because you about to be okay. You hear me?"

"Yes," I answered him. I did need a man to reassure me, to tell me that it's going to be okay.

"The minute I get out of here, you not going to need anything. I got you. You hear me?"

"Yes." I was confused. If he came home, he would really want me to leave Malik.

"I need you to do me a favor."

"What?"

"Do you think you can take some money past my people's house?"

"Where is it?"

"Myrtlewood Street by Twenty-ninth. Go give my son some money."

"I'll do it after work," I said.

"Okay, good—I love you," he said.

"All right, 'bye."

"You supposed to tell me you love me too!"

"I have to go."

"You not going to tell me?" he said, looking disappointed.

"I love you, too!"

I have a husband and I'm telling a dude in prison that I love him. But I do feel like I do love him. I miss him when I'm not near him. I had to talk to somebody about Ocho. I hope Tae understands. I didn't have anybody else to talk to. I needed her to give me some insight about my relationship with Ocho. I went to her place to ask her for advice.

"Where is Kenneth?" I asked as I looked around her apartment.

"He is at his second job, getting that money," she said, rubbing her thumb across her fingers. "He's got to, though, 'cause I'm trying to save for a house so I can decorate my bunchkins' room."

"You're pregnant?"

"No, not yet, but I can't wait to be. Our plan is to get married by September, be in our house by Christmas, and have the baby by our first anniversary."

"So you got everything all planned out."

"Yes."

"This was quick."

"I know, Shonda, but it is so right. So tell me your news."

"Well, Tae, I met someone."

She jumped up and said, "Oh shit, where? Malik is going to be hot. Who is he?"

"He is at my job," I said.

"At your job. You know job romance never works out."

"I know, but he doesn't work there." It took a few minutes for it to sink in, and then she said, "Shonda—an inmate!"

"Yes, he is an inmate, but listen, I didn't think it would lead to sex. I was getting to know him and one thing led to another."

"You cannot lose your job for some bum-ass niggah in jail."

"He is about to get out, and he is not a bum. His name is Ocho."

"Ocho? What is he, Spanish?"

"No, he's black. He used to get money down Susquehanna."

"I can't believe you are risking your job and marriage for an inmate. Do not cheat on Malik with some convict."

"But, Tae, you are not listening."

"I am listening—you shouldn't be doing this to Malik."

"Are you taking Malik's side?"

"I'm not taking his side, but come on—if you not happy, then get a divorce. Don't let some thug-ass inmate convince you that he is your soul mate, Shonda. You can do better. You should try to work on you and Malik's relationship."

"It's not that simple. I think Malik is already cheating on me."

"I can't cosign on this, Shonda—this is just dumb. You are too old for this stupid shit."

I didn't even say anything else to Tae. I just got up and left her apartment. Ever since she met Kenneth, she does not call me at all. I'm not jealous of her happiness because I don't have my own happiness. It's just now she thinks she has all the answers. I mean, yeah, you engaged—yeah, you getting married—so the fuck what. When he starts hanging out late, cheating—I hope he doesn't—but when he does, I hope you have somebody else to turn to, because I won't be there. Maybe I'm being self-centered. Just a little, but when I was with Malik, I didn't front on her. I didn't hang out as much, but I always took her phone calls and I didn't get self-righteous on her. I hope he dumps her, and when she is ready to become friends again, I'm going to tell her to suck my dick.

I grew up in Philly, so I knew what street life was like, but I had never seen anything like Ocho's son's block. My car barely rode down the tiny block, and I was scared to get out. There was an empty lot filled with old soda bottles, tires, and soiled mattresses. I got out of my car and looked for the house. I pulled the address out of my pocket and located the house. The address was painted on the brick wall with white paint. The door handle was broke and hanging off a little. A handwritten sign that read KNOCK HARD was faded and barely hanging on with a thin piece of tape. A faded blanket was acting as a makeshift curtain. I knocked hard, like the sign said. A woman with gray, matted hair answered.

"Can I help you?"

"Yes, Ocho sent me."

She then invited me in. She had an old-time velvet sofa and love seat with wood on the armrest.

I handed her some money and she said, "Tell him I said thank you, and I'll bring the boy up to see him."

"Okay."

Jahan came down the steps—he was five. "Mi-ma, who is that?"

"A friend of your dad."

"Tell my dad I want to live with him."

"Boy, you live with me. Go upstairs or I'll take you up there."

Chapter 37

Kim

Andrew was holding my hand as we walked down scenic Penns Landing. Boats were at the dock and the water was flowing back and forth. Across the river you could see Camden, New Jersey and the Aquarium. The sun was just setting as we walked passed it all. I was enjoying the moment. Andrew asked me to blow in his eye because something had flew in it. He bent down and I tried to see what was in his eyes. I blew and blew and then he said it's out, thank you. "What was it?" I asked.

It was this, he said, holding a white gold, emerald-cut diamond ring.

"What is that, Andrew?"

"Kim, I know we have only known each other for a couple of months, but when it is right, it is right. I never felt like this about another woman—will you do me the honor of becoming my wife?" he said as he bent on one knee in front of me.

"Andrew, we just met."

"I love you, Kim. And nothing is going to change that. We have the same goals, and I want to marry you."

I didn't even care about the ring or its size, but it was huge.

"Yes, I will marry you," I said as we kissed without thinking about it.

A day later I told my mother that we were getting married and heard the first "Congratulations. Oh my, how soon? When do I have to start planning?"

The thought of going with my mother to get a dress again, and looking at banquet halls, began to feel like déjà vu to me. My mom took over my first wedding. I can't go through that again. I mean, I got the pretty dress, my sisters had their dresses, everybody showed up with money and gifts, and I walked down the aisle—and the wedding never happened. All types of thoughts overloaded my brain and the one that stayed was *I can't marry him—not yet.* I got in my car and drove straight to his house.

"Andrew, we need to talk," I said, as I rushed past him and took a seat on his sofa, covered with Barbie and her accessories.

"What's wrong?" he asked.

"We can't get married. We need to talk about us. We never got basic things out of the way. Like, where are we going to live? Then, how about kids? Do you want more? I don't want any—I want my tubes tied. I love my boys, but I don't want any more kids. Will Cianni be enough for you? Will I be good enough for you for the rest of your life? Why do you want to marry me? How do you know you won't get tired of me? Huh? Do you know I was raped in college and Kevin just met his dad? Do you know, right before we met, I was seeing a psychiatrist. You still want to marry me?"

"I don't care about any of that Kim. I'm not leaving you, for any reason or any thing. I love you. I'm here.

How about we sell both houses and buy one big, pretty house with a pool, and a two-car garage, with chandeliers in every room and a big kitchen with an island in the middle," he said as he comforted me.

"Can we afford a house like that?"

"Yes, we can. I make enough money to take care of us."

"Andrew, you didn't say how you feel about kids."

"I'm fine with not having any more."

"How do you know that won't change?" I asked.

"Because it won't. Kim, what's up with you?"

"Nothing. I just, I just have my mom and everybody planning our wedding the moment I told them we were engaged."

"Kim, don't be nervous. Listen, if you don't want this big, grandiose wedding, let's cancel it."

"Cancel it? You mean not get married?"

"No, I want to marry you. I mean cancel the big wedding. We don't need a big parade—we both have been married before."

"*You* have been married before," I said, correcting him.

"You know what I'm trying to say. We both spent money before and had that big party. I think what we need to do is just jump on a plane and go get married."

"Like where, Jamaica. Everybody does that."

He thought for a moment and said, "Let's take the kids with us. Let's get married in Disney World."

I laughed. I'm not getting married with Mickey Mouse."

"No, it will be real informal. The kids will come, I can get my parents to come, and you can have your mom and dad. We'll get them suites and invite our sisters and a few close friends and family."

"How soon?" I asked.

"As soon as you like."

* * *

We decided that we were going to start everything immediately. I called my mother to explain everything to her.

"Mom, we have changed plans. We are getting married in Florida, and we are going to buy you and Daddy tickets. There is not going to be a lot of hoopla like there was before at the last wedding. Just us, just family."

"But what about all my planning?" she said disappointed.

"Mom, I'm sorry, but I want to do it this way. I'm still paying you back for the first wedding," I said, reasoning with her.

"Okay, well, when are we leaving?"

"This weekend—start packing."

Chapter 38

Nadine

Even though me and Malik are hot and heavy, I find myself thinking about Erick all the time. I guess I should be happy that I have someone that is so good to me, but I think I still love Erick. I'm going to give Erick one more chance—if he don't go for it, then fuck it. I love him. I want to get with him. I picked up the telephone. I was about to call him and tell him how I felt and how I think we should be together, but before I had a chance, a text message from Malik came through. He was saying that he missed me and wanted to see me. I messaged him back that I missed him, too. I have to admit that it feels good to have someone in my life that is about me. I decided not to call Erick—instead, I dialed Malik.

"I want to see you. You going to stay with me tonight?" he asked.

"Yeah, I'll stay with you tonight. I'll be over," I said. I took a shower, lotioned my body, and rode over to Malik's house. He had all the lights out. I knocked on the door and he pulled me in. He had a comforter on the middle of the floor, surrounded with candles, white wine, cheese, and crackers. He opened a bottle of wine and handed me a glass. I took a sip.

"What's this for?" I asked.

"I was just thinking about you."

"Thank you. That was so thoughtful."

"You're welcome," he said.

I thanked him again by kissing his lips. He kissed me back, and laid my body on the comforter, and devoured every inch between my legs for an hour. It was so enjoyable, I couldn't even move or speak. He then just held me, and told me all he wanted to do was please me. That is, so what's up? Erick who?

I awoke in the middle of the night, and Malik told me to be quiet. He was hunched down, peeking out the window.

"What's going on?" I said, wondering why I had to be quiet.

"It's my ex-wife—she is crazy. She is knocking on the door."

"Well, go answer the door," I demanded.

"No, if she knows I'm home, then she will break out the window." It seemed strange that Malik was hiding from his ex-wife, but he said some people don't know how to let go. After about ten minutes she left and we went back to sleep.

Chapter 39

Shonda

I was so suspicious of Malik "Mister Creep-Creep." He hadn't come home yet. I called his phone and he didn't answer. I talked to Ocho for a little while, then I went to sleep. I awoke around three in the morning. He wasn't home yet, wasn't answering his phone, and hadn't called. I decided I was going to ride over to Jarrod's to see if he was there, so he couldn't lie and say he was over there. I drove up to Jarrod's house—all the lights were off. I tried peeking in, but it was pitch-black and I couldn't see anything. I knocked on the door a few times. Nobody came to the door. I thought I heard somebody, so I knocked again. Malik could not tell me he got drunk and spent the night over at Jarrod's, or he was helping him move.

The next day I went through my day like nothing was wrong. Malik has to come home and explain where he has been and what he is doing. And when he does, I'm going to cuss his ass out and then find out what is going on with us.

I wasn't going to stay home and sulk over him. I decided I was going to do something for me and went to the hair-and-nail salon. I called and called, and still he didn't answer—he was treating me how he used to treat Kim like a nut jawn, sucker, a nobody and I'm not feeling that. He got to be messing with somebody else, but who?

After my nails were dry and my natural hair was done, I felt better about myself. My hair was growing back nicely and I looked good. If Malik couldn't appreciate that, then Ocho or someone else could. I entered the house and I saw some of Malik's mail sitting on the kitchen table. He must have just left, because the television was on and the cordless was off the charger. I was so mad that I'd missed him. I ran up the steps and saw a bag full of his dirty clothes. I opened the bag and saw a note that read, *You are a special man. I am enjoying our time together.* It was signed *Nadine Clark.* I stared at the note. Who the hell was Nadine? I ran back down the stairs to call Malik, but instead of calling him I pushed Redial on the phone to see if he'd used the phone. A woman answered the phone and said, "Thank you for calling John Master Middle School. How may I help you?"

"Excuse me, what is this?" I asked. The woman replied a John Master Middle School.

I hung up the phone. Who was Malik talking to at a middle school? I thought about the name on the note and pressed Redial again. "Excuse me, is there a Ms. Clark there?" I asked.

"She is in class—I can't disturb the class. I can take a message for her." I got the address and went up to the school. I didn't stop at the office. The hall aide assumed I was a parent, because I asked her which way to Ms. Clark's room and she told me second floor, room 207. I walked right into her classroom. There was another woman and her talking—they were eating lunch, reading magazines. I looked at them for a moment, trying to decipher which one was dealing with my husband. It couldn't be the older one—it had to be the young, big girl.

Before I could say something to them, the lady wiped her mouth and said, "Can I help you?"

I said, "Yes, hi, I'm looking for Ms. Clark."

"Oh, you have the wrong room—she is in room 209, the next classroom over."

"Okay, thank you," I said. I walked in the room—this time my heart was up.

"Are you a parent, because I have to pick up my class from gym. I set conferences up before and after school," the woman said, writing something on the board and dismissing me.

"No, I'm not a parent."

"Then who are you and how can I help you?" she asked as she paused from writing.

"You can help me by leaving my husband, Malik Moore, alone."

"Your husband?" she said, frowning.

"Yes, my husband. Don't act like you don't know. I know he has been staying out with you. You are so wrong. You're in here teaching kids, and you are involved with married men. They should fire your ass. I will tell you one thing—you better stay away from my husband," I yelled as I moved closer to her and she backed away.

"Malik never said anything about being married. He told me his ex-wife was giving him a hard time with his visitation of his son," she said.

I had to laugh. "Well, let me tell you something. I'm Malik's wife and we don't have no kids together. His baby mom has a baby for him. I'm his wife, not his baby mom, or girlfriend, so leave my husband alone or—"

"I didn't know Malik was married. I have been to his house and he spends the night out with me."

"That's because I work at night. And you're spending the night at his friend Jarrod's house not my house!"

"Well I didn't know. I find that real hard to believe that you are still married to Malik," she said with an attitude.

"So you are saying I'm lying?"

"No, I'm saying, can you leave my class? You said what you had to say."

I thought about choking her for trying to play me. She was dealing with my husband. I was ready to choke her when I heard the two teachers come into the room.

"Are you okay, Ms. Clark?" they asked.

"Yes, I am," she said, embarrassed.

"You sure?" the older woman asked.

"Do you have a pass? You stopped at the office, right? If you didn't, you are trespassing, and I'm going to call the cops and you are going to get locked up," the younger one said.

I looked them all over and decided it was time to go. I left the school. No need to hit her or get arrested. She seemed like she really didn't know that Malik was married. I called Malik as soon as I got a few blocks away from the school. He finally picked up.

"Malik, where are you? You have to come home," I cried.

"What's wrong, baby? Are you all right?"

"No, just come home. It is an emergency."

"What's wrong, baby?"

"Just come home *now.*"

"I'll be right there, baby," he said.

I beat Malik home, I was so mad. I wasn't going to give him a chance to explain himself. Here he was, fucking around with some bitch and shit, and our house is not in order. He must be out of his damn mind. I went to the closet and grabbed all of Malik's suits and threw them down the steps. Then I took a handful of shoes and threw them down—they fell and rested on top of the suits. I didn't even get a bag to put his shit in. As I threw his belongings down the steps, I stumbled upon a duffel bag. I opened it and in it was a digital camera with pictures of naked women in all types of positions. A cellphone, handcuffs, a phonebook with all these women's numbers in it. Letters, receipts for strip clubs and hotel rooms. Malik had been cheating all along. The moment Malik came home, I blasted his ass.

He took a look around at all his stuff at the door and said, "What is goin' on, Shonda?"

As calmly as I could, I said, "Malik, who the fuck is Nadine?" He had the stupidest look I'd ever seen on his face.

Then he said, "Nadine who?" His face was telling on him.

I was so aggravated with him, I just said, "Listen, Malik, I went up to her school. I already know everything."

"I don't know what you are talking about."

"You don't know what I'm talking about."

"No, I don't. Why do you have all my stuff down here on the ground like this?"

"Because this marriage is over."

"For what? What are you talking about? Shonda, listen," he said, grabbing my arm.

"Get the fuck off me. Malik, it's over. You are a liar and a cheat. Look at all of this that I found," I said, dumping the duffel bag.

"I'm not a cheat. That stuff is not mine, it's Jarrod's. I don't know any Nadine. Plus, you know what? You're not all that innocent either, Shonda. You been doing shit, too! I'm not stupid."

"No, I haven't, and we're not talking about me. We're talking about your cheatin' ass," I screamed.

"I'm not a cheater," he yelled.

"Yes, you are, and I don't want to be married to you no more. You are a lying bastard. I want you out of my house, Malik. You have to roll. Right now. Take your shit and get out."

"Fine—we don't have to be married, but this is my house—I'm not moving anywhere. You move," he said.

"I'm not moving. You are going to get out!" I screamed as he walked toward the door.

"Shonda, whatever," he said, throwing his hands up at me and walking out the door.

"That's all you got to say is *whatever*?" I said.

"Yeah, whatever. You say I'm cheating and I know I'm not, so whatever."

"So you just going to leave while I'm talking to you, bitch."

"Stop calling me names, Shonda. Ain't nothing else to be said. You don't want to be married, fine." And he walked out the door.

I was so mad. Malik is lying, saying he don't know the bitch. Then he tried to say this bag doesn't belong to him. Then he's just going to leave out while I'm talking to him. Oh hell, no. I'm done. I can't take his shit no more. No more. Malik wants to cheat on me, I got something for his ass. I got to get his ass out. I called Tae up, filled her in on today's details, and then asked, "How I'm going to get this bitch out of my house?"

"I would change the locks and put his stuff out."

"That's what I am going to do. Okay, I'm going to call you back. I am going to call a locksmith."

The locksmith came and changed the locks. I paid

the man and started taking all Malik's stuff and placing it on the pavement in front of our house.

Malik came home. I heard him put his key in the door and that's when I screamed, "I changed the locks, bitch."

"Let me in, Shonda," he said, bamming on the door.

"You don't have nothing else in here. Everything you own is out there."

"Shonda, open this damn door or I'm going to break this door down."

"No, go move in with your teacher. Go live with that bitch or one of the other bitches you deal with. I got a man, anyway—how you like that? He got money too unlike your broke-ass."

"It's okay—I know you was out there. I don't know why I even married your ass. You ain't nothing. Don't nobody want you," he yelled.

"That's what you think. I got a good man."

"Where he at? Tell the dude you about to get fucked up. Open this door."

"No, leave or I'm going to call the cops."

"Call them—my name is on the lease, too! You can't just kick me out the house."

"Oh yes, I can and I did." Malik stopped knocking, so I peeked out the window and saw Jarrod pulling up, helping Malik gather his stuff.

"I told you not to marry her ass. That she wasn't shit. Look at what she's putting you through. Leave this crazy bitch alone. She's not worth it man," Jarrod said.

I was ready to cuss his ass out and tell him to mind his business, but I wasn't about to open the door. Malik collected whatever could fit in his car and left. I dialed Tae back, and she told me that I could go and get a restraining order on him and he would get kicked out immediately.

I made sure Malik was gone before I walked out the door. I got in my car and went downtown to the Justice Center to get the protection order from abuse. Tae called me back and said, "Shonda, if you want them to give you an emergency protection order, you have to tell them that Malik is kicking your ass or is not going to work."

"Okay, so what should I say? He punched me in my face?"

"No, they're not going to believe that because you don't have any bruises. Just say he's been threatening to kill you and punched you in the stomach."

"All right."

"Listen, Shonda, you can tell me to mind my business, but you're not doing all this for that dude in jail, are you?"

"No."

"Just making sure, because it wouldn't be worth leaving your husband for."

"Tae, this man is cheating on me. I only started cheating on him because I knew he was cheating."

"All right, girl—be careful. Call me when you get out of there."

A guard told me I had to go downstairs. I was acting like I was so upset when I entered the room. A woman with a gray suit and red, curly hair asked how she could help me.

"I need to speak to someone about my husband," I said.

"Yes, I can help you." I sat down and told the lady a made-up story about how Malik hit me all the time and how he violently told me he was going to kill me.

"What did he say he was going to do to you exactly?" the woman asked.

"He said, 'Bitch if you leave me, I'm going to kill you.' And then he bammed the door and I called the cops. I'm scared—I think he might kill me." Then, just to make sure she knew I wasn't playing, I told her that he has a gun.

"He has a gun?"

"Yes," I said. Then she wrote something down and said, "I'll be back." I sat nervously—I hope she believed me. I think I sounded right and believable. The woman came back and said, "Mrs. Moore, I need you to sign this."

"Sign what?" I said, grabbing the paper.

"It is the statement that you just gave me. The judge is about to approve it." I signed the form and moments later, the woman came back out and said, "Here's your protection order. It will go in effect immediately. Be careful."

I thanked the woman for her help. I called Malik and told him that he could pick up his restraining order at the 19th District police station, and if he came anywhere near my house, I would call the cops and have him arrested.

Chapter 40

Kim

As I packed our clothes for Orlando I was looking around the house to see if I forgot anything. I made a checklist. I had everything, I was so excited, but nervous at the same time. I was able to make our reservations online and got a good rate for staying at a Marriott in Grand Lakes, Orlando. Everything and everybody was ready except for me. The boys were running around the living room, excited about our trip. I felt like I couldn't keep my emotions together. I was happy, then I was sad. I kind of felt like I was marrying the first man that asked me, but I really do love Andrew. However, I still had a little doubt about us. I paused for a few moments, thinking everything over until Kevin yelled that Andrew and Cianni were at the door. I guess whatever doubt was in my mind, I had to let go of it.

"You ready?" Andrew asked, as he came up and hugged me around my waist.

"Yes, I have to get a few more things together," I said nervously.

"Are you okay?" he asked, studying my face.

"Yeah, I'm fine."

"You don't look like it! Kim, we can't start our marriage off wrong. If we have problems or issues, we have to be able to come to each other. We have to be honest. Now tell me what's wrong?"

"I don't know Andrew. I love you but I feel like we are rushing."

"So, you're not ready to get married or you don't want to marry me?"

"I love you Andrew but I don't want to rush marriage. I want us to get to know each other more. I just don't feel comfortable marrying you after only five months."

"Okay, Kim that's fine with me, I just want to make you happy. Let's go to Disney World, have fun and plan for a wedding at the end of the year. How does that sound?"

"Great, I love you." I said as I kissed Andrew and finished packing.

Chapter 41

Nadine

I called Malik for two hours, but he didn't answer his phone. I had to talk to his ass. I wanted to know why his crazy ex-wife was coming up to my job. How did she know where I worked? How did she know my name? She didn't seem that crazy. Maybe she is not crazy and she is still Malik's wife and he is lying. I have to get in touch with him. I dialed and dialed, but no answer. I finally got Malik on the line. I only had one question for him.

"Malik, are you married?" I blurted out. Malik stumbled over his words, and then said, "Nadine, hear me out. I am married, but—" he stuttered.

"Hear you out? You liar! Why didn't you tell me? You fucking bastard. I don't want to date a married man," I said as I hung up on him, fuming mad. Malik dialed me back.

"What, Malik?" I said. Malik was still stumbling for words and an explanation. Then he said, "I'm in love with you, Nadine."

"No, you are not. You are crazy. I don't have time for this. I don't need people coming up to my job, asking me if I'm dealing with their husband. Malik, we are so over," I yelled as I slammed the phone down in his ear. Malik called back again.

"What, Malik? What can you say to me? I trusted you and you are nothing but a liar. And to top it off, your baby mom and your wife are two different people."

"Nadine, I was going to explain it all to you."

"When? When were you going to tell me?" I yelled.

"I swear I was going to tell you, Nadine. I didn't mean to hurt you. I left my wife a long time ago, but she won't give me a divorce. So I didn't want to tell you all that, then tell you about my son's mom. It was just too much. I really liked you and I didn't think you would give me a chance if you knew all that. I swear to you, Nadine. I'm really in love with you. Let me come over there so we can talk. I'm on my way."

"No, don't bother. I'm good, Malik." With that, I hung up on him and turned off my ringer. I had heard enough. I don't need Malik, and I definitely don't need no drama. I cried very briefly about Malik, and then I realized the tears I was shedding were not for Malik, but for Erick. I had to try to talk to Erick again. This is going to be my last time. I'm going to put it all on the line. I'm going to say everything I want to say to him. If he don't come back to me, I'm moving on with my life. Me and Malik are over, and I just want my man back. I didn't call Erick's house. I grabbed my handbag, got in my car, and drove over there. The whole ride, all I could think about was what I can say to Erick to get him back, make him understand that I made a mistake, that I love him, that I miss him. I couldn't think of anything that I could say. I was on his block and I saw his car. I called from my cell phone, blocking my number so he would pick up.

"Hello," he said.

"Erick, I'm outside your door."

"What are you doing? What do you want, Nadine?" he said, annoyed.

"Just listen, Erick. Please hear me out."

"Make it quick—I have to do something," he said.

I wanted to tell him to go to hell for his last comment, but I wasn't going to let pride interfere with me telling Erick how I felt about him.

"Erick, baby, please listen. I love you. I always loved you, I never stopped loving you. We have been apart for all these months, and I thought it would be easy to go on. But it hasn't been. Each day we have been apart I have thought about you or somewhere we'd been. I know I wasn't ready before, but now I am ready to make a serious commitment to you and us. I'm ready for us to be one and start a family. I'm ready to be all you need, I don't care about anybody else or who you were dealing with while we were apart."

Erick hadn't hung up on me yet—that was a good thing. He was listening, so I kept talking.

"Erick, nobody is going to take your place in my life. I was so wrong for breaking up with you, but I was confused. I didn't know what I wanted. But now I definitely know what I want in my life, and it's you. And I understand you are angry with me. Be angry, but don't block me out anymore. Let me back into your life. Stop acting like you don't have feelings for me. Let me back in, Erick. Please stop pushing me away. Let me in, Erick, let me back into your life," I said as I began banging on his door. I banged and I banged and my phone went dead. Erick hung up. I guess everything I said meant nothing to him. I was still banging on his door, then I stopped and I stood on his steps, crying. He didn't even come to the door. He doesn't love me anymore. I have to move on. I wiped my face on my shirt and began walking down the steps.

Just as I was walking away, I heard Erick's door unlock. I went up to it and turned the knob. The door opened. I couldn't believe it. I walked in and Erick was sitting on the sofa. Tears were running down his face. I walked over to him and hugged him. It felt so good to hold him. I didn't want to stop holding him. I held him so tight. He tried to pull away from my hug, but I wouldn't let him. He then hugged me back. He looked at me and said, "It's okay—stop crying. Nadine, stop crying."

"I can't stop—I love you, Erick. I love you—please take me back. I don't care about anybody you was dealing with. I just want us to be together again."

"I don't know, Nadine. I don't know how I can know you might not leave me again. It's been hurting me not to take you back. I didn't want to deal with anybody else. I wanted to get back with you just as much as you wanted to. I just thought we both needed space and time to see if we were right for one another."

"We are right for one another," I said. We continued holding each other and just sat talking. Erick told me not to cry and that he wasn't going anywhere. "I love you Erick, so much."

"I love you, too, Nadine." After all these months, we were back together, back in each other's arms. And it felt so good.

Malik kept calling me. I put my house up for sale and moved in with Erick and I also changed my cell phone number. We're getting married next summer. Malik can go call his wife or somebody, or the next girl. I'm back with my man. I learned a lot while we were apart. The biggest lesson being you don't miss your water until your well runs dry.

Chapter 42

Shonda

I haven't heard from Malik. I think he's staying at Jarrod's house. I did get a message on my phone from the attorney that represents him, asking me to call him back. I didn't bother. I don't have the time to worry about our divorce. For the time being, I was satisfied with having a ghetto divorce. We can take care of the paperwork later. All I have been concentrating on is Ocho.

Ocho was supposed to be coming home on house arrest, but his attorney advised him that he should just remain in custody. He only had three more weeks before he went to court on the attempted-murder charge. The other assault case was already thrown out. As soon as he got out, he told me, I could quit this job and I could just run his businesses with him. I couldn't wait till he got out. It's been so difficult dealing with him being in jail, Malik cheating, and just not knowing how everything is going to pan out. My daughter hasn't even been home in a few weeks because of all this bullshit.

* * *

I went to work and Hicks told me Wilson was about to have a meeting.

"Why?"

"I don't know," he said, looking concerned.

I followed him and a few other guards into Sergeant Wilson's office. We all remained standing. Wilson came in and said, "We are having this informal meeting tonight because it has been brought to my attention that somehow inmates are getting access to outside food, cigarettes; and a condom was found on Unit E last week. Now, this means somebody is bringing it in. We will find out who it is, because it will not be tolerated. We are starting an investigation into the matter." The first thing that came to my mind was, could they do a fingerprint? Was it that serious? Hicks was on Unit B tonight, and I didn't want to look suspicious by going up there, talking to him. Actually, I knew the best thing for me to do was to stay away from him.

Today was the first day of court for Ocho. I had been praying for everything to go okay with him. Ocho was on the stand with a crisp black suit on. He was confident and answering all the prosecutor's questions.

"Mr. Johnson, isn't it true that the night before your sister was allegedly raped by Mr. Parker, you attempted to shoot and kill him?" the prosecutor asked.

"No," Ocho said.

"Well, why does the 7-Eleven have footage of you getting in his car and shooting him?" Gasps were heard all over the courtroom. "You want the court to believe that the attempted murder of Mr. Parker was not premeditated, that you were the victim? But the victim is still here, trying to cope with one eye. Because you tried to kill him, isn't that true?"

"No! That is not true."

Ocho turned to his attorney and his attorney shouted, "Objection."

"Order in the court," the judge said as he banged his gavel on the block. The judge called for recess and said that we would continue tomorrow. I don't know about Ocho—I can't be dealing with a killer. I mean, he didn't kill the dude, but he tried. The drugs is one thing—he said he was stopping that and cleaning his money up.

I snuck in to see Ocho—I had to. I was risking getting caught, things were so tight now. Everybody was looking and snitching. But I had to talk to Ocho.

"Ocho, did you try to kill him?" I asked as I walked up to his cell, looking around.

"Yeah, Shonda, I did—but my man was supposed to pay him off," he confessed.

"What?"

"He's not supposed to show up. If he comes to court, I'm going to get found guilty. I can't believe this shit," he said, holding his head down. I didn't know what to say. This shit was crazy and over my head. I couldn't let him do more time—there had to be something I could do.

"Well, where is your friend? I can call him and see what is going on."

"See if you can talk to him. Tell him I got double that when I get out. Call this number." He gave me the number and I remembered it.

"He'll know what I mean." I gave him a quick peck and left his cell.

On my lunch I called the number. "Yo, who this?" the voice said.

"I'm a friend of Ocho—he said to tell you, make sure you don't do that," I said.

"Yeah, well, tell him I got to do what I got to do. Because his man was supposed to come and see me and make sure I was all right."

"What you need so you will be all right?" I said, trying to choose my words carefully.

"Ten stacks and I would be good." *Ten thousand. I didn't have that money,* I thought. I tried to reason with the guy and said, "I don't have ten stacks right now, but Ocho got you when he gets home."

"Nah, I'm not doing any of that." Then there was silence.

The next day the prosecutor called the witness and victim, Mr. Sharif Parker, who took the stand. He pretty much sealed the deal for Ocho. He described in detail that he used to hustle for Ocho—they had an argument and Ocho tried to kill him. He said the next day he went to talk to him to squash everything, and Ocho tried to kill him again.

"That's not what happened, nigga. Don't lie," Ocho screamed.

"Silence your client," the judge said.

The rest of the day, the prosecutor kept trying to portray Ocho as this killing, ruthless criminal, and that wasn't true. There was a strong possibility that Ocho was not coming home. I don't know what he was going to do if he got sent upstate. I waited, praying and hoping when the verdict came in.

The juror stood up and said, "We, the jury, find the defendant, Edward "Ocho" Johnson, guilty of attempted murder." They told Ocho he would be sentenced in thirty days. I broke down in tears. He turned and he looked at me and lip-synched *I love you* as they took him out of the courtroom.

I reluctantly went into work the next day after Ocho's trial. I couldn't get myself together. The life that I was hoping and wishing to make with Ocho was not going to happen. I was planning to quit when Ocho got out—I'm glad I didn't. Now that's all I got—this dumb-ass job. I'm going to try to stay here as long as I can. I got to be able to put some money up. I walked in the jail and I went to see where I was reporting today. I saw Angie.

"What's up, girl?" she asked.

"Nothing."

"Me and you are working Unit C tonight."

"Okay. Let me go to the bathroom and I'll be right back," I said.

"Yeah—hurry up, because I got something to tell you."

"Tell me now," I said.

"Well, they are pressing charges on Hicks. One of the female inmates is pregnant, and they found out he was bringing things in."

"Are you serious?" I asked Angie.

"Yup, and he is getting charged with rape."

"But he didn't rape her—it was consensual," I said, a little too defensive of him. I checked myself and rephrased it. "She didn't tell them that she wanted it, too."

"It didn't matter. She is an inmate and he was supposed to protect her. As far as the state is concerned, he didn't protect her. He had a position of power over her and he violated it."

"Where is she now?" I asked, alarmed.

"They let her go—she will be on house arrest until her court date.

As Angie finished telling me what was going on with Hicks, Riddick came up behind me and said, "Wilson wants to see you."

"I wonder what he wants," I said, like I had no idea. I was busted—I might be going to jail. I didn't know if I should run out of there or what. I was scared to enter his office—instead, I went into the restroom. Again I contemplated my next move. I didn't know what he wanted, so I didn't run.

"Yes, what's wrong?" I asked, walking into Wilson's office.

He turned around in his swivel chair and said, "Robinson, come in and close the door. I'm giving you a heads-up. You know everything that's going on. I don't want to see you go down with Hicks. I know you have something to do with everything. Internal affairs are investigating you and a few others."

"I didn't do anything."

"Listen, I know it is you. You have to quit before the investigation goes any further. If you don't quit, the state might bring charges against you. Here—I already typed a resignation letter up for you," he said as he grabbed the paper off his printer. "Sign here."

I read the letter. It said, *I, Shonda Robinson, am resigning of my own free will.* I signed the letter, then Wilson asked for my badge and told me to clean out my locker.

My life was ruined. No husband, no job, and Ocho was in jail for who knows how long.